Uncommon Miracles

Julie C. Day

TABLE OF CONTENTS

Acknowledgements

THIS COLLECTION EMERGED after years of support and encouragement from those around me. I've been incredibly lucky in the people who have entered my life.

To my partner Tom, who knows when it's time to hold my hand and when it's time to send me out the door with my laptop. If not for you, none of these stories would have made it into the light. To my children, Fina and Holden. You are both such amazing humans. I wish you could see yourselves as I see you. I couldn't be more proud of who you've become.

To my parents for setting me on this path all those years ago and for providing child me with an unrestricted library of books. To my brother, Andy, and Pam Long for being my co-conspirators when we were kids. Duck detectives and tunnels to the center of the earth require more than one person's belief.

To Linda Lewis who nudged me out of my cocoon and into the world.

To my writing mentor, Jim Kelly, who still takes my phone calls after all these years and to Liz Hand, whose belief in the possible extends far beyond her own work. The generosity both of you offer to aspiring writers says everything about the quality of your hearts.

To the amazing people in my critique group, the Post-Apocalyptic Writers' Society (PAWS), including Bonnie Jo Stufflebeam, Sarah Read,

Acknowledgements

Emily Cataneo, Kat Köhler, and C Liddle. These stories are far better for your insights. I love each and every one of you.

To Gavin Grant and Kelly Link. Thank you for taking a stray intern off the streets and letting her run loose in your aisles. Your encouragement still takes me by surprise.

To Aaron Hamburger, who reminded me that daydreaming is as important as written words and Scott Wolven who preached the power of hard work.

To Keith Potempa, Adam Gallardo, Will Ludwigsen, Joe McDermott, Amy Tibbets, Derek Hoffman, Adam Mills, Karen Bovenmeyer, Allister Timms, and all my many Stonecoast friends. You are my fellow creators of misfit toys. You gave me the confidence to believe that my mad writing voice needed no alteration.

To the Day Drinkers and one special bear.

To Margot who has helped me find the uncommon miracles within myself.

To all the editors who have published and believed in my work, especially Andy Cox who for years has given my stories a friendly port away from the disinterested storm.

An immense thank you to Nicky and Peter Crowther at PS Publishing for taking a chance on this book. It's like a rainstorm of chocolate and fairy dust. Neither feels entirely real, though both are extremely welcome.

And finally to anyone and everyone who has helped me. Thank you. I know you are legion. I wouldn't have managed this without you.

Uncommon Miracles

To Tom, Fina, and Holden.
You make me happy when skies are gray.

Everyone Gets a Happy Ending

"Baby bunnies," Steph says, "herald the apocalypse. Kendra, you know that, right?"

"Painful truth," I reply, even as I luxuriate in the soft fur pressing against my arms. The heat is oppressive. Sweat soaks the back of my shirt, drips from the fine hairs at the nape of my neck. It's dusk in southwest Arizona, and Steph and I are far from home. Spring is supposed to mean daffodils and tender shoots of Chemlawned grass. Instead, the Arizona air pulls the moisture right from my lips—the dark reverse of a lover's kiss.

Steph and I should be hanging at my condo or, even better, in Steph's room at her parents' house, trying to ignore the new reality that is Ohio. But no. We're sitting behind a tiny cottage at Sister Francis's New World Sanctuary, staring out at the desert plateau and the mountains beyond, distant peaks that bisect the sky. Besides Sister Francis's compound, there isn't a building in sight. A truth I don't share with Steph: I like it here.

Steph looks like hell with a sunburn and a scowl that seems permanently etched on her face. I'm sure I don't look any better. Two weeks post-birth and we're both exhausted. Beyond Sister Francis's sanctuary, the bunnies have us surrounded. They're hard to pick out among the cacti and dry underbrush, but I know they're there. The landscape of Arizona, Ohio, and the rest of the world overflows with rabbits. Steph's babies are just a drop in God's vast ocean.

3

Now that they're born, I don't know what comes next. Which feels like yet another apocalyptic betrayal. My dreams, like my human self, are beside the point.

"Kendra, we need a plan. A better plan than this." Steph grimaces as one of the babies tries to wriggle off her lap. Meanwhile, I'm handling a couple myself. After two weeks, I'm well and truly schooled. Baby bunnies are big daytime sleepers, but God do they start moving once the sun goes down.

"Ohio wasn't all that bad," Steph presses when I don't immediately reply.

The bunnies' eyes opened a week ago, and despite their tiny size, in the last couple of days they've gotten curious—and bold. The minute one makes a break for it, a second and maybe a third are likely to follow suit. So far the escapees haven't managed to get very far. Sister Francis says we've got another week, tops, before they manage to kick their way free. Steph's not wrong. We need a plan. At the same time, she's not right. Ohio doesn't take kindly to women with bunnies in tow.

"I don't know. Ohio was never great. And our favorite people aren't even around anymore," I say, avoiding one painful truth only to bump up against another: the mass of dead and disappeared.

"Jesus, Kendra. I actually liked our friends." She pauses, her frown deepening. "And my parents."

"Sorry," I say, meaning it. Apocalypse is such an overdone excuse for assholedness.

Steph and I are stretched out on plastic recliners, our laps full of her offspring: six desert cottontails, and for some unknown reason, one of the English Spot variety. After all my careful care—changing the bedding in their crate, cradling them when Steph disappears from their sight—the English Spot is still the only bunny who greets me when I come near. I've named him Cole. A fact I don't share with Steph, though I whisper it to him like a lullaby when she isn't near. He has soft shiny fur and gentle eyes. During the day, when Steph goes on another one of her exhausted-and-needing-to-pretend-this-isn't-happening walkabouts, I carry him around with me, tucked into a homemade sling. It's not his fault God has decided to kill off the people. He doesn't even know God exists.

Forget the Four Horsemen, the plagues of boils and locusts. Forget whatever the priests and ministers used to say. These days everyone knows the truth: Bunnies are God's unknowing, apocalyptic emissaries. His plan is brilliant: Shift one thing in an ecosystem and an unstoppable multitude of other changes follow. Never one to fuck around. When God made his move, he went straight-up global. And showing us humans just how off we can be, his change agents were cottony-tailed bunnies. Mosquitos would have been less of a curve ball.

Our road trip from Ohio to Arizona started with the best of intentions. Change always comes slower to the Midwest. Sacramento, California, had lost power months ago: bunnies in the substations and gas pipelines that had run dry. Meanwhile, DC had emptied of its politicians and any semblance of nation-wide emergency management.

The Ohio version of the apocalypse mostly involved Pilates classes and running clubs filled with other women of childbearing age. Bunny fever, people called the new birthing paradigm, and not in a good way. If you were a woman, you better be a skinny woman with no possible baby bump in sight. Nothing like impending group hate to motivate. Regular exercise had never been so popular.

Even after the fall of both coasts, in Lakemore we had streetlights, local news, and reliable refrigeration. And staying healthy wasn't such a bad thing. Compared to most everywhere else, it was actually a good place to live. That's what Steph and I and all those other women told ourselves. And why not? We had nowhere else to go.

When Steph showed up on my doorstep that Sunday morning in May, I realized two things. First, after all my failed attempts—my application to the University of San Francisco, my job as chaperone for Semester at Sea, my boyfriend Joseph out in Oregon—I was finally going to leave Lakemore, for real this time. Second, people, even people you think you know, are hard to understand, hard to read anyway. Maybe it's because we humans take so much longer to mature than rabbits.

Day ten of our Ohio-to-Arizona journey. "We're almost there," Steph said, looking up from the AAA road map.

"Awesome." My enthusiasm was totally sincere. It was only a couple of hours since we'd left the last motel and already Steph's silence was grating on me. Bunny bump or not, I was sick of her moods. You'd never guess she was the one who used to dream of motherhood. Swollen ankles, raging hormones, and two rabbit-scared parents who refused to even meet up and say goodbye had taken their toll. Steph's parents had given her a 1998 Honda Civic for her sweet sixteen. In high school, Mr. and Mrs. Meyer had gone to all of Steph's softball games. Unlike my own checked-out parent, her mom still made Steph's breakfast. Or she used to. Bunnies really do change everything.

From the corner of my eye I watched Steph carefully fold the map and place it in the glove compartment. Cell and satellite signals had disappeared months ago, taking Google Maps and GPS with them. Paper was back. Meanwhile, the North American power grid had crumbled into pockets and fragments.

Road trips, however, were still very much in play. In the end, roadside motels might be the last thing to go.

On our drive south, Steph and I saw cities with rabbits so thick on the ground that even the highways were blocked. You either drove over them or took the more forgiving side roads with their wide verges and nearby fields. Not really much of a choice when your bestie has been knocked up via Immaculate Conception. Side roads all the way. We saw cornfields rustling despite the lack of a breeze, unseen bunnies moving along the ground. We saw the piles of bodies, both rabbit and human, at the edge of too many towns, the burning pyres like beacons in the night. When we reached Arizona, one of the first areas hit by God's new plan, it felt like we'd entered a quieter—and yes, hotter—world. Not that the rabbits seemed to mind. The mass of cottontails blended in with the brush and the dusty ground. Unlike the suburbs and paved cities of Ohio, the herds of rabbits just seemed to fit. Herds, one of those fun facts you learn when the world is ending. It's not just cows and horses. Rabbits come in herds too. And while they may not bite or claw, a herd of anything is hard to stop.

"There." From the passenger seat, Steph pointed to a collection of buildings about a half-mile off. "I think that's it. It matches the address on the card."

"Right." For some ridiculous reason, I'd been imagining some dystopian movie–style miracle. Rebar reinforced concrete walls and tall fences. A Compound with a capital C. Instead, Sister Francis's New World Sanctuary consisted of two rows of tiny, graying whitewashed cottages and an office that pressed up against the road. Next to the office was an unlit neon sign with the words Jerry's Motel. Sister Francis and her supposed salvation compound didn't even have its own sign. Two thousand miles is a long way to go for an unlabeled roadside miracle.

I parked the car next to the motel office, tried and failed to find a reassuring smile.

"Now what?" Steph said.

I shrugged. "I guess it can't be any worse than home."

Still, neither of us got out of the car.

The motel office had a wilted space-age enthusiasm, circa 1960. The building's upswept roof extended over the parking lot, held up by flaking blue pillars. The front wall of the office was made up almost entirely of glass. I could see half a dozen chairs upholstered in mustard yellow, a stack of wooden crates, and a long countertop with one of those wooden brochure stands.

"Hungry," Steph said. "Again." She took a slug from her water bottle, her eyes fixed on the windshield and the desert landscape beyond. Steph, new tougher bunny-pregnant Steph, was not going to cry. At least not if she could help it.

"Yeah, tacos with extra guac."

"And a Sprite float."

"No way. Root beer or nothing." The same old argument we'd had when we were ten. It felt good, like a well-worn blanket.

Inside the office a stout woman in a nun's wimple appeared from a doorway behind the counter. She waved and strode out toward the car.

"It could be worse," I repeated, thinking of the fertility lists our local ob-gyns were mandated to keep, and the rage that erupted when seemingly regular people were faced with a pregnant woman or a nest of living bunnies.

"I guess." Steph rolled down the window.

"Welcome." The woman peered inside the car. "My name is Sister Francis."

"Stephanie," Steph mumbled, tugging at her tunic as though that would cover her bunny bump.

It was then that Sister Francis performed her first miracle. She smiled at Steph and patted her hand. "The cottages all have swamp coolers—and power to run them. Being pregnant in the Arizona heat is such a burden."

Sister Francis had iron-gray frizzy hair that slipped out of the sides of her wimple. She wore sensible shoes, no stockings, a white button-up shirt, and a black skirt that hung just below her knees. Despite the clothes, the supposed holy woman didn't give off a bride-of-God vibe. Underneath that wimple I could see at least one neck tattoo, a snake with a face that looked like a longhaired Jesus. I'm Midwest Baptist, not Catholic, but even so, I had my doubts. A single woman dressed in a wimple and an abandoned motel did not scream Papal God to me. Not that I gave one little fuck. This woman was the first person I'd met in months who didn't seem scared.

"I'll help in whatever way you need, Stephanie," Sister Francis said as she opened the passenger-side door.

"Okay," Steph said, actually returning the woman's smile.

And that seemed to be that. I grabbed our gear from the back of the car while the two of them started to unload the trunk.

With Sister Francis's help, Steph and I hauled our bags of groceries and bottled water into the motel office, exchanging them for our very own one-room cottage. "Lucky eleven," Sister Francis pronounced as she handed over the key. "Meals and linens included at no extra charge."

"What about prayers?" I said, trying and failing to hold the attitude at bay.

Steph turned her frown in my direction. "Kendra, what the hell?" she said, then raised a hand to her mouth, looking suddenly embarrassed.

Sister Francis seemed unfazed. "If you like" was her only reply. The woman even managed an understanding smile.

Our cottage had vinyl flooring and twin beds with a large wooden crate set between them. Sister Francis hadn't lied. The swamp cooler kept the place reasonably cool. Despite the handful of cars in the parking lot, some with plates from as far away as Virginia, our neighbors remained elusive. Like us, they mostly remained inside, waiting or hiding or whatever the hell you do until your quota of newborn bunnies arrives.

Sister Francis brought us fresh towels each morning. She checked in with us after lunch. She fed us and somehow she kept the generator running. What Sister Francis didn't do was talk about God, salvation, or the coming rabbit births.

In the daytime the motel seemed almost abandoned. At night, though, the sounds of the other residents slipped into our room. I heard the occasional bang of a closing car door, the scuff of shoes on gravel, and behind it all was the hammering that arose at unexpected moments, muffled but clearly coming from the direction of the office.

HOURS BEFORE THE FALL

God certainly moves in mysterious ways, especially in Ohio during the End of Days. Saturday night Steph's out with Danni and Maryanne, two of her besties she met in her weekly spinning class. Sunday morning her stomach has a suspicious bulge, so it's the pharmacy, peeing onto a stick, and then a visit to my place.

It's almost noon, but I answer the door wearing a robe over my jeans and sweatshirt. Like most nights, I fell asleep in front of the TV. Might as well enjoy it while it's still around. On the coffee table sits a collection of Heinekens and a soot-streaked glass bowl. I used to be the planner. The success. The one who could be counted on. Getting things right feels less important than it used to.

Steph is a foot shorter than me with a dimpled chin and curly brown hair that she straightened each morning our entire high school career. Four years of straight hair must have burned the need right out of her. At twenty-six she likes to go to bed early. She keeps a suitcase in the back of her closet full of hand-stitched linens from various lady ancestors. She does not show up at my doorstep on a Sunday morning still wearing heels from the night before with remnants of mascara streaked across her face.

"Kendra, I'm in trouble," she says, not even waiting for me to close the door.

"How?" I know. Of course I know, but I pretend just the same. One final moment of sanity.

Steph waves her hand, pointing to the form-fitting North Face jacket she's thrown over her shirt and leggings. Despite the spinning class, and the ten-plus pounds she's lost since the apocalypse began, Steph's stomach bulges. There are weird patches of dried skin along the backs of her hands. Lakemore and the surrounding towns have been swarming with rabbits for over a year now and the medical advisories are on the TV 24/7. I know the signs.

"We can figure this out," I lie. I am the fixer, the friend with the car and the working landline phone, one of the few who have managed to make it to the End of Days with extra cash in hand.

I push aside the empties, tuck Steph in on the couch, and make the call to Tapestry Healthcare up in Akron, well away from any prying eyes. I do not call Steph's God-fearing parents or any of our other supposed friends, though before we head out I do manage one final thing. I change my days-old clothes and brush my teeth, as though making myself presentable will somehow change the outcome.

It doesn't.

"Positive. Six maybe seven," the ultrasound tech says in that carefully neutral voice medical professionals use when something is terribly, awfully wrong.

Steph's legs are up in the stirrups. The paper cloth is across her lap. She is not looking at the monitor and all those black-and-white blobs. That's my job. Steph's job is not crying. In that moment mine seems a whole hell of a lot easier.

"Right," I say. "So what's next?"

"A follow-up appointment is advised within forty-eight hours." The tech keeps her head bent over her computer screen as she talks. "We'll also add you to the monitoring list, just in case you need some extra support. Sometimes, after the initial procedure, the issue returns."

"Are you kidding me? The bunnies just grow back?! I thought that was an urban legend." Steph sounds angry. No, she sounds furious. She is a 4-H girl. Repeated Immaculate Conception is not on her list of acceptable methods of reproduction.

"Unfortunately not. The receptionist will help you with the follow-up plan." The tech looks over at Steph. She suddenly seems weary and uncertain. "Take care," she says before she exits the room.

And then Steph and I are standing at the receptionist's desk, waiting to book Steph's "follow-up appointment," as the receptionist carefully terms it. Extraction prior to birth is the only option for women carrying bunnies, no matter what official monitoring list it puts you on. Back-alley bunny abortions might be a thing, but they are also an easy way for a woman to disappear without too many awkward questions.

The receptionist has purple hair fried from too many dye jobs and deep circles under her eyes. Tiny silver crosses traverse the length of her left ear. "Good luck," she says as she hands me Steph's appointment card. "With all the backlog, it takes a few days to get people into the system," she adds. "For the first forty-eight hours it's paper in, paper out."

"Right."

It's only after I unlock the car doors and watch as Steph carefully places the seatbelt beneath her bulging belly that I realize something strange has occurred. The appointment card is clear enough: a "follow up" for Tuesday May 14th, two days from now. It all looks very straightforward and official. However, attached to the underside of the appointment card is a second card. The heading "Sister Francis's New World Sanctuary" is printed in bold black letters. Underneath in smaller font are the words "Every family in its own way." The logo shows a pregnant woman in silhouette. Little rabbits surround her. The bunnies seem to be playing some sort of game. It's as though the artist had no idea what these particular creatures signify.

New World Sanctuary. Okay. Steph needs sanctuary. Steph and everyone else. But that's not how the world works. Thanks to the receptionist and her business card, Steph has two days and one road-trip alternative before the electronic records are updated and the surveillance begins.

We pack my car that afternoon. Steph sits in the parking lot while I load up a shopping cart with ramen and water and all the rest. I don't go near the vitamin or skincare aisles. Pregnancy is hard enough without some mob trying to corner you before you manage a mad dash out of town.

"Bye, honey," Mom says when I call her on the phone. "Enjoy." As though Steph and I are heading on out on some girl's weekend. It's 10 a.m. and Mom's voice is already three-drinks slurred.

11

"I never wanted a rabbit," Steph screams.

Which is true enough. Even when she was in 4-H, all she ever wanted was her very own horse.

"It'll be over soon," Sister Francis soothes.

Bunnies may be smaller than human babies, but the contractions seem no different from those I've seen on medical shows. There's water on the floor and sweat-soaked sheets and Steph's knees are wide apart. She looks all sorts of pissed off when Sister Francis tells her to push harder. Me, I just stand there wishing I could be anywhere else. Whatever those medical dramas used to pretend, childbirth is stinky and painful, and at least for the person watching, pretty gross. Then again, I'm the friend who never wanted babies.

"It hurts. Goddamn it!"

"You need to push." Sister Francis sounds calm, but it's a practiced kind of calm. The kind that only comes after dealing with enough shitty experiences.

"I. Don't. Care."

"Stephanie, I know it's hard, but you need to push. It won't be over until you push."

In the end, Sister Francis is the one who cuts the umbilical cords and washes the newborns in a basin of warm water, while I stand by with the towels. After four hours and seven baby bunnies, it's over.

Even as we're swaddling the babies, I can sense some new goal on the horizon, still too far away to see clearly. Since Steph and I arrived two weeks ago, three of the other cars have driven away. I can't think of a single town that would take a family with rabbits in tow.

As with caregivers of all new babies, quiet time is scarce in the Arizona desert. Two weeks into Steph's parenthood and we still don't have a post-birth plan.

Mornings, Steph wanders the desert once the sun rises and the babies settle in for the morning. Sometimes I think I can see her red bandana, a slow-moving dot out toward the horizon. Other times I wake up to find her gone and untraceable. I've taken to checking the car first thing, making sure it's still parked in the space outside our cottage door. I pretend I need to restart it each morning, not that anyone ever asks me for my justification.

The Virginia and New Mexico plates are still in number ten and fourteen, but their owners never emerge during the day. Sometimes, as the car engine sparks to life, Sister Francis pops out of the office door and waves. Sometimes she doesn't. Those are the mornings that the thrum of the car engine competes with the banging sound of Sister Francis's hammer. From the driver's seat, through the office's glass wall, I can see her sweat-stained white blouse and the swaying movement of her wimple as it picks up speed with each downward swing. Crates and more crates. Despite all her hours of work, it seems her crate-building is never done.

"What happens now?" I finally ask Sister Francis one morning as she leaves yet another set of towels.

"Take all the time you need," is her only reply. "Seven isn't so much." But the glance she and Steph share, it's like they're carrying out a second silent conversation I can't decipher.

"Seven isn't so much," Stephanie repeats after Sister Francis leaves, and then we're both laughing, lips held tight, trying not to wake up the bunnies.

Cole's nose twitches, but he doesn't wake.

Five weeks is all it takes for bunnies to grow big enough to leave their mother's nest. I'm pretty sure I'm not the only one counting the days.

All those grasses Stephanie has been collecting from her desert walks and the bits of rabbit fluff she finds and brings back. It's like she can't help herself, lining the second wooden crate Sister Francis provided sometime in week three. It sits in the corner of the room: four walls, an enclosed top, and a door that latches.

Sister Francis doesn't comment when she walks in with the day's clean towels and helps reswaddle Stephanie's fast-growing young, but there is no way in hell she's missed it. One of them, not Cole, has hopped out of the lidless baby box and is busily moving about the room. They might not be full grown, but Cole and his siblings are no longer babies.

"They're getting so big, right?" I say.

"They are beautiful," Sister Francis declares. She picks up the adventuring bunny and attempts a smile. I can't help but notice how she avoids my eyes.

"What happens now?" I say, refusing to let it go.

She pats my hand, but "Pray on it" is her only reply.

Steph and I are sitting like we always do at the end of each day, watching the sunset and the vast arid plain. I don't know why Steph's words are such a shock. Steph's babies don't wake in the night to nurse anymore. They've discovered their flat herbivore teeth. Now they love grass and clover and dandelion greens. Their ears turn and twitch, listening to every little sound. They always seem to be scrambling out of their walled wooden bed.

"Let's set them free." These are the first words Steph has spoken since we came outside.

In Apocalyptic Arizona, "set them free" is just another bullshit euphemism. Even with God's blessing and all that, most wild rabbits don't make it to adulthood. And Arizona, minus Sister Francis's New World Sanctuary, is a hard land.

"I didn't ask for them," Steph continues as though reading my mind. "And it's not like they're mine. Not really."

"Steph." I'm not sure what she sees on my face, but it can't be good.

"Forget it. Never mind, let's just go to bed, all right?"

Forgetting is one of the many things I'm not capable of doing.

I'm laughing as my spotted almost-nephew twitches his nose just inches from my face. My breath creates momentary patterns in his fur.

"Don't do that," Stephanie snaps. She's lounging on her bed, staring at the wall, the ceiling, staring at anything that's empty of rabbits.

"What?"

"Pretend like he's a real baby."

"He is. He's your baby." I stare at her, saying nothing more. It seems we're finally going to do this.

"It's a fucking rabbit, Kendra. Just a fucking rabbit."

"He came out of your fucking body. Look, I'm the one who drove you all this way. I'm the only one who—"

"You're so holier-than-thou. Like that's going to change your real problem, Miss Perfectly Unloved."

"Shut the fuck up, Stephanie. Now."

But she doesn't.

"Mom felt sorry for you and your fucked-up family. Told me Christians make an effort." Stephanie's expression is an unholy mixture of rage, guilt, and worst of all, pity.

"I am *not* killing your babies. Most of them will die out there. You realize that, right, Ms. Christian Charity?"

"Along with the millions of others. If you're so hot to play rabbit mama, you keep them." And then with that Steph is gone, car keys in hand, leaving me with all seven of her blessed offspring. I'm pretty sure she's not coming back.

Sister Francis and her towels arrive sometime afterward.

"The thing about rabbits," Sister Francis says, "is that they make good eating." She isn't smiling this morning. Worse still, she's looking me directly in the eye.

"What?"

"Not people, dear. Other creatures: coyotes and hawks and such. The Lord knows that I've prayed, but it seems like the world keeps getting darker each day. I wish God could have found a different way."

I look down at the spotted bunny cradled in my arms and say nothing. I just want this conversation to end. But it seems Sister Francis hasn't finished.

"Have you ever seen baby owls, owlets, with all that fuzz, and that funny way they have of tripping about on their oversized talons?"

"Yeah, on YouTube maybe."

"Did you know those fuzzy baby owls will kill a mouse or a mole, tear them apart, and eat them while they're still alive? It shouldn't be a big surprise, but somehow it always is: killing is the way of our Lord."

I don't disagree. But I want to. The baby is twitching in my arms, hind legs thumping against my forearm as he dreams of running or leaping in some field. He's not frightened. He has not even a raindrop of fear.

"Here, let me take him," Sister Francis says, reaching for Cole with practiced hands. I let her take him and watch as the baby settles for a moment. "A rabbit is a blessing, just like every other new life. A few bunnies in the right place can change everything, Kendra. And sometimes the world needs to change." Sister Francis pauses, hands Cole back to me, wipes the tears from my cheeks.

My hands tremble, just a little, as I hold Cole close to my chest. I used to go to Steph's house on Saturday mornings. Sunday mornings the Meyer family went to church, but on Saturdays Mrs. Meyer would always make me waffles. On Saturdays my own mother slept, or wept, or wandered in from wherever smoking her Virginia Slims.

"I don't think the Lord wants to be cruel," Sister Francis says. "People call it the apocalypse, but it's nothing more than another Godly act of global re-creation. All these bunnies are guiding a vast new web of life across the land. Unlike the Flood, I just don't think God wants us to be a part of it anymore."

"Cottontails breed the fastest." Sister Francis reaches over and strokes Cole's soft head. "The kindness of a quick human death. Perhaps that's what the Lord had in mind."

In the end I keep one of the bunnies. Fair or not, it's Cole. He's just not suited to this new wild world. Maybe that's what Francis was praying for all these weeks.

I stand in the open doorway of cottage number eleven, Cole in my arms, and watch as Sister Francis loads her truck and heads out into the desert with the latched rabbit cage. And in some wordless manner I try to pray. I wish all those rabbits well.

Cole shifts in my arms, trying to press even closer. Despite the heat and the broken friendship and the impossibility of the world ever going back, the Lord has provided. I've somehow found a companion to keep me company in this new rabbit-blessed End of Days.

The Woman in the Woods

Papa's Death and the Orphan Train

NO MATTER HOW MANY TIMES Horace told her different, Eliza knew her brother was wrong. The woman in the woods didn't look the least bit dead. The woman in the woods looked beautiful. With her long flowing hair and a leaf-gold cape, she made Eliza think of an ancient Irish queen. Of course, the woman didn't speak as she made her way along the trail. The woman was communing with her subjects, the dead and dying trees.

Sometimes Eliza suspected her brother's heart was an ancient stone, rigid as a dead man's body. "You don't try hard enough to remember," Horace accused whenever he caught her following the leaf-cape of the woman in the woods. "I think that's why Mother still hasn't come."

Horace's fingers were skeletal thin and oh so hungry. His eyes dark as empty holes. Once upon a time, before the scream of metal against metal had mixed with all those other screams, before she and Horace and the Orphan Train had arrived in the woods, Horace had been different. Back then, Horace had loved the hills on the west side of Manhattan almost as much as he loved these woods. He'd loved rolling barrels through the alley next to their apartment and yelling at the top of his lungs. One autumn day he'd tucked one of their father's many hand-rolled cigarettes behind his ear and chased a wooden barrel down the steep hill on Strathmore Street, grinning and making Eliza swear she wouldn't tell, even as he flipped and fell and lay sprawled across the paving stones at the bottom. Eliza had screamed then too despite Horace's laughter, wrapped her arms round his neck.

"It's all right, Eliza." Horace had that sweet smile slipping across his face, the one he saved just for her.

"It's all right," he repeated. "I promise. I'm not gonna die."

And, being little, Eliza had believed him.

Horace, it seemed to Eliza, had stopped smiling once they reached the Iowa woods.

Cholera, Horace had called it when their father died. "Old Mr. Goehle looked just like that," Horace said as he leaned over the straw mattress, looking at the skeletal man who used to be their father. Horace the truth teller. Horace the unflinching. Horace dragging Eliza down the stairs and away.

"But Momma is still—"

"Orphans," Horace cut in, ignoring the way Eliza pinched at his hand. "Good as, anyway."

That was the beginning.

Memories, Horace said, were the important thing. Memories stopped you yearning. Memories kept you from forgetting who you really were.

The women at the New York Children's Aid Society gave Horace and Eliza black, shiny shoes. They made sure both Eliza and Horace were scrubbed clean. Then they proclaimed Eliza and Horace ready for their new lives. Some kids waved from the train's many windows. And why not. Goodbye dead Father. Goodbye teary-eyed and raging Mother. Goodbye strangers who ignored your hunger and walked on by.

New York, Pennsylvania, Michigan, Illinois. And then came Iowa and the lightning storm. Everything a blur of screams and tumbling limbs and sudden flashes of color against the night.

Some memories Eliza wanted to forget: the freshly fallen corpses that had littered the clearing, the splinters of yellowish wood and twisted lengths of bark. Just beyond the train, Eliza had recognized the bodies of the two matrons, still wearing their special matron capes. Though eventually they were gone—or "decomposed," as Horace repeatedly explained.

After that came the winter snow and the silence with only the groan of the leafless trees. Until the woman appeared.

The woman in the woods was nothing like the matrons on the train or the mother Horace kept talking on and on about. No matter how often the woman and her golden cape wandered away, she always returned.

HORACE AND THE PASSAGE OF TIME

Before the trees and the night sky, there had been a city train station, soot-stained. Some kids, like Horace and Eliza, had a parent in tow. Most did not. They all wore clean clothes, black shoes, combed hair. A few kids had a valise or a cloth bag. Horace and Eliza sat together in a corner of the train car, pressed tightly together, holding nothing but each other while some of the bigger boys pressed their heads through an open window waving goodbye. Only the matron spoke to them, checking their names off her list. Eliza hadn't wanted to talk to anyone besides Horace anyway.

When the train first arrived in these woods, Horace used to cook roots they dug up in the coals of the fire. He used to make forest tea in an old tin can. Now the tin can sat unused.

No more train station clocks. No more conductors with watches. No more New York City time. And yet they kept waiting. Horace had explained so many times that Eliza could recite the reasons herself: When something disappeared, rotted, floated away, it was gone and could never come back. That was why they had to wait for Mother. That was why mist and floating and following those matrons wasn't right.

In the woods, Eliza relied on the sun to reveal the time of day. The maples, the sumac, the ferns helped out with the season of the year. And Horace confirmed how old she was. "You're such a baby, Eliza," he said. "You still need someone to take care of you," he said her. "Eliza, when are you going to grow up?" Who needed calendars and birthday candles? Eliza had Horace.

Time pressed against Eliza's shoulders. Time sucked the last gasp of air from Eliza's lungs. Time, Horace said, kept flowing even if no one watched. Mother, he promised, would come.

Eliza was no longer so sure. Time, it seemed to Eliza, was the only powerful magic left—that and the woman in the woods. Though with each day the woman's magic seemed less real. The woman couldn't even open her eyes. Some days she seemed more gray than golden, a smoke phantom among the trees.

ENDURING

Some moments are about enduring. Some about forgetting. Other moments have to be re-explained.

Once there had been a man and a woman. They lived in a tenement in the west end of the city. Horace and Eliza lived with them too. The man wore a black cap. His faded trousers weren't smeared with forest dirt. A hand-rolled cigarette hung from his lips. When the man talked, his cigarette moved up and down.

The conductor had held out his watch, showing Eliza the time. Still, Eliza refused to go alone. The man said he understood how Eliza felt. Of course Horace could go too.

People rushed across the platform: frowning people and tear-stained people. Children filled the train cars, leaned out of half-open windows, pressed their faces against the soot-speckled glass.

And all the while the conductor was holding out his watch, showing both Eliza and Horace, explaining why the train had to pull away. "You kids are the lucky ones. A new home. A new life. It's way past time."

Silently, Eliza disagreed. Lucky was finding a silver dollar on the sidewalk. Lucky was catching your mother laughing somewhere nearby. Lucky was noticing your father's smile.

Lucky was not riding an over-full train away from the man and the woman and everyone else Eliza had ever known—everyone except for Horace.

ELIZA BECOMES TIME

Time endured. Time forgot. Time played and watched the woman in her golden-leaf cape walk the woods, her eyes closed. Some days the woman's face seemed to vanish into mist or smoke, no different from Horace's campfire when they first arrived.

Watching the woman didn't feel lucky anymore. The woman in the cape made Eliza feel sad.

Eliza trailed the woman round the birch with its split trunk, through the stand of pines. No matter how many times they looped through the trees, Eliza always kept a little less than three feet away. Horace would approve of her careful distance. But Eliza wasn't so little anymore. Eliza had her own thoughts.

"Hey," Eliza called. "Hey," she repeated when the woman didn't answer, didn't falter, didn't change in any way. The woman's pace was as steady as a train on a track that hadn't yet broken.

Until now.

Eliza sped up. Despite the cape and the hidden face, Eliza knew the woman's hair was pale white-blonde and that her lips were a silent pink slash that cut across her face.

Eliza was less than an arm's breadth, less than a tree trunk's width away. She could see a dense network of raised veins like maple leaves running across the woman's cape. And the scent. The woman smelled of sadness and ash. She smelled weary, like someone who'd been walking for a very long time. She smelled like Eliza felt.

Only a single footstep left, less than a foot. Eliza reached out and felt the brittle veins and warm, heavy smoke. Felt her hands moving through the woman into nothingness—the relief of it—not ever coming out on the other side.

Once, long ago, there had been a woman who had worn a green woolen coat. As the conductor closed the final door, Eliza had seen the woman elbowing her way through the crowds to the train car. The woman had called out words Eliza couldn't recall. Horace said the woman in her green woolen coat had promised—cross-your-heart promised—"soon enough" and "won't forget," but all Eliza could remember was her face looking all crinkly and strange.

Eliza had been little then. But everything changes. Even the woman in the woods with her closed eyes and her ashy scent. All changed.

In the empty Iowa woods, Eliza and Horace sat on the softened remains of a pine tree. Mildewed remnants of bags lay tumbled across the clearing, along with other things, white and hard. The train cars with their shattered windows lay on their sides.

And still no mother arrived to claim them. Eliza was tired. The trees were dark shadows in an even darker night.

"Horace, when is Mother going to show up?"

"Soon, Eliza."

"But, Horace, there's no one—"

"When you're truly dead it's even worse," Horace said.

Eliza stared at the narrow pricks of starlight and the looming trees, only half-listening to the other things Horace had to say. The wind wrapped its way through the rustling autumn leaves. And still Horace kept on talking, explaining why she was still so little, explaining why they needed to wait for Mother, explaining the meaning of hope, and family, and the end of time.

"It'll be better tomorrow, Eliza. I cross-my-heart promise."

Horace sounding like Mother yet again.

A Pinhole of Light

Waiting

LIKE THIS LIFE, the afterlife is unfair. A woman dies at twenty-nine and leaves her infant daughter behind. Eight years later she is still trapped on the other side. When I'm in my happiest frame of mind, I imagine Veronica searching for my darkroom each time I turn on the blood-red light. In my darkest moments, I know I'm failing her. She still hasn't arrived.

I'm an experienced photographer. I should be able to do better.

Forget ghost stories and the spiritual emanations reported at places like Gettysburg and Edinburgh Castle. Forget death's cricket song: the sound that slips across no matter what we living humans do. True paths between this world and the next appeared less than two hundred years ago when Joseph Nicéphore Niépce developed the first photograph. Niépce exposed a specially treated sheet of pewter for eight hours. The image was hard to make out, but it was a photograph all the same: a view of Niépce's estate from a second-story window. Niépce's photograph was the first physical pathway between the living and the dead. It wasn't the last. After Niépce came Louis Daguerre with his daguerreotypes and Henry Fox Talbot and his paper-based process. Miraculous—all of it. With each developed print another physical doorway appeared.

Long before Veronica's death and everything that followed, I understood the power of film. The one secret that all photographers know: Only physical images offer an actual path to our living world. It is the chemicals—the darkness—the photographer's intention—that cuts through death's wall. No photographer is ever really alone. When we're working, our darkrooms are like crowded railway stations: the dead passing through with each developed frame.

At night in my darkroom, I soak my limbs in developer, fixer, rinse, and then stare—hopeful—as the ghosts rise from the pictures I've imprinted on my arms: a longhaired child with stick-thin limbs, a scowling old woman with a limp, a village, a traveling horde, a forgotten family, the father carrying their smallest child. No matter what I try, it is always dead strangers who follow my guideposts back to the land of the living. My wife Veronica's face is never among them. And so, each night after our daughter, Jenny, goes to bed, I turn on the blood-red light, submerge my arms, and try again.

OUR AKSNES FAMILY

After my parents died, my Grandmother Henrietta raised me. Henrietta Aksnes and her orphan grandson Geir, I overheard a neighbor say, as though we were misplaced characters from a Dickens novel: *David Copperfield* or *Oliver Twist*.

Black-and-white images of Aksnes ancestors lined the hallways and parlor walls of Grandmother's home, a timeworn brownstone near the center of town. Those pictures, with their egg-white-treated albumen paper and the brownish black-tea highlights, were my first introduction to photography— dead eyes following me from the house's many corners.

In my own home on Lyman Street, all the photographs are of a single face, that of my wife Veronica. It's eight years since Veronica's passing. These days the Aksnes family is down to three people: me, my daughter Jenny, and my cousin and oldest friend Peter. He moved in soon after Veronica died and, thank God, he stayed

Peter with his blond Nordic hair and long limbs. My sunny, sunny cousin. I don't know where he got the knack, or how he passed it on to Jenny.

"Beets don't mean Christmas, Uncle Pete," Jenny declared at our family's annual Christmas dinner. At nine years old, she had no trouble stating her opinion.

I watched as she pushed the salad, with its gherkins and cubed vegetables, to a corner of her plate.

"Jenny, Uncle Pete went to a lot of trouble," I warned, though I understood where she was coming from. The dish, with its beets and apples and boiled carrots, wasn't exactly kid fare.

"Not much Santa in that particular salad." Peter nodded his agreement and pushed his own portion to the side of his plate. "Or reindeer. They're both too chewy." He grinned, clearly anticipating her response.

"Uncle Pete, eating Santa is not funny."

"Reindeer are delicious though, right? Super delicious." Pete snorted and shook his head, pantomiming a reindeer shaking off the snow.

Jenny's glare lasted maybe a second before she gave in and grinned. Peter had charmed her. Of course he had. Jenny is our family's baby. The living light of our lives.

Peter and I have no one else. Our parents and grandparents are buried less than two miles away in Farsdale's Forest Glen Cemetery, along with Veronica. Veronica's grave is easy to find. At Jenny's insistence, a small teddy bear is taped to either side of the gravestone.

Fear. Love. Obsession. Take your pick. Teddy bears and good intentions aren't enough. Since that final night, that hospital phone call, I've known exactly what this family was missing, Veronica.

Of course, I wasn't the only Aksnes on a mission.

An Incomplete World

Like any obsession, the mural in Jenny's bedroom started small. In fact, it took two fighting squirrels for me to realize what was going on.

Five-year-old Jenny and I knelt before the bay window at the front of the house, pillows under our knees, looking onto the street, our usual Sunday morning routine. Or Jenny watched the street. Mostly I watched Jenny, her expression so much sunnier than more hesitant me. My daughter smiled her crooked smile as two squirrels chased each other across the street, over a wooden fence, and into our neighbor's yard. Suddenly, she busted out laughing. One of the squirrels had scampered up a maple tree and onto Mrs. Tomasics's roof. The other squirrel, smaller than the first, remained below, chittering with anger, but unwilling to risk a rooftop fight.

"You know, Daddy, the ghosts like it better on Mrs. Tomasic's roof too," Jenny said, glancing up at me. "That's what I told Uncle Peter when he tried to sketch Mr. Tomasic inside his house."

"Ah."

The mural project wasn't exactly a surprise. Peter is a painter, a sculptor, and an all-round crafty guy. Since Jenny first started walking and talking, the two of them had spent their time on clay creatures, collages, and papier-mâché. The mural was their most ambitious project. Peter and Jenny had been putting in long hours, slowly sketching images across the wall facing Jenny's bed. I'd expected Jenny would lose interest. Five years old generally means enthusiasm without much follow-through.

"You guys are still working on that?" I finally managed, trying to not frown. Sunlight streamed in through the window. Jenny's head was bathed in light. She tilted up her head, her eyes meeting mine.

"Come see, Daddy." Jenny grabbed my hand and tugged me toward her room.

What could I do? My girl actually sounded happy and Peter wasn't even around.

What Jenny and Peter had managed in the month since they'd started the project was amazing. That was my first thought. Some areas of the mural were painted while others were just sketched. On the right side of the mural was a miniature version of the east end of our town, Farsdale. A red-hued barrier divided the town from the emptiness of the unpainted left. Peter's faint pencil marks indicated that the non-Farsdale side of the barrier was unfinished rather than intentionally blank.

As I stepped closer, I noticed something new; the picture had extended to a second wall. On the wall that divided her room from my darkroom, Jenny had drawn a thick line with a charcoal pencil, identifying where the red barrier would wander next. Next to Jenny's line, Peter had marked a few preliminary sketches with faint, careful pencil. One reminded me of Grandmother Henrietta's old house. It seemed they were recreating our entire town.

"More?" I asked

"Of course, Daddy. It took me a while to figure out where the red barrier should go," she continued in a rush. "I drew it out all by myself. Uncle Peter said it was really good." Jenny sounded just a shade concerned. The beginning of a frown line had appeared on her forehead. I wasn't showing the appropriate parental enthusiasm.

"Jenny, it looks terrific."

Aksnes. Obsession is our natural territory. For whatever reason, Jenny and Peter were determined to recreate our world, and the next, one paint stroke at a time. Who was I to say no? Glass houses and all that, or in my case closed darkroom doors.

And by some mysterious alchemy, in our house mural and photograph have always been linked.

FLESH WORK

For four years, after my wife's death, I pulled the paper images from their chemical baths and watched as the ghosts rose up through the images and wandered through my home. Mere strangers, none of them were invited to stay.

That night was different. I'd finally recognized the need for deeper sacrifices and put the photographic paper away.

It was long past Jenny's bedtime. I'd finished my darkroom work. My body hadn't yet recovered. Point of fact, I was still trembling, waves of hot and cold crashing against my skin. Peter had gone out, though I knew he'd be back before Jenny woke up.

But Jenny wasn't sleeping, instead she stood in my bedroom doorway— all skinny limbs and large brown eyes. Between her outstretched arms hung a piece of paper almost three feet long. The paper has been cut into a series of paper dolls: eight identical figures in white dresses, with white stockings, white shoes, and paper-white skin.

"Daddy, look at my ghost people."

"Paper dolls, honey, not ghosts," I corrected. Why wasn't she in bed? It felt like a phalanx of tiny angels were hard at work beneath my skin, carving me apart one nerve ending at a time. Each sharp jab of pain pulled at my attention. Tears welled in my eyes. It was all I could do not to claw at my arms and pull away the skin. Despite the burning, I noticed Peter's scissors dangling from Jenny's left hand. Jesus. He'd forgotten and left them out again. Five year olds aren't supposed to play with sharp things.

Sometimes parents are only, barely, good enough. I didn't take the scissors away. I didn't tell Jenny to put those scissors down. Instead, I bent over my bed and started to straighten the quilt. If I was lucky the distance between us would camouflage my trembling, bloody arms. If I was fucking lucky Jenny would put the scissors down and go back to bed.

Jenny remained in the doorway, that stubborn look on her face. "Daddy, we don't collect paper dolls. We—"

"And we don't collect ghosts." I tugged the top of the quilt and didn't let go. Teeth. Or a knife. The pure clean pain of a naturally occurring wound. Anything would be better than this.

"But we let them visit, right?" Jenny replied, her mind still on her row of paper ghosts.

"Right." I took a staggered breath, exhaled, and then started in on my bedside table, stacking the books into a careful stepped pyramid. Sweat trickled down my back. More sweat rested above my upper lip. And still Jenny didn't budge.

"Ghost mommies," Jenny reiterated, rattling her sheet of paper women. The look she gave me—even at five years old.

"Okay." I attempted to keep my tone even. "Though only one ghost mommy, Mommy Veronica. All right?"

Jenny nodded. "Daddy, what did you do to your arms?"

"Oh, just a darkroom thing." I should've just dealt with the fucking scissors. Of course she was going to ask.

My four-year epiphany: that night I didn't use tongs to handle the developing paper. After four tediously obsessive years, I finally had the necessary revelation. Flesh. If a photographer's intent is necessary to bring the dead back, how much more powerful is the effect when you use that photographer's actual body? That night, for the first time, the Kodak XTOL Black and White Developer and the Ilford Rapid Fixer were busily opening doorways directly into my skin.

"Daddy, can you tuck me in?"

"Sure. Of course."

The ghost horde would carry my Veronica up through my bleeding flesh ready to try again. Dear Lord, let that be true.

Technical Limitations

True miracles are as ephemeral as a child's paper doll. When Veronica and I stood before that priest, my wife pledged her love "until her dying day." Niépce and Talbot performed their own miracle with pewter and paper, but they never promised they would last forever. Now, after just two hundred years, the gaps in death's wall are sealing up again.

Digital cameras and smartphones have infested this physical world. Each month we lose another brand of film stock as yet more film cameras sit unused on some collector's shelf. Meanwhile collection after collection of photographs moves from the physical domain into the digital world. With each digital image we lose another opportunity to guide our loved ones back home. It is the physical that draws the spirits back. Digital images all have the same basic limitation. They're incapable of connecting us to the dead.

It's been eight years. Veronica has missed our daughter's first steps, her first words, her first day of school. Meanwhile, I still crave Veronica, her skin and lips, that moist warmth as I pressed my body into hers, but most of all I crave the way she used to look at me, as though my eyes carried her paradise.

When I'm alone in the house, Jenny at school or out with Peter, I find myself scanning their mural. These days the twisting images that stretch across Jenny's bedroom walls seem to change almost overnight. The red barrier has become more complicated over time, a swirl of burnt orange and brilliant poppy that binds the world of the living from the land of the dead. On one side of the red wall is our town of Farsdale, including Lyman Street. Across from our house, huddled against the chimney, I recognize the face of our neighbor, Mr. Tomasic, an elderly man who died years ago. Stretched along the soot-stained exterior of Our Lady of Perpetual Hope High School is the face of Jack Nevinsmith, the kid who slit his wrists when Peter and I studied there. So many lost faces are scattered across our town. Not one of them is Veronica. It's almost like Jenny and Peter are trying to keep her out. But I know that can't be true.

In the last few months, a drab, haze-filled land has appeared on Jenny's walls. Beneath the haze is a painted city with a multitude of crystalline towers. A pale ocean extends past the horizon, surrounding the city, while a wide swath of field leads from the city to death's red wall. When I look closely at the field, I see scores of bent necks, tangles of arms, a mass of torsos and legs. I try not to glance at the field too often. I keep my eyes on Farsdale instead.

PHOTOGRAPHIC DEVELOPMENT

My grandmother is long dead, and no afterlife doorway is going to bring her back. Still, each night as I work in my darkroom, I can hear Grandmother Henrietta's voice somewhere nearby: "Not too much, Geir. Tone it down. You're scaring all the good people away."

No doubt, she's right. Even my hands are revealing: orange-and-mustardtinted cracks burrow deep into my fingers. Burn marks pockmark my arms. But my damage goes so much farther. A single monochromatic photograph is permanently etched along each arm. From a distance the photographs are likely mistaken for tattoos. It took me nights of darkroom work, calibrating the developing images until I heard the faint *shhrushhhhh* sound of death slipping through the newly opened doors.

Each night I redevelop both arms, helping through the spirits desperate to return. On one arm an empty highway edges up from my wrist, and then is lost in the bend of my elbow, the California coastal road near Big Sur. An Ansel Adams print from 1953. The image on the other arm follows a set of broad stone steps—the Mills College Amphitheater—as they curve around my shoulder and across my chest. The original picture was taken by one of my favorite photographers, Imogen Cunningham, in 1920.

I'm not the first to understand the power of architecture and landscapes. Adams's photographs of McDonald Lake and El Capitan were full of empty space just waiting for the dead's hurried footsteps. Cunningham's architectural work is much the same. My body aims to repeat the trick: a photographic bridge that traverses the barrier between life and death. Lately,

I've started wondering. Architecture and landscapes. What about the power of love and passion: Jenny, Peter, Veronica's broken self?

Grandmother, I'm sure, does not approve of any of my darkroom theories.

Turns out the dead don't have to travel back in order to haunt you.

NIGHT PATROL

It's 3 a.m. and the ghosts are busting through.

"Dad, the lonely people woke me up again," Jenny calls out. At nine years old, my jaded child doesn't even bother to get out of bed. If it's midnight, she knows I've already pressed through the barrier.

"Just close your eyes, sweetheart." I'm holding my arms submerged in a vat of rapid fixer. I try to take shallow breaths, fail, and take a big gulp of air, feeling the familiar bite as the fumes burn the back of my throat. My hands have more than the usual quantity of sores. I try not to think about what will happen if they start to pop, revealing the raw skin underneath. Over all these worries, I hear the soft *shhrushhhhh* sound that signals death has found its way through my doorway.

Jenny will fall back to sleep. Please, let that be true.

"Daddy! The ghost people won't stop whispering. And the baby one is stinky, like that milk you spilled in the car. I need Grandmother Henrietta's glass."

"All right. I'll be right there." I use my gentle voice, will myself to stay calm while a multitude press against my forearms. I can feel each spirit trying to force itself to the front of the line. The pressure is like a needle pumping liquid into already-bursting veins. These souls are angry or desperate or simply stubborn. Whatever. I'm closing the door. After six hours of trying and failing, the lonely fuckers have woken up Jenny.

Four years of practice has made me careful. I wait until I'm sure the *shhrushhhhh* sound has died away completely and the path is completely clear before I pull my arms free of the metal canisters. Even then there is more to do. I rinse the fixer from my arms, towel off, and wait for the pain to quiet before finally turning off the red safety light.

When she was alive, Veronica said things I wish I could forget. "I can't stand the way you look at me." "There is nothing that would compel me to return." Death is supposed to make everything different. That's what I've been pretending. But Veronica, my Veronica, what if she wants to stay lost?

"Dad?"

"Milk's on its way."

I pad down the hallway toward the kitchen. Our house is a single-story bungalow. Veronica loved the iron railing fence and the brick steps that led up to the front door. The rust and crumbling brick were all part of the charm. That first summer Veronica and I set some geraniums, all fuzzy, pale-green stems, on the sill behind the bay window's curtains. Grandma flowers, we called them. Our ironic shrine to all those women who were dead and gone. The geraniums no longer strike me as funny, but they stay. Like so much else—the roses, the bedroom furniture, the toppling collection of books on the living room mantel—I worry one of them might be the necessary key that guides Veronica back home.

Jenny. I pull Grandmother Henrietta's old tarnished tea glass from the kitchen cupboard and warm a saucepan of milk and honey. Back in Jenny's room I prop her up in a nest of stuffed animals and pillows, just the way she likes it, and watch her sip from her special cup, the one that is supposed to mean I love her—which as it turns out I do, a surprising truth I still don't know what to do with.

"You're going to stay. Right, Dad?"

"Yes. Of course, I'm going to stay." I move the teddy bears, Mr. Cuddles and Fuzzy Bear, off the bed, and settle myself in their place. Fuzzy Bear is the toughest of bears, the one set closest to the bedroom door at night. At nine years old Jenny still has a nightlight and a horde of stuffed animals, including the two teddy bears that guard the perimeter of her bed.

"Dad, what if Mommy tries to visit and Fuzzy Bear won't let her in? The ghosts are always telling me how tired they are, and Fuzzy Bear is really strong."

"Jenny, it'll all be fine." I refrain from mentioning that the other spirits have managed to make it through. I know my kid. She's got something specific on her mind.

"But what about you, Dad? You could die? That could happen, right? Fuzzy Bear might not trust it's really you."

"Jenny" I pause. "Fuzzy Bear has known me his entire life. Even if I were dead, that wouldn't change." I smile at her, adjust my position on the bed, and try not to wince when I bang my arm against the wall.

Jenny smiles back, but that worried crinkle still runs across her forehead.

"How about a password?" I ask with sudden inspiration. "Words only Fuzzy Bear and I know." I grab Fuzzy Bear from the floor. He has a worn and stained stomach and a tiny drop of dried glue at the edge of one of his button eyes. He can see in the dark with those eyes; that's what Jenny tells me. Things can get rough at night. Peter has had to stitch his tongue back on at least twice. But Fuzzy Bear is the King of Calm. He is the Emperor of Secrets. Jenny is no fool. She chose well. Fuzzy Bear is the friend you can trust to keep you safe when the monsters arrive. I whisper in his ear as Jenny looks on. I watch as the worry crease smooths away and her smile widens. I can see her left eyetooth, the one that twists a little to the side.

"Now he'll know for sure," Jenny declares.

"Yep. Even if I sound funny or have a cold or lose my face or some such thing."

"Or die." Jenny likes to be specific. She takes a sip of milk, waiting for my response.

"Yes. Or die." I take a slow breath. Right now at least, I'm alive and sitting at the bottom of Jenny's bed, talking with my favorite girl.

"What was Grandmother Henrietta like?" Jenny asks. I don't talk about my childhood much. My own dead parents. The glass is the only memento I kept from Grandmother Henrietta's house.

"Dead," I reply, seemingly not answering her question at all, but making her laugh—just a little—and roll her eyes. Death does not frighten my Jenny, not in the way it frightens most people.

"Dad." She glances at me. "You know Cousin Peter says Grandmother wasn't all that bad." She gives me a stern look over the top of her cup. "You shouldn't be so hard on her."

"Cousin Peter didn't have to live with her." Then I make my Grandmother face—squinty eyes, twisted lips, hands held up like crippled and grasping claws—and Jenny snorts, milk froth flying up and landing on her nose. Subject dropped.

Show Time

It's Friday night, not late, maybe 7:00 p.m. Peter is wrapping my arms like he does at the end of each week. But he keeps glancing at his phone as the buzz of yet another text rises up on the screen. A smiling woman's picture shows up: long hair, heart-shaped face, and woolen mittens she uses to frame her happy face.

"Soooo who's the friend?" I ask, trying to hold my arms still. These days even the gentlest of handling is hard to take.

"Her name's Fiona."

"Looks like she's been in your phone for a while. That's a winter pic."

"Yeah. A while," Peter agrees.

"Linen shirt and skinny jeans. Peter, man. I should have known something was up. Don't let my arms keep you. Really."

"This won't take long. Keep still, Geir. I'm trying not to hurt you."

"Why don't you ever bring her over?"

"You know why."

"What? No, I don't."

"Jenny already has enough competition. You and your Veronica. She doesn't need to see Uncle Pete slipping away as well."

"Peter, that's not—"

"Just drop it, Geir. It's okay. Fiona isn't expecting me until Jenny goes to bed."

I open my mouth, close it again, hold in my sudden flash of anger. But Peter and I both know it's there.

In silence, Peter finishes tying the bandages across my arms. When he's done he's careful not to pat my shoulder or arm, no different from any other week. Even without anything touching my skin, my entire body prickles with fire.

"I better go help Jenny," Peter says. "I promised her we'd finish the hospital section before bedtime."

"Sounds good." I feel like a shit. There is no way I can blame my sunny, sunny cousin. The golden boy who just visited Grandmother's house. Despite my blunders, Peter stuck with me during my marriage and stuck with me after it as well. He camped out on the couch for six months when he realized Jenny and I weren't managing all that well. And then he moved in. Of course, he has his own life. Eight years is a long time—for both of us.

I never start work until Jenny is in bed and asleep. But tonight, despite Peter's date, Peter and Jenny seemed determined to outwait me. I try surfing the web, looking at the digitalized version of the George Eastman Museum's permanent collection, but it just makes me antsy. Depressed. How many people will print these ghost-empty digital copies? How many people would even care if the originals disappeared?

It's now 10:00 p.m.

"You guys still at it?" I'm standing in the doorway of Jenny's room. The bedroom lamp throws both light and shadow across the mural. The figures in the City of the Dead and the surrounding land look like warriors or battling monsters, depending on where you stand. No doubt Peter intended them to come out that way.

"Just a few more minutes, Dad. I think we're really onto something," Jenny says. Tonight the two of them seemed to be concentrating on the Farsdale side of the mural. In fact, it looks like they're both focused on Lyman Street. Jenny's body blocks my view of whatever she's painting.

"I think I'll just get started in the darkroom." I can't wait any longer. My body itches and thrums, demanding its share of pain.

"I can tuck her in." Peter turns and tries to smile. It's not convincing. I probably look like some strung-out junky, waiting for his corrosive fix. I feel like one.

"Thanks, man."

"Night, Dad." Jenny doesn't even turn around.

Moments later I'm inside my darkroom, the door locked. My arms are submerged in a vat of developer. It takes less than a minute of waiting for the ghosts to crowd into my flesh. Each desperate spirit takes its own tiny bite. Eight years of punishment. More and more my arms feel like virtual facsimiles of a living man's flesh. I no longer bleed when I submerge my arms. My skin itches but nothing more as the first wave of sound crests, high enough to slip across my living photographic bridge.

Shhrushhhhh. The sound rises over the whirring of the darkroom's vent. *Shhrushhhhh.* I'm coming, that sounds says. I'm traveling over. I'm almost here. The dead rush along the steps of Cunningham's amphitheater, race down Ansel Adams's road. *Shhrushhhhh.* The sound compresses my eardrums. Fills my skull. The song has never been this loud before. Veronica. After all this time I still can't stop myself from hoping.

When the first spirit appears, biting into the bone of my left forearm, it's just another stranger. "Damn it." The words leak out.

I hear a knock on the door. "Geir?"

"Yeah?" My voice sounds rough, even to my own ears.

"I thought I'd stay in tonight, after all." It's Peter. Jenny is probably just behind him, the two of them covered in a rainbow of splattered paint.

"Okay. Sure," I say, but what I really mean is why. Peter loves both Jenny and me, but Peter has plans. Skinny jeans and a linen shirt. Peter's in love, or lust, trying for some sort of connection anyway. His heart is a multitude compared to my one.

I am thinking about Veronica's rage, how she was that last time I saw her—and how I was—which is probably why I don't move my arms from the developer to the stop bath. And why I forget to set the timer.

THE END

That last week, I sat next to Veronica's bed, just another useless spouse, determined to follow the script. I was a photographer. I could sense the ghosts slipping under Veronica's skin, jabbing shots of rage and despair along her brain's neural network. Didn't mean I knew what to do about it.

"I've been doing some research," I babbled on. "You know there's other options besides meds. I read this really interesting article on TMS, transcranial magnetic stimulation. It lets you create new pathways in the brain."

"Jesus, Geir. Stop trying to fix me. Just because I'm not happy doesn't mean I'm not happy with who I fucking am."

My wife looked pretty, even with the meds and the fluorescent hospital lighting. The long fine strands of her hair clung to her face and spread outward like an ill-defined halo. I itched for my camera. For something to do.

"You should have just brought your rig and taken a few shots," Veronica said. She frowned and then turned her head away. "You could title the piece

'Woman in Psych Ward: Day Number Fifty-Two.' You could do a whole fucking series."

"I didn't come here to take pictures." I said, and then fell silent. We sat like that for the rest of the visit.

Of course Veronica was right: the lighting, that brutal look on her face. It would have made the perfect shot. Rage Against the Dying Night Day Number 52.

THE UNVEILING

Pain, sure, but I'm used to that. It's what I see in the metal canister that holds my attention. Cunningham's amphitheater and Adams's coastal road both show something new. Instead of a horde of desperate souls with wavering faces, a whole world is moving along my flesh-built bridge. The will-o-wisps are hard to make out, but I recognize the crystalline city with its towers and the ocean shrouded in fog. Peter and Jenny's mural with its blood barrier breached. It's like a collision of tectonic plates never meant to touch. The *shhrushhhhh* sound is missing, replaced by a sensation I haven't felt in all my darkroom years. It's like a multitude of fingertips moving across my body, their touch both soft and insistent, pressing in then abruptly pulling away, until another wave of seeking hands crowds in.

There's no smell. No spoiled-milk baby ghosts. No stink of sweat. Even the vinegary scent of my darkroom has disappeared. The living world is somewhere behind me. My body feels like it's stretched via a series of fishhooks attached to my back. I can't turn around. Veronica, a faded Veronica made up of a swirling shimmer of lips and hands and eyes, but Veronica all the same, is standing atop the field of bent necks and outstretched arms. It seems the only way she'll cross my bridge is if her world comes with her.

"You always were a selfish asshole," she says. The first words I've heard her utter in almost a decade. "Eight years and you still won't take the hint."

"I'm sorry. Veronica, I am just so sorry."

"You traveled all this way so I could make you feel better? Really?"

Veronica is a head shorter than me. When we were first together, I liked to slip my arms around her while she tucked her head against my chest, and then we would both hold on: thirty seconds, ninety, two whole minutes. That's how it went for a while anyway, and then she stopped, turned away first, complained about my "Geir drama," as in "Jesus, Geir. Just this once could you act like a normal human being." Which, of course, I can't—even now.

"I miss you, babe. Jenny does too. We want you to come back." The words sound all wrong, even to me.

"Jesus, Geir. Jenny doesn't even remember me."

I'm bad at love, that's what Veronica used to say. Looking at her now, my will-o-wisp wife, the bits and pieces of her body moving in and out of focus, the field's carnage rising up through the haze, I know she's right. Whatever or whoever she is, she's not the person I've been carrying in my mind.

"Veronica, life isn't so—"

"Shhh, God is singing," Veronica says, but being alive, even on the bridge, surrounded by the City of the Dead, I hear nothing.

"Veronica, I can get it right this time. I know I can."

"What are you talking about?" Her expression, her wavering, non-corporal expression is not that different from those last days in the hospital bed. Cold. Distant. Impatient.

"Don't you love me?"

"Geir."

"Admit it. We had something special."

"Had."

Veronica's body keeps shifting. It's hard to keep my eyes focused as sections of skull appear and then submerge again. Basic features like eyes and lips and nose fade in and out. It's as though Veronica doesn't remember how a body works anymore, what parts go where.

"I don't—"

"Geir, of course you do. It was over long before I used that razor blade." The expression on her face. After all these years, it's just the same, the irritation holding in check something far more primal. And then it seems the rage is unwilling to be tamped down any longer. I watch as Veronica pushes against the tarmac road and the stone amphitheater, as she pushes against my oh-so-human bridge. I can feel the power of the haze-covered ocean and corpse-strewn field gathering behind her. She speaks one final time: "No more." And then I'm tumbling, untethered.

Bile rises in my throat, my stomach rebelling as my body unravels back across the bleeding-red barrier, across the years of hiding in my darkroom, the years of no. The images on my arms, the Cunningham and Adams, slide off like the raw skin Grandmother used to remove before tossing the rest of the chicken leg into the cooking pot. And still my shorn body tumbles, through the rent, back to the living land of Farsdale.

Shhrushhhhh. Death's thrumming sounds like a slow-moving wave finally pulling away. And beyond it, a chorus of voices rushes out to follow. For a moment, I can hear God's song, death's entire composition, and then it's gone, replaced by silence.

"Geir? What the hell. Geir?"

When I open my eyes, there are no more translucent towers. No more haze. There are no finger fronds trying to stroke my still-living flesh. Veronica has discharged me back to our house on Lyman Street. Our house no longer.

Both Jenny and Peter are kneeling over me. Peter isn't smiling. He looks worried. Jenny looks plain scared.

"Geir, say something, or I'm calling a goddamn ambulance," Peter says.

"Uncle Peter, you said, you promised. The paint was supposed to fix things." My daughter, my Jenny, is crying, tears spilling down her cheeks.

I can feel moisture on my face. It seems I'm crying as well. I never do that.

I raise my left arm, my Cunningham arm, pat Jenny's cheek. The amphitheater steps have vanished. Instead, my arm is covered in paint, not just any paint, but a rendering of Jenny and Peter's blood-red wall. The painting continues on beyond the wall to the pale ocean and the crystalline city. Traversing it all is a multitude of lost, of dead, of will-never-travel-back faces.

"What the hell?" Every one of those painted faces looks like Veronica, her eyes unblinking as she says goodbye.

Eight years is enough. More than enough.

Truth time: It wasn't just that I couldn't make Veronica happy. What I was really good at was driving her to despair. The words might as well be chiseled on her gravestone: Geir Aknses drove me to this. I am the widower of a suicide. Of course, I got things wrong.

A PINHOLE OF LIGHT

After rinsing and rewrapping my arms, Peter heads out to meet Fiona, leaving me to tuck in Jenny.

"Mommy Veronica doesn't love you," Jenny says when I hand her the warm glass of milk. Her expression is calm. Veronica is just the name of someone she never really met.

"Yes," I say. I set both teddy bears on the edge of the bed just in case. Not that I'm expecting any more visitors. I've locked up my darkroom. And underneath the paint, my arms are covered in nothing but scars. The desperate ghosts are stuck on the other side now, along with Veronica.

"Dad, can you paint with me this weekend?"

"Sure."

"Uncle Peter says winter paintings send up dream flowers that last until spring."

"Huh. That sounds like Peter."

Stare at an image. Rewatch a movie. Retell a story. Do it often enough and the subject's power evaporates. Instead of darkroom-time, I tell Jenny a new story, holding an old photo album between us, pointing out the pictures. "Once there was a very wise and beautiful woman named Veronica with long brown hair and eyes that looked like a cloudless winter sky."

I am the camera, the lens, the opening through which all light must fall. I am a true photographer. I can let go of a broken image and move on.

One Thousand Paper Cranes

October 2026: Remembering the Past—Part 1

THERE IS A STORY Elijah likes to tell himself. This story is set long before the fire, more than ten years ago, back in 2015.

Elijah was the younger brother, only eight years old, and Callie was the older sister who sent handwritten notes to the dead. Callie had long curly hair that frizzed in the summer till it was just like Elijah's. Her skin was pale Irish, shades lighter than Elijah's. Elijah had never met his father, though their mother claimed he was Caribbean-American. From Antigua, she always added, as though that last detail made it magically true.

Callie and Elijah's mom paid the rent close enough to on time, bought the food, and slept in the largest bedroom in their apartment. But it was fourteen-year-old Callie who tucked Elijah in at night and told him bedtime stories. She told him stories when Uncle Eddie, or Uncle Arthur, or Uncle Whoever stopped coming round. She told him stories when Mom stumbled through the house, tinfoil and lighter in hand, already too high. And when he wanted to go outside with her and see the plasma-fueled stars, Callie told Elijah stories about how each one of her younger selves had found her place "somewhere up in the sky."

Call it basic neurobiology. Call it cellular death and chemical rewiring. The brain is constantly rewriting memories and cutting off unnecessary neurochemical connections, allowing the next version of a person to step

41

forward. Dried lizard skins. Caterpillars forgotten in a flurry of butterfly wings. People are never who they were before. Callie's story of star-bound younger selves was as good a description as any for the part that is lost.

And at eight years old, Elijah needed his bedtime stories.

"Some people believe if you really want something all you have to do is wish on a thousand paper cranes," Callie told Elijah. She adjusted his covers and settled herself against his feet. Elijah could hear Mom crying, the noise traveling through the closed bedroom door. This time the guy hadn't even made it to Uncle status.

"Yeah?" Elijah replied. Wishing paper sounded pretty good. And Callie knew all about folding cranes.

"All bullshit," Callie said.

"Callie!"

Callie waved away Elijah's little-boy gasp of outrage. "Point is, even if we fold a million cranes, fate still wins. It's biology that makes us who we are, Elijah. It's our very own bodies that force us to change. Not even the most powerful wishes can fight that."

Elijah couldn't remember a time when he didn't know this particular bedtime story. According to Callie, genetics was a slow-growing slime monster inside each and every brain. No matter how much Mom decided or learned or tried to feel better, the monster had its own plan written in little squiggles called DNA. Biology, Callie said, was merciless. In the end, the body was "DNA's bitch," pruning away memories and dreams, constantly warping the mind into something new.

"Those old Elijahs and Callies are gone," Callie said. "We can't change that."

It made Elijah's head hurt to think about it: All those old versions of himself lost for good no matter what he did.

"But then why do you keep making all those wishing cranes?"

"Jesus, Elijah," Callie's tone was full of well-practiced disgust. "Hopeless doesn't mean you shouldn't try. Sometimes, you know, that's kind of the point."

"Okay." Elijah often found Callie confusing. He was tired. Maybe in the morning it would all make more sense. Or maybe the version of Elijah who worried about understanding would have already floated away.

June 2021: Remembering the Past—Part 2

Callie hit her genetic fate when Elijah was fourteen and she was twenty. Scabs under her toenails, missing teeth like shadows in her mouth. Her skin yellowed, as though she'd been shooting iodine rather than Mexican ice. Life and her addict-prone biology knew just how to fuck things up.

It was 10:00 p.m. Callie lay stretched out on the bathroom floor while Elijah brushed his teeth. "Help me, Elijah," she whispered. "My old selves are dying faster than mayflies. Poor things hardly have any memories to keep them company."

"Callie, people change. Cells die. End of story." Elijah's eyes were on the mirror, the toothbrush grinding its way across his teeth.

"Bullshit. Look at you. Your brain is reworking a goddamn million neurons. This you is definitely gonna be dead by morning."

"Callie, can you please, just this once, shut up?" All those library books and *NOVA* specials Callie had made him sit through, and this was what the two of them ended up with: bullshit fantasies about dead sky-bound selves.

"Elijah."

"I'm tired." Elijah headed down the hallway, locking his bedroom door behind him.

A shuffle of feet and then a fist. "Elijah, goddamn it! Let me at least say goodbye before this you flies away."

Elijah could hear Callie's pounding fists slipping down toward the ground. He could almost see the accompanying slide of her body, her forehead now pressed against the cold wooden floor as she tried to peer through the inch-high gap at the bottom of his door.

And then the first paper crane sailed through the opening.

"Elijah," Callie murmured. "Please, don't be afraid."

A flurry of paper landed against the sky-blue rug, the bed frame, the bottom of Elijah's faded Star Wars curtains. Elijah closed his eyes, pressed his head against the doorframe. But the tears came anyway, Elijah crying as he stuffed those paper cranes under his mattress, behind his bureau, inside the winter boots that didn't fit him anymore. Broken Callie with her paper cranes and Elijah not that far behind.

43

OCTOBER 2026: THE ALMOST MIRACULOUS FUTURE

Elijah isn't a kid anymore. At nineteen, he listens to the news reports and reads the blog posts. He even pays attention when Callie's caseworker comes to call. A few months later when his own court-appointed lawyer makes her pitch, the story is a well-worn favorite.

The medical community, in tandem with the State of Connecticut, has a solution for Elijah and Callie and every other scramble-headed sinner. Chemical reclamation is the official term. Helpful, the newspapers and talking heads say. An actual solution to societal ills and personal pain.

Scientific advances happen all the time. Five years ago, Connecticut and Massachusetts, along with Vermont and New York, came together to fund the Emotional Literacy Project. The goal of the project was rehabilitation through chemically regulated, restricted-environmental-stimulation therapy (CR-REST).

In this world there is no magic. Instead, through the miracle of designer drugs, the state could now provide the equivalent of years of psychotherapy in just a few days. As everyone kept repeating, this was most definitely not a punishment. It was an insta-cure.

People are always trying to fix electrical devices and eradicate the unwanted glitch. Of course they think they can reboot a person and fix the world. Elijah knows he's nothing special; with a little help from his court appointed medical team, Elijah's Anger+10 / Despair+15 rating will disappear. New Elijah will be more than happy with the results. All those hard and ugly feelings—gone.

Bureaucrats like their processes and procedures. Even with all the evidence of Elijah's crime—the smoldering remnants of the apartment building and the sirens and all the rest—the court-appointed doctors are thorough. They write reports and present findings. Elijah has no brain lesions, no neurochemical imbalance. His microbiome—his gut flora—is of a recognized type. Elijah is on the negativity spectrum, but close enough that intervention is statistically likely to have an effect. Intervention, Dr. Kensington states from the witness stand, is key. Intensive therapy will help both Elijah and society.

Neither Callie nor Mom is sitting in the courtroom. Too traumatic, his lawyer explains. Instead, Elijah stands alone in front of the bench, determined not to cry.

It only takes two words for the judge to pass down his sentence: chemical reclamation. As far as the court is concerned, Elijah is just another stupid asshole who likes fire. Just another asshole who refuses to fly like one of Callie's paper cranes and find his peace.

2015: Elijah's First Flying Lesson—Part 1

A paper crane takes thirty-two folds. A few are unique. Most are nothing more than careful repeats of a previous step. In a house full of overflowing trash bags and almost-empty cupboards, in a neighborhood full of neighbors screaming through thin apartment walls, Callie learned the quiet art of folding from one of their mom's revolving door of boyfriends.

That Saturday in early May, eight-year-old Elijah sat curled in his usual corner of the couch. His legs were folded up against his chest while a rerun of his favorite cartoon, *Teen Titans Go!*, danced across the TV screen. Cyborg and Beast were singing—all bright greens and bold grays—while they taught Starfire the Pee Pee Dance.

"Step to the left, then step to the right."

"Put your knees together, and squeeze real tight."

A few feet away, Callie sat at the kitchen table, her head bent over a notebook. Behind her stretched the apartment's hallway with its closed bedroom doors. Even with the TV volume turned up past twenty, Elijah could hear his mother's side of the latest phone call. "Ray. Please, Ray. Don't be like that." And then she was sobbing, again.

"Mom always could cry like a boss," Callie said, loud enough to be heard over the song.

"Shut up, Callie." Elijah's eyes were on Cyborg and Robin, his ears trained to Beast Boy's laugh. Mom's sobs were nothing but background noise. Mom's sobs had nothing to do with Elijah at all.

"Elijah, you twerp, did you even hear me?" Callie wasn't working on her notebook anymore. She stood next to Elijah, bending down so that her face was level with his.

"Huh?" Callie's face was so close. Her curly black hair was tipped flame-

45

bright orange. Her lips were a matching shade of neon pink. Callie was brighter than any Teen Titan.

"Come on, Elijah. We've got crane work to do. Go get me the scissors."

"Okayyy." Elijah let a smile slip out, and miracle of miracles his teenage sister actually smiled back.

But sitting at the kitchen table wasn't all that great, even with Callie's notebook lying open in front of both of them.

Callie frowned as she chewed her pen. "It's hard to get the words right. Our old selves don't always carry a lot of memories. They can be easily confused."

"Yeah?" Elijah glanced at the notebook full of Callie's cramped swirls. He could tell they were actual words, but none of it made much sense. He tried. He waited, he kept still, and then another "I love you, Ray. Oh, God" erupted from behind Mom's bedroom door, followed by gut-ugly sobs.

Elijah reached for Callie's pen.

"Quit it." Callie didn't even look up as she pinched his upper arm, twisting the flesh tight.

"Callie—"

"Don't fucking whine."

Elijah started to scratch at his skin, a hard back-and-forth, new red welts crisscrossing older scars. The pain felt good, filling up his head and pushing out all those other feelings.

"Jesus. Elijah." Callie tore a sheet of paper from her notebook, slipped it into his hand. "Here. Why don't you draw us like we used to be? Help me remember who I'm talking to."

Elijah nodded his head and made his best serious face. Then he drew the fuck out of those old selves: sad Elijah, raging Callie, a superhero duo— brother and sister—with big muscles and monster faces. Callie continued working on her blue-ink, swirly words.

"Done," he declared after some unknown number of minutes.

"Okay." Callie slipped an arm across Elijah's shoulders and carefully looked over at his work. "Perfect. Just awesome. Hand me those scissors, little dude." Then layering the drawings underneath her own paper, she carefully cut her double-stacked notebook pages into squares.

"Now, it's magic time." Callie smiled for the second time that day.

Even at eight years old, Elijah knew enough to make damn sure he smiled back.

October 2026: Medical Rituals Help Us All

After the judge pronounces Elijah's sentence and all the lawyers clear out, Elijah finds himself in the back of a sheriff's van. It is a Tuesday morning. Eight a.m.

Elijah lies on a gurney with metal rails, wearing a hospital johnny and a pair of cuffs attached to his ankles. The officer who escorted him to the center's examination room stands by the door, careful not to make eye contact. The room is a study in contrasts: white johnny, white sheets, putty-colored floor against the red scars that run along both of Elijah's arms, a history of self-inflicted scratches. The scars look like shooting stars that have lost their way, wavering back and forth even as they travel forward.

Elijah's face is pale and creased with deep shadows. His sentence may last only a couple of weeks, but with the CR-REST chemical alterations, it will feel like years. He'll be alone with himself for a chemically subjective ten years. CR-REST therapy is like a series of scratches deep inside the brain. The scars will be deep enough that this version of Elijah will have no choice. He'll have to let go, fly away—just like his Callie did a few months before.

The medic inserts a needle into the crook of Elijah's left arm and attaches a second tube at the base of his neck. The guy is maybe twenty-two, just a couple of years older than Elijah. He has wispy brown hair and hazel eyes. There's a tiny patch of missed stubble on his cheek.

Elijah watches blood trickle out of his arm and through the tube, disappearing into the medical pump that sits next to his bed. The machine hums gently as it pumps the chemically altered blood back into his body. It doesn't hurt. Not really. But Elijah is sweating. Goosebumps rise along his arms.

"Can I get a glass of water?" Elijah asks.

"Sorry, man. The water would mess up the ratios." The medic attempts a smile.

"Sure."

And then they both are silent, watching the last of Elijah's recycled blood return to his body.

A second medic enters the room, pushing a trolley with bottles and assorted clippers. This one is wearing gloves.

"You'll need to stand and strip," he says after the guard unlocks Elijah's ankle cuffs.

Elijah's caseworker has been very thorough in her explanations. CR-REST relies on "meditative isolation without any external stimuli." In other words, before he enters the reclamation cell, every organic way of marking time must be removed.

The medic moves the clippers over every inch of Elijah's naked body, even his balls, and then follows up with some sort of depilatory cream. As the man focuses on his task, Elijah can see a small bald spot peeping through the hair on the crown of his head. The guy probably doesn't even know it's there.

Elijah is hairless and once again cuffed to the gurney. Like a chemo patient, even his eyelashes are gone.

It's the caseworker's turn. She looks at Elijah with her brown limpet eyes. "I'm here for you," she murmurs.

"Okay."

She sighs and then, after a pause, continues. "Is there anything you want to discuss?"

"Nope."

"Are you sure?"

Elijah doesn't even bother to respond.

"Then it's time."

She holds out a paper with a blank signature line and far too many words. Elijah shrugs, signs, hands the woman back her pen.

Primed. That's the word the medic uses when he hands Elijah over to the guard. "Primed and ready to go."

2015: SCIENCE CLASS

At fourteen, Callie was the girl who demanded answers. Weekend mornings, while Mom was still asleep, she dragged eight-year-old Elijah out of bed to look at glossy library books with titles like *Cosmos*, *Portraits of the Mind*, and *Neurobehavioral Anatomy*. The illustrations were alive with glowing synapses and webs of gossamer filaments.

"Elijah, remember when I told you about supernovas and black holes?"

"Yeah." Not angry but not looking Callie in the eye. It was Saturday. They were sitting on the couch. The Cartoon Network was waiting.

"Yeahhh, dummy." Callie smiled and flicked Elijah's cheek with her thumb and forefinger.

"Yeahhh," Elijah repeated, this time dragging out the "eh" sound at the end. He only managed to half-stifle his grin.

Callie pressed herself against Elijah's side and kissed his forehead. "Pay attention, fool." She pointed at the picture in the book. Glowing blue and orange brain cells with all that black space in between. "Our brains are just like the night sky, Elijah. Exploding, reforming, tossing aside neurons along with their store of emotions and memories."

Whether it's due to chemical reclamation or life scars, in the end it doesn't matter. Like all discarded selves, the Elijah that cares about his storytelling big sister will soon be cut loose. The loss of feelings will make everything so much easier.

OCTOBER 2026: LOCKUP

Elijah's cell in the State Reclamation Center is small, no more than ten feet in either direction. The air smells of sour sweat—Elijah's—and an intense minty scent—the guard's, used to cover up whatever the guy huffs on his breaks. Not that Elijah blames him. The guard spends his days setting up not-always-entirely-willing reclamations, and walking out yet another post-procedural result. Elijah would huff too.

"Are you ready, Elijah?" the guard asks from the doorway.

"A cakewalk," Elijah replies, feeling it, really feeling it for the first time. This guy and his graying, walrus mustache will be the last face he sees for ten years. "Will I be awake the whole time?" The words slip out.

"A kid like you?" the guard said. "You'll be fine." His gaze is not unfriendly. "Best thing for your type sometimes." Then the man and his mustache are gone, the door locked. There is a hum that wavers for a moment, followed by something even stranger—absolute silence. Elijah's sentence has begun.

The cell is a CR-REST version of a sensory deprivation tank. But despite all their research and reports, they somehow forgot about the smell. Most of the time it hovers between antiseptic swabs and bathroom cleaner. But every once in a while it shifts to burning leaves on a gray, autumn day. Sometimes Elijah can feel the heat from the burning paper cranes that he and Callie used to toss into the night sky. It's at those moments that Elijah knows that he is almost ready.

Stay inside, Mom used to say before leaving for wherever it is moms go.

Stay inside and I'll stay with you, Callie would repeat. Pink streaked hair, or black nails, or later, brands along her arms: the outline of a pipe or fleur-de-lis. Even when she sat with Elijah folding her cranes, it was as though Callie were preparing her body for what was to come.

"Pretty cool, huh?" she'd ask, nodding at the latest oozing wound, as though anyone could see the smooth shiny shape waiting to appear.

"I guess," Elijah muttered. Those flaming crane wings hurt his fingers, and they didn't even leave a mark.

Years and years of staying inside with Callie and her scars, sending signals to all those lost selves. Making sure they knew they weren't forgotten and entirely alone.

"She'll be back," the caseworker promised just before she drove Callie away to the Reclamation Center. As though this new version of Callie with her court-mandated therapy would love her broken, little brother just the same.

AUGUST 2026: CALLIE RECLAIMED

When the doorbell rings, it's Elijah who opens it, even though Mom is sitting on the couch. She's stayed home just especially.

There are two people in the doorway. One of them is Callie's caseworker. The other has dark, curling hair and a fleur-de-lis on her right bicep. She is twenty-five years old, six years older than her brother.

"Hey, Elijah!"

Her enthusiasm makes the caseworker grin.

"Callie. Hey." Elijah doesn't like the look on his sister's face. The way she smiles at Mom as much as she smiles at him. The way she glances at the stacks of dirty dishes and piles of trash, the lip-gloss and forgotten notebooks. She looks so content. After her treatment, she looks like someone else entirely.

September 2026: One Thousand Cranes

Back before she was reclaimed, Callie and Elijah had a mantra they repeated as they launched each of their paper cranes. "Burn all you want. I'm never letting go." Callie inked those words on each of the cranes, along with all the other things she needed to say. As Callie repeatedly explained, wishes only work if you commit—"really commit"—to your one true wish.

Reclaimed Callie might be finished with her little brother and paper cranes, but Elijah had a plan, and following his sister's original advice, he was going to commit the fuck out of it.

Step one was simple: unlock their apartment door and let himself in. Once inside, Elijah set down the two red, plastic containers he'd picked up at the gas station. He'd waited until dark to fill them up. If the neighbors noticed, they could ruin everything; he only had this one sliver of time to get it right.

Inside the apartment Elijah could feel the slither of history. Mom and Callie were at some court-mandated, post-procedure review, but their discarded memories were stamped across everything. The couch, the scratched-up coffee table, even the glass-topped kitchen table with the big chip in one corner all had stories to tell. And then there was Elijah's eighth-grade art project hanging on the kitchen wall. He'd spent hours sketching himself, Callie, and Mom into a family tableau. If he looked carefully, Elijah could still see the grid marks that he'd tried to erase once the sketch was done.

No time for that now. Elijah pulled the picture from the wall, pried open the frame, and pulled three of Callie's flattened cranes from the back.

"One, two, three," he muttered. He needed to be certain. The count had to be right: He needed at least one thousand cranes to leap into the void.

Underneath all the mattresses, taped to the bottom of the kitchen drawers, tucked in behind the mirror that hung on Callie's bedroom door. It took Elijah over two hours to track down and count all the cranes: 1,254. Another two hours to make sure the right words were scrawled on each and every crane.

And then it was time for the final step: the one that would force the scientists and courthouses and all those special therapies to give him wings and finally set him free.

Elijah poured the gasoline, knocked the smoke detector off the wall. He locked each window and made sure the bars were secure. Finally, he flicked the lighter and lit the 2,508 wings scattered throughout their home. Committed. Despite the smoke and the ache inside his throat, Elijah screamed the right words straight at those flames: "Don't worry, Callie. I'm never letting go." He watched as the fire rose up along the living room's polyester curtains. A handful of cranes rose up on an updraft created by the heat and swirled about the burning room. "Never letting go," he chanted under his breath, even after he stepped back into the hallway and locked that apartment door.

OCTOBER 2026: ELIJAH RECLAIMED

The cell door opens, though it takes a few seconds for Elijah to notice the change. New Elijah doesn't track things like he used to.

"Ready to go home?" Walrus mustache asks, peering round the door. The guy's eyes look bloodshot. For some reason he avoids looking at Elijah directly even as he holds out a scrap of notebook paper. "Someone left this for you."

"For you," Walrus mustache repeats. He waves the paper impatiently in Elijah's direction. "Take it."

Poor guy. He's starting to look angry or maybe nervous, one of those worry creases rising between his eyebrows. "Sure. Okay." Elijah reaches for the piece of paper. It's a piece of notebook paper, flat and uncreased. Blue-inked words are written across it in straight even lines, each word completely legible.

Elijah knows that at some point the unfolded paper and block print would have bothered him. But that feels like a long, long time ago.

"Welcome home!!!" the words say. "Call us when you get in." Below the words is an address: 83 Belmont Street Apt. 3G. It's not the address of their old apartment. Of course not. That apartment is gone.

"Guess you got people meeting you at home," the guard murmurs. "That's good."

"Yeah, I guess so." Elijah smiles. Callie will be there, probably Mom as well. After all this time, it'll be great to have the three of them together again.

2015: Elijah's First Flying Lesson—Part 2

"Callie, how many more?" Elijah asked. He could hear the creak of Mom's door opening and the sound of her feet shuffling down the hall. He and Callie had been folding squares of paper for what felt like forever, the results piled into an open Shaw's grocery bag.

"Soon. We'll leave soon." Callie was frowning, but Elijah knew the frown wasn't meant for him. It was meant for Mom.

Mom stood, swaying in the middle of the kitchen. Her hair was pressed up into oversized waves and bumps. Black flakes of mascara and eyeliner trailed down her cheeks. "Any food around here?"

"Nope." Callie's eyes remained trained on the inked paper in front of her. Thirty-two folds per messenger. At least one thousand cranes for one true wish.

"Right." Mom opened the refrigerator door, then stood, staring at the empty shelves.

"Maybe you should go back to bed, Mom," Elijah offered when the silence got uncomfortably long.

"Good idea, baby. Well, goodnight…?" She stood for a moment longer, then closed the refrigerator door, turned, and wandered back toward her bedroom.

"Callie, I'm hungry," Elijah whispered.

Callie placed her final blue-inked crane in the Shaw's grocery bag, stood, and then seemingly magicked a box of Pop-Tarts from one of the kitchen cupboards. "Here. Take one. Then go put your coat on. Quick! Quick!"

The best dinner ever.

It was night now. Elijah clutched the grocery bag while Callie locked their front door. The street was all dark sky and puddles of light that spilled from uncovered windows. A couple of guys stood near the 7-Eleven a half-block down, but other than that the street was empty.

Wishes, he could feel them pressing in from light-spilling windows and flickering TV screens. All those trapped wishes. At least he and Callie knew what to do. He and Callie knew just how to make things right.

"Let's go, kid. Those cranes are itching to fly." Callie slipped the key into her back pocket along with a lighter, and the two of them started down the street in the opposite direction of the 7-Eleven.

Laughter nearby. The slam of a car door and the heavy tread of male feet moving quickly along the sidewalk. Two men Elijah didn't know headed straight in their direction. One of them was smiling.

"Hey, baby," he said.

Elijah could feel Callie stiffen and reach for his hand. He couldn't see her face, but he could tell something had happened. "Fuck off."

The guy stopped smiling. "What the hell?"

"Come on, Denis. Leave it," the second guy said.

The men moved on. And so did Callie and Elijah, walking quickly, three blocks north and five blocks east, finally stopping at an empty lot surrounded by parked cars and blank brick walls.

The lot was like any other discarded space, full of tall weeds and a scattered collection of objects: faded candy wrappers, Miller High Life bottles, gloss bits of latex Callie called condoms, even the occasional forgotten shoe. Elijah thought that the shoe wearers were probably like Callie's cranes, flying up into the air, but somehow losing a sneaker as they launched themselves.

Forget the shoes. It was time to launch their own messages to all those lost and lonely selves.

"Thirty-two folds and one lighter full of fire," Callie cried as Elijah held out the first crane. Then she flicked the lighter and ignited the tail and both wings, tossing the bird toward the sky.

Instead of flames, the wings started to crumple into ash immediately, the crane barely taking off before it hit the trash-strewn ground.

"No problem, we just have to get the message right. That's all." Callie smiled encouragingly at Elijah. "We have plenty of cranes."

Another flick of the lighter, another set of wings smoldering their way back to the ground. And then another. Each messenger to a lost Elijah or forgotten Callie was blessed with different Callie words.

"Our one wish: We hope you are well."

"You were special and strange."

"You are magic, even in the sky."

"We miss you. Please come back." For a moment, Elijah was sure that last message would work. He watched as the wings flickered with orange flame, the crane rising ten or fifteen feet before tumbling back down. The grocery bag was almost empty.

"We're going to figure this out, I just know it. Elijah, it's your turn." Callie wasn't smiling, but she didn't have that worry frown that creased up her forehead either. She looked fierce. "Got your message ready?"

"Ummm…" Callie was the one who always knew exactly what to do. Now, she needed Elijah. He wasn't going to let her down. "Got it. Yeah."

In seconds the lighter sparked again.

"Burn all you want. I'm never letting go," Elijah howled. Callie's voice joined his, repeating the incantation as he heaved his arm back and up. He didn't let go of the crane right away. Elijah waited until the fire caught against his fingers and his skin began to sting, then he released that bird straight up into the sky. Instead of smoldering, the crane and its message shot up on flaming wings, traveling upward even as the wings curled into dark sheets of ash.

Still, Elijah and Callie took no chances. The two of them jumped up and down, chanting "Never letting go" until the crane was completely transformed. Then Callie grabbed Elijah's hands, spinning the two of them round and round as her flame-colored hair streaked out behind her.

Without knowing it was going to happen, Elijah tilted his head back toward the spinning night sky and started to laugh. They'd done it: that fire-lit crane was flying somewhere up and beyond, carrying their message. Bringing some measure of hope to all those forgotten Callies, and all those forgotten Elijahs as well.

THE THIRTEEN TUESDAYS OF SAINT ANTHONY

May 13, 2017

Navae Olsson
Grants Committee Chair
Farsdale Arts Council
City Hall, Office of the Mayor
212 Dwight Ave., Suite 203
Farsdale, MA 01007

Dear Ms. Olsson,

COMMUNITY ARTS ACCESS GRANT PROPOSAL
THE THIRTEEN TUESDAYS PROJECT

I AM WRITING TO APPLY for a 2017 Farsdale Arts Council grant following the application guidelines provided on the Farsdale Arts Council website.

Abstract:
    There isn't a city in the world that generates more prayers per capita than the city of Farsdale, Massachusetts. Yet, despite the hard work of Farsdale's city council, its teachers, and its many outreach workers, most citizen prayers

remain unanswered. Broken marriages, despoiled innocence, shattered trust—it smothers our city's streets. In some neighborhoods the air is so thick with grief and prayer, inhalers and hospital masks are a necessary accessory. The weight of Saint Anthony's failure hangs heavy over Farsdale's streets. No one seems to know if our city's entreaties to Saint Anthony are on hold, abandoned, or simply unheard.

Among the more than eight hundred Catholic saints, it is Saint Anthony who is assigned the task of providing aid to the lost and the stolen. A young girl's heart, a straying husband's soul, that feeling of trust between a mother and a child—Saint Anthony is responsible for recovering it all. No wonder Saint Anthony used to weep from the strain. But in the end the impact of this backlog goes far beyond Saint Anthony himself. Unanswered novenas and prayers have become the new norm for the people of Farsdale. We suffer longer, more deeply, and with less hope of even the slightest reprieve. Some days life feels pointless to each and every one of Farsdale's forty-three thousand residents. Some days I barely manage to breathe.

As the report of the Mayor's Citizen Advisory Committee makes clear (Hope and Inter-heavenly Cooperation Survey—Analysis and Conclusions, April 4, 2014), despite these systemic problems, less than 10 percent of Farsdale's citizens blame Saint Anthony himself. Most understand. Sometimes even the blessed are powerless, are deaf and blind to the simplest entreaty.

The city council, at least, has noticed our festering scars and our failures to "just forget." Over the last two years, they have responded with a series of educational programs. The citywide 2015 Power of Organized Prayer Campaign and the school-based 2016 Importance of Tracking Your Tears Campaign are the most well known. But the council has gone far beyond these initiatives. Informational pamphlets in Spanish, Vietnamese, and Saint Anthony's own language, Portuguese, now litter our neighborhoods. In an attempt to reach out to Farsdale's homebound citizens, council members have also partnered with Victory Home Health and Mercy Hospice.

Thanks to the foresight of our city's government, the people of Farsdale know that Saint Anthony is most accessible via ritualized communication. They even know that thirteen novenas over thirteen consecutive Tuesdays is his particular sweet spot.

And still Saint Anthony fails to answer our prayers. With each breath we are forced to take in our neighbor's burden along with our own. A punctured finger, a bruised thigh—physical pain of any kind is a welcome relief. These days I smile whenever I see a child's savagely skinned knee or feel a cold sore erupting across my lips.

The Thirteen Tuesdays mural project is more than an expression of our citizens' need. It is an actual solution. It aims to resolve the issue of pending prayers and Saint Anthony's broken system of reclamation through the mechanism of thirteen carefully crafted murals. The Thirteen Tuesdays mural project will harness the power of our citizens' own memories and pain, amplifying our cries one thirty-by-fifty-foot mural at a time.

There must be someone out there ready to listen. There must be a way to ease this pressure on my chest, bearing, always bearing down.

Introduction:

The collapse of the Essex House was not the first sign, but it was the first to catch our city fathers' attention. For years the five-story tenement stood empty. Apartments, businesses, and a neighborhood daycare resided just feet away from the block-length landmark. Yet despite a committee of neighborhood residents praying for thirteen weeks, midday last December, the building cast off its southern wall, showering mortar and bricks across Jarvis Avenue, Essex Street, and the surrounding structures. A few citizens claimed that the lack of any human injury was a sign that Saint Anthony was not entirely negligent ("Editorial: Saint Anthony's Mercy During this Holy Season," *Daily Farsdale Gazette*, December 13, 2014). However, to most citizens the destruction of the Essex House demonstrated a fundamental shift in Saint Anthony's responsiveness; Saint Anthony had failed to heed a single prayer. The Essex House incident also marks the moment when our city's ongoing tally of pending intercessions became formalized ("Announcements: Intercession Count," *Daily Farsdale Gazette*).

Each day the evidence of Saint Anthony's lack of attention mounts: the flayed and mutilated body found behind Our Lady of the Cross; the missing girl, Cecile Johnston, whose picture, twelve months later, is still plastered across our city's telephone poles; along with images of so many other vanished souls. The weight of our city's suffering poisons every living

59

creature. Pigeons and sparrows no longer nest in City Hall's eaves. Feral cats no longer wander the streets.

The Farsdale Senior Center now offers breathing centers with tanked oxygen at strategic points throughout the city. However, that alone is not enough to counterbalance the absence of Saint Anthony and Our Lord. In recent months the citizens of Farsdale have also had to contend with a multitude of disembodied voices wandering almost every city block. In the North End and Canal Street neighborhoods, the voices are most prevalent. Some voices scream as though through half-collapsed lungs while others echo the never-ending whimpers of a dying child. Despite the NyQuil and Ambien, I can't remember the last time I slept through the night. I know am not alone.

The Thirteen Tuesdays Project aims to solve all these problems at their source, galvanizing Farsdale's citizenry to come together and request the assistance of someone who can, and will, actually help.

Statement of Need:

I have a C-section scar along my lower abdomen from the birth of a child I knew for less than a year. I have three ruptured discs and a steel rod in my upper spine from a spinning-car crash that sent me through a windshield. At least I survived. I walk. I stand. I run. Faster every day, though I never get away.

The accident sits like a putrefied knot of flesh beneath my skin, a hematoma of hardened blood and nascent infection. Soon it will be too late.

As far as I can tell, Saint Anthony and his Lord are unable to solve a thing.

Objectives:

The Book of Ezekiel states, "A new heart also will I give you, and a new spirit will I put within you: and I will take away the stony heart out of your flesh, and I will give you a heart of flesh."

No people need divine assistance more than the people of Farsdale. As an artist the conversion of actual physical flesh has always been at the heart of my creative work, and the Thirteen Tuesdays project is no exception. As the attached portfolio shows, prior projects have included cleansed skulls in the woods of Sre Leav, Cambodia and hand-sewn flesh capes in the desert just outside Mexico City. If funded, the Thirteen Tuesdays project will be a culmination of these and other works, incorporating the two crucial steps required to find grace: rigorous cleansing and transformation. It is one thing to erase. To take the hardness within a human heart and change it, that requires art.

Methods:

Thirteen murals in thirteen weeks. Each week for thirteen consecutive weeks, the project team, along with local volunteer artists, will paint a mural across one of the buildings of Farsdale. As artistic director, my role will be to guide the artists. However, the heart of the creative process will come from the volunteer artists themselves. To make sure the entire city is included in any resultant grace, a special effort will be made to include volunteers from each of the city's six neighborhoods. To maximize the power of the project's communal prayer, the first mural will start on Tuesday, June 13th, the date on which Saint Anthony died, and will be completed on midnight of the following Monday. All thirteen mural initiatives will begin on a Tuesday, Saint Anthony's actual death day. Death is always the first step. And the last.

Materials for the project will include supplies acquired by myself and my core project team, along with those collected by the volunteer artists. Potential volunteers will be required to apply at one of four confessional booths that the project team will set up around the city in the weeks prior to the start date. The following locations have been identified as applicant locations and the appropriate permissions obtained for booth placement: the intersection of Lyman Street and Canal Street, next to the bus stop at the northern end of Jarvis Avenue, Babolla Road just south of Ashley Reservoir, and most fittingly, the end of Hospital Drive.

For the nine weeks preceding the project, a team of eight interrogators will man the four booths on a twelve-hour rotation. The booths will follow the pre–Vatican II design and will contain both a privacy wall and a grille, along with the most modern soundproofing. Inside each booth potential volunteers will be interrogated, and if found to be suitably attuned, will be provided with a sketch pad, a knife, a paintbrush, and a stub of leaded pencil with which to draft their early inspirations.

Once an actual mural is begun, it will be the responsibility of that volunteer artist to render the most effective visual entreaty without hesitation. As artistic director, my responsibility will be to breathe, to watch, to listen to the screaming voices, and still to guide him to the end.

Survey Data:

The scars tighten whenever the rain draws near. The hollow feeling lingers after I open my eyes each morning. Some days it feels like nothing I do will ever be enough.

Over the last few months the core project team has conducted a series of anonymous surveys concerning the proposed project. For the project's success, it's important that the Thirteen Tuesdays Project represent the needs of all of Farsdale's citizens. Community feedback has been specific and spirited. Clearly, the project has already engaged the imagination of Farsdale's citizens.

A representative sample of survey responses is included below. As much as possible, this feedback has been incorporated into the final proposal. However, while the project includes suggested guidelines for its volunteer artists, no form of creative expression is proscribed. As Father Xavier tells us, the purity of a penitent's heart has by far the most influence on a novena's outcome. Perhaps the girl on Jarvis Street would have fared better if her older brothers hadn't forced her to make that single, life-altering cut. A forked tongue could have symbolized so much if the slash of the blade had been freely offered.

Sample Responses:

Please note, a full report on the survey, including all respondent comments and a statistical analysis of these responses, has been attached to this application.

"Vivisection is the provenance of the Lord and his disciples and should remain constrained to veterinary colleges and monastic retreats."

"Mixing tears and tempera paint creates a very unstable substrate. It'll never weather even one winter."

"Medical professionals should be present for all self-directed aspiration. You never know how people will react to the sight of blood."

Budget:

The importance of filming each mural's seven-day creation using physical film rather than a digital medium cannot be overstated. As each of these murals will demonstrate, it is the physical act that separates the human idea from the actually divine. Thirteen Super 8 cameras have already been reserved and will be purchased as soon as this project is approved. However, each Super 8 cartridge is only expected to capture three minutes of artistic sound and motion. For each mural, this translates into twenty cartridges an hour for seven days. By far the most expensive item for this project will be the acetate film.

With the assistance of our camera crew, each nuance of our penitents' creative journey will be recorded. The inspiration this footage will provide future penitents in their creative design is incalculable, well beyond the initial 1.4 million dollar investment. No digital camera, no smartphone, no pixelated image can capture the blessed touch of God-hungry inspiration.

Aside from the film, the four confessional booths and the scaffolding are the only other significant expenses. No financial compensation is expected for any project participants, including the eight interrogators, the artist volunteers, the camera crew, and myself. Additionally, as will be made clear during the interrogation process, the cost of any materials provided by the volunteer artists, along with any resultant post-mural expenses, will be borne entirely by the artists themselves. The only human expense associated with this project is the de-sanctification ritual that the diocese requires before selling the confessional booths.

Materials

Purchases

Four confessional kneelers with privacy screen . . . . .$1,053 each
Twenty-four acoustic wedges . . . .$60 each
Four de-sanctified confessional booths . . . .$1,800 each
Bauer S108 Super 8 sound camera with extendable mic . . . .
. . . .$74 each

Kodak VISION3 color negative Super 8 fil . . . .
. . . .$34 per 50 foot cartridge

Rentals
14-foot fiberglass twin stepladder . . . .$168 per week
Two scaffolds . . . .$160 per week

Donations
Art materials . . . . .Free
Interrogator materials . . . . .Free

Labor
Artistic Director . . . . .Free
De-sanctification ceremony by an archdiocese-selected priest . . . .
. . . .$1,200 per confessional
Interrogators . . . . .Free
Volunteer Artists . . . . .Free
Camera Crew . . . . .Free

Final cost to the arts committee $1,508,034

Other Preparations:

Long before anyone noticed the thickening air and the screaming voices that consume the edge of everything, Saint Anthony blessed me. In his final act before his Great Disappearance, Saint Anthony chose me to spread the new truth. One day God and his saints ruled this physical plane; the next day Saint Anthony and our Lord were gone, disappeared. Death is like that.

The car's crumpled door, half-open. The dome light, flickering and dim. Blood dripped down into my eyes. I could taste the choking scent of powder from the still-inflated airbags. Icy midnight air rushed in through the shattered windshield. Saint Anthony had done his best to reach me.

The car's seatbelt warning system *ping-ping-pinged* as I screamed. And those sobs from the backseat kept on rising for a second, a minute, an hour before dying away, and then it was just me. I remember my arms shook. I remember I couldn't turn my neck. I lay sprawled across the dashboard, another abandoned and ungrateful sinner.

Despite my tears, I understood nothing. I had been blessed; despite the Lord's incipient migration to parts unknown, Saint Anthony had reached down and interceded one final time. Of all the people in all the world, he had chosen me as his vessel. Saint Anthony's message was as clear as the crack of my skull against the too-hard steering wheel, as clear as my shattered jaw and the pins and wires that came afterward. Only the body—the flesh, the bones, and all the viscera—carries the correct moral weight for heavenly supplication.

The Lord has vacated his realm and taken all his heavenly host with him; Farsdale's only hope is to scream, to writhe, to act as a human beacon, guiding the new gods close. Every town needs its blessings.

Even as I plan the Thirteen Tuesdays project, I practice the truth of Saint Anthony's message: a broken nose, a shattered collarbone, the long flap of skin that rubs and bleeds, constantly seeping up into whatever shirt I wear. And still our new gods fail to notice a single one of my bloody prayers. My own voice is not enough to create an actual path, though I understand the seriousness of my charge.

When the time comes for each Thirteen Tuesday's artist to create one of the city's murals, physical film will record the sounds and sights of their 168-hour entreaty. Physical film will replay that entreaty to the gods.

I am the last artist blessed by the hand of Saint Anthony. Thirteen novenas over thirteen Tuesdays. Even in this new world, how can the new gods fail to look favorably on a people willing to transform the taint of our own flesh into a light capable of guiding the heavens themselves? It is time the people of Farsdale steered the gods toward their duty. It is time the new gods blessed each one of us with their eternal grace. It is time our screams rang from the city in a clarion of prayer.

Raising Babies

EVEN THOUGH IT WAS SPRING, God's time for new life and rebirth, beneath three feet of hard-packed dirt, the baby wouldn't stop crying.

Unlike back in Asheville, real flowers were hard to come by at Grandma Charko's house. But they were necessary. Two weeks ago, Sylvia had grabbed a handful of zinnias from the neighbor's garden. Last week she'd lifted roses from the top of a shiny gravestone. Yesterday she'd even sacrificed the carnation Grandma received at church, pressing it down into the dry, unyielding ground.

"See, baby? See what a seed can do?"

But still the baby kept crying.

Momma's garden sat in a corner of the backyard, not far from the chain-link fence and the looming shadow of the neighbor's sagging porch. Sylvia could hear a dog bark followed by the frantic scrabble of large paws against an unknown door. The garden was a lonely place for newborn things.

"It's okay, baby." Sylvia crouched down and patted the hard earth. "It's all right." When Sylvia was little, Momma used to sing those nursery songs with the hand gestures. Maybe that was why the baby cried all the time—it couldn't move its arms.

"The itsy bitsy spider," Sylvia began, her spider fingers laddering upward, "climbed up the water spout..."

The dog had finally quieted; Sylvia could hear the whoosh of cars speeding along Third Street and out of town toward the East Fork White River. One block in the other direction stood Columbus's historic district. Grandma's church, St. Peter's, was on that street, by all those houses with the fancy wrought-iron fences. Beyond this little stretch of Fourth Street, it was almost like Grandma's faded-wallpaper house didn't even exist.

"... And the itsy bitsy spider climbed up the spout again." Sylvia's hands reached high overhead, then dropped quickly as yet another whimper rose up from the ground.

"Mma. Mma. Mmaaaaaaa."

"Shhh." Sylvia scuffed her Mary Janes against the late-spring ground. "Shh, you stupid, cranky baby." The bad baby-seed was ruining everything. And she and Momma had both worked so hard. They had started working as soon as Grandma pulled into the driveway of Grandma's house and hauled their suitcases up the stairs. Grandma may have dragged the two of them, Sylvia and Momma, all the way from Ashville, North Carolina, to her own home in Columbus. She may have even driven Momma to some doctor and made sure to collect all those medicine bottles with the hard-to-open caps. That didn't mean Momma had given up on her dream.

Sylvia and Momma arrived in Columbus at the end of summer, just before school was supposed to start. The air conditioners stuttered and droned, and the grass was patchy from weeks of August heat. But at night the air cooled, and Momma pulled the thin cotton blankets around Sylvia before she kissed her goodnight.

"Now that summer's over," Momma said before she closed the bedroom door, "it's time to prepare for the spring rebirth."

"Like Grandma's baby Jesus?" In her nightlight's glow, Sylvia could see Momma's smile.

"Yes. Exactly like that. Goodnight, my little gardener."

Somehow Momma never mentioned her plans to Grandma Charko or to anyone at Grandma's church. Even though all those old people were always talking about rebirth and resurrection. And for some reason, now that they lived with Grandma, Momma's smile looked all wrong to Sylvia—different, all teeth and stretched skin.

Back before Grandma Charko showed up at their old apartment in Ashville, it was just the two of them. Sylvia and Momma. No God. No doctors. No Grandma Charko. Back then there had been no smiles; Sylvia's days were all about sad Momma and anxious Momma and not-even-able-to-walk-Sylvia-to-school Momma.

Gazing at yet another Momma smile, Sylvia was reminded of those germs Grandma Charko kept talking about; no matter what Grandma and the doctors did, no matter how happy those Momma smiles made everyone else feel, underneath her smiles, those big Momma-feelings were still spreading and spreading, getting ready to burst yet another cell.

Just like every other morning, Momma sat with Sylvia and Grandma in the dim, wallpapered kitchen. Momma sipped her coffee and Grandma ate her oatmeal one careful bite at a time. Sylvia could almost count the seconds between each mouthful.

Three. Two. One. Swallow.

Meanwhile, Momma smiled and smiled.

"I thought I'd plant a few flowers, Mom, to get my mind off of things. You know, therapy."

From the center of the table, two salt-and-pepper-shaker girls in yellow dresses watched Momma and Grandma Charko. Nearby a crowd of wallpaper ladies stared at them with faded, gone-away eyes. Momma's own eyes were wide and shiny, like all those nights in Asheville when Momma didn't bother to sleep, swallowing stuff she took out of that small wooden box. Momma took a different kind of pill now. Grandma and her days-of-the-week pillbox made sure of that.

"Flowers?" Grandma's voice was calm enough. Still Sylvia noticed that Grandma had clenched her spoon in one claw-like fist.

Momma noticed too. "It'll be glorious, Mom. Transformative. Like the hands of God himself." Momma tossed her head and stretched her lips extra wide, then stood up and quickly unlocked the sliding glass door. "Sylvia.

Little Sylvie, come dance with me!" she cried, darting down the back steps and out into the yard.

Carefully not hearing Grandma's "wait," Sylvia followed. Of course she did. Momma needed Sylvia's help.

Momma and Sylvia covered the flowerbed with leaf mulch. They snapped off the dead flower heads. The two of them cleared the ground of weeds, revealing the curling grubs and worms underneath.

"Autumn's not the right time for planting," Momma said. "We waited too long." As though Momma had known Grandma was going to drive out to their apartment in Asheville and collect the two of them. As though this move back to Indiana was an actual Momma-plan.

Sylvia bent and picked up one of the worms. The worm wriggled against her palm, not even trying to escape.

Why weren't people more like garden worms?

"The ground has to be prepared just right for plantings to survive the winter." Momma's eyes were on the undulating worm or perhaps just the bits of dirt coating Sylvia's hand. "The season's not entirely lost, though we have a lot of work to do." Then Momma knelt down and laid her ear to the ground, listening, she said, to her worm friends loosening the soil.

Whatever that meant.

Sylvia glanced toward the house. Grandma stood in the kitchen window, her arms crossed, her expression hidden by the comparatively dim light. Sylvia couldn't even see the ladies with their pretty parasols and wide skirts that covered Grandma's kitchen wall.

It was better, Sylvia decided, if she didn't show Momma any more worms.

Even without Sylvia's help, Momma remembered.

Grandma and Sylvia stood at the kitchen window watching the water run down Momma's face: Momma's cloud tears making all the world gray.

"Don't you go crying," Grandma said.

"But, Grandma..." Sylvia started. Momma lay stretched out on the soggy ground. And she hadn't moved for an age, not even when Sylvia came inside.

Momma needed the worms' help to calculate the optimal planting time. That's what she'd said.

Worms cared for all buried things, she'd said.

"Now, hush, little Sylvie. I'm listening," Momma had said just before Sylvia ran to find Grandma.

"Grandma?" Sylvia tried again. Grandma looked round and sturdy underneath her loose, flowery dress, but Sylvia didn't feel the slightest urge to lean in for a hug.

"I'll talk to the doctor about her pills. Got cleaning to do right now. You coming?" Grandma Charko pulled her cardigan more tightly across her shoulders, then walked back into the interior of the house, not even waiting for Sylvia's reply.

Sylvia stood next to the fading wallpaper and the worried ladies, staring at the too-full woman sprawled out under the too-gray sky. Some seeds needed more help than others to find their way. Some people too.

Momma didn't garden anymore. The January wind rattled the windows. The wallpaper women seemed to huddle beneath their parasols. These days it was just Sylvia and Grandma Charko and yet another Sunday dinner table set for two.

It was ice cold outside. Hopefully, the ground was warmer underneath.

"Can't believe they still haven't found your mother," Grandma said, spooning green beans onto both their plates. "Bet she planned this right from the start." Grandma Charko's lips were all puckered, as though Grandma wasn't the one who had herded both her and Momma into her car and all the way back to this very house. "Hopefully, blood won't tell," Grandma continued with what Sylvia thought was a certain lack of Christian charity.

"Change is really, really hard work," Momma had whispered all those weeks ago, on that cold November night. But Sylvia wasn't going to share Momma's secrets with an angry Grandma.

"It's okay, Grandma," Sylvia said instead. She tried not to smile or frown, tried not to look all droopy with feelings.

What if Grandma started hearing the worms? What if Grandma asked

Sylvia to help? Sylvia already had enough to care for in the garden. Though Grandma had known Momma for a really long time, much longer than Sylvia. Grandma Charko, Sylvia decided, was probably immune to Momma's feeling-germs.

All those winter prayers at St. Peter's church with Grandma, all those candles Sylvia lit in the hidden garden shrine didn't help. Neither did the lullabies, the roses, or the carnations.

Spring had arrived and still God and the worms hadn't transformed a darn thing.

"Stupid, stupid baby." Sylvia scrunched her nose at Momma's flowerbed and kicked at the spring-softened dirt. The other green sprouting things were rising up from the ground, and yet no newborn Momma wriggled out, wrinkled as a garden worm.

"I'm ready, Sylvie," Momma had said as she looked up at the autumn sky. And Sylvia, holding that cold shovel in both hands, had tried really hard to believe her.

But Momma's plan wasn't working.

Sylvia looked down at her scuffed leather shoes and the bunch of brown tea roses. Grandma would be so mad. She liked to sit with Sylvia and count the wallpaper ladies on the kitchen wall before heading off to services. But Sylvia had promised Momma she would help. And Sylvia always kept her promises.

The April air was night-cold. The stars hung overhead as Sylvia took two paces to the left of the garden plot, pressed the sharp edge of the shovel into the dirt, and began to dig.

It had all gotten muddled somehow: the baby cries and all those tears. But this time Sylvia had a plan, a real plan. This time Sylvia would get it right. Soon that lonely baby-seed would be sprouting up all green and freshy new.

Momma's baby-seed just needed someone to hold its hand.

Sylvia sighed. Grandma's Bible Study would be over soon. She needed to finish up. Grandma wouldn't understand about all the dirt.

A few months in the earth was a small enough price to pay for a freshy-green rebirth. Soon enough, Sylvia and Momma would finish their new baby bodies, and together they would rise up, ready to face the sun and the wallpaper-dim world.

HOLES IN HEAVEN

IN ADDITION TO ITS OTHER POWERS, the Arizona heat compels decay. My forty-year-old apartment building with its Class C construction and Title Eight clientele didn't stand a chance. The stench had overtaken my bedroom months ago, the epicenter of my carefully assembled physics experiment. Even with a bandana tied around my face, the room stank like clam bellies festering in the desert sun.

I tossed another stack of torn and stained newspapers, *Gila Bend Suns* and *Arizona Republics,* onto the edges of the enormous trash heap and then angled my metal grabber, dropping Tuttle's typed letter on top of the pile. At this point, my self-constructed stellar nursery was taller than me, taller even than my twin brother, Agustin, or any other full-sized man.

I'd done my best to get things right. Under all the carefully selected trash was a mattress, a small side table, and two of our most precious family heirlooms: the Pointer Sisters' album *Energy* and a polished circle of pyrite. Mama's favorite song, "Fire," was on that album.

Didn't matter. I still had only ten days left.

My hand wobbled and the grabber dipped into a syrupy pool of sludge about one-third of the way down the room's molding heap. "Christ," I muttered. Bok globules might be the smallest sites of star formation, but building one in your bedroom was filthy work.

I needed that plastic claw for more than nursery care. Being a little man, a little person, in a hick town like Gila Bend meant everyone noticed when

75

I couldn't reach the bread shelf at Sunrider's Grocery. It also meant no one lifted a finger to help. I was just that "little Jack Rodriquez with the asshole chip on his shoulder."

I shook the worst of the sludge off the claw and watched as one corner of Tuttle's letter fluttered against the eddy of air that followed. I couldn't see the actual words. I didn't have to. This was just the latest in a string of official notifications. They all boiled down to the same two words: ten days. I had ten days to transform this mound of trash. Ten days to beat Agustin through my yet-to-be-completed portal door and chase down Mama and Papa. In less than two weeks, Mrs. Rhonda Tuttle, the complex manager, and her squadron of cleaners would dismantle all my work and toss it into one of the green dumpsters at the edge of the parking lot, even if I wasn't done.

Out beyond our solar system, Bok globules are the cottage industry of star creation, the backyard vegetable patch, as compared to the industrial-scale star formation found in places like the Orion Nebula. And like actual garden patches, Bok globules are far more numerous than those massive corporate farms. Mama and Papa weren't the galaxy's only small star farmers, but they were my only parents, and I wanted them back.

Of course I wouldn't be making any stars down here on earth. I was enough Papa's child to know it just wasn't possible. Didn't matter. All I needed was sufficient energy to find my way to all that black space between the stars. A hard enough task, though I refused to use the word *impossible*. It's just that it takes a hell of a lot of energy to leave this world behind. And now, as Rhonda Tuttle and her letter had reminded me, after all my work, after all my failures, I was almost out of time.

I held my breath against the stink as I stared at the still-transforming bedroom. Let my brother chatter on about solar masses, molecular clouds, and hydrogen-to-helium conversion. I knew the truth; portal creation was spirit magic, shamans, and fermented cactus juice unlocking the bonds of mere human flesh.

Joni Mitchell and Mama said it best:

We are stardust.
We are golden.
And we've got to get ourselves back to the garden.

Lots of people collect things. Lots of people build things, homemade things. Of course, most people involved in bedroom trash collection would be diagnosed with a psychiatric disorder. In my case the diagnosis would be wrong. I was creating just enough energy to return to that quadrant of the sky where Mama and Papa now resided.

Everyone treated Mama and Papa's disappearance as a death. "Angels in heaven," the funeral director said as we sat in his office, making the arrangements.

"Angels in heaven my ass," I muttered. "Mama and Papa are in the heavens, not Heaven with a capital H."

The man ignored both me and my glower.

"And the ashes, Mr. Rodriquez?" the funeral director, Mr. Avenidas, asked, as though I hadn't even spoken. He looked at my brother, Agustin, from across the wide desk. "How would you like to handle the ashes?"

"Agustin," I said, louder this time. "Agustin, you planning on buying a casket for Mama's cat, as well? Or are we going to pretend it ran away?"

Agustin grunted but said nothing more. He still couldn't believe they'd left without him.

"An urn, perhaps?" Mr. Avenidas persisted.

"For crematorium burnt wood?" I protested.

"It's okay, Jack," Agustin said. "Perhaps an urn..." Agustin was always better at the human stuff: the college boy, the honors student, the son who played the clarinet in the school marching band. Once he even had a girlfriend, Veronica, though Mama and Papa hadn't liked that much. A girlfriend, or any kind of friend, was far too earthbound for their two children.

"Christ, Agustin." I slipped down from the leather armchair and stalked out of the office, slamming the door behind me. Agustin might be the brilliant brother, but I was the hot-tempered Rodriquez, the one prone to regrets.

I started building my own sacred platform mound—or gravitation sink, as Agustin and Papa termed it—that very day. My indoor structure didn't quite match the old Tonaj mounds found at the edge of town. Still, I knew my training was sound. I placed Mama's polished pyrite mirror in the center of the room along with her faded macaw feathers. The pyrite might not open the door, but it could at least show me the way. These were the old relics Mama pulled out at the height of summer, when the saguaro fruit ripened and she and Papa danced on wobbly legs, drunk, long after Agustin and I fell asleep.

You don't grow up with Claudio and Isabella Rodriquez without learning a few things. By day there were songs—the Pointer Sisters, Joni Mitchell, older tonal songs without any actual words—and harvesting trips into the Sonoran Desert. As well as the saguaro fruit, there were prickly pear pads and the saltweed and dried mesquite pods Mama ground down for flour. At night our family TV was the backyard and the darkened sky. The stink of creosote and a sweeter scent, like oranges, filled the air. Sometimes you'd hear aircraft from the nearby Air Force training grounds. In early summer, the sound of cars from Interstate 8 competed with the chorus of frogs and crickets that emerged after sunset. The sounds didn't really matter and, it seemed, neither did the light from the houses on our street. Agustin, Papa, and I stood looking up at the sky, scanning for those holes in heaven, the small dark patches that signified a Bok globule. We looked for other things too: galaxies, nebulae, even individual stars, but in the end Papa always returned to those same little masses. Both Agustin and I learned the basics of astronomy on those TV nights.

"The universe is filled with little star factories, mijos. Tiny families, waiting to release their energy out into the universe," he'd say. "All you have to do is look."

"Multiples, Papa? What about binary stars?" I pressed one night as Agustin fiddled with the telescope, a Dobsonian reflector, his back to both of us.

"Binary systems are the worst. Tricky anyway," Papa amended, glancing at me. The light from the waning moon illuminated both of our faces: a small brown-skinned boy and a taller man staring at each other through the surrounding darkness. "Sometimes the molecular cloud fragments into two protostars," he continued. "But the minute you get two, the possible problems rise exponentially. A hypergiant often captures mass from its smaller companion. You might even end up with a brown dwarf."

"Brown dwarf?" I scowled at Papa. "Well if I'm a brown dwarf, you're a brown jerk. All you care about is Agustin, your big, giant star!"

Agustin shifted his position at the 'scope but remained silent.

"Kiâ'hâd," Papa said, using my proper name instead of the usual "Jack." His voice had a sudden edge to it. "We're talking stars here—astrophysics, not people."

"Go on, Papa," Agustin said. He'd turned to face us both. Even in the dark, I recognized that look. He loved it when Papa told us something new, as though it were yet another proof of Papa's love. Agustin was a fool, despite all his brilliance, that's what I thought. Mr. Langlois, our science teacher, told us stuff in school all the time. Didn't mean he liked us. Never saw how love even came into any of the things Papa explained. Agustin, though, always blamed me for Papa's moods, as though I'd chosen to be born this way. As though Papa would ever hold either of us the way Mama did.

"Let's just look for the damn space station, all right?" I said.

Papa frowned, looked over at Agustin and the dark night sky. Even in profile, I could see his frown disappear as Agustin smiled up at him. Of course, I didn't care, not one little bit.

"A brown star occurs when the core fails to ignite, Agustin. No atomic collisions. No star. Got it?"

"Yeah, Papa," Agustin said. "Plus you've—"

I didn't hear the rest. Agustin and Papa could talk about brown dwarfs, but they'd be doing it without me. I headed back into the house, slamming the glass door on my way inside.

In my memory, my childhood is a series of dark nights and slamming doors.

Rhonda Tuttle's first letter declared her determination to inspect my apartment, something about the smell and the flies. She delivered it in person.

"Hey, Miss Peterson," I said through my cracked-open front door. Rhonda had been an ass back when she was just a teased-out blonde cashiering at Sunrider's. Forty pounds and one husband hadn't changed a thing.

"My name is Mrs. Tuttle, not Peterson," she replied. Why Rhonda had shown up on my doorstep was beyond me. It was the weekend, for God's sake—Sunday even. I'd been about to head out for my weekly dinner with Agustin.

Despite being over one hundred degrees, "Mrs. Tuttle" was wearing a pantsuit, bright press-on nails with swirly designs like tiny spiral galaxies, and melty makeup in a shade of off-orange that she'd matched with thick clumping mascara. She could have been Tammy Faye Baker's Western cousin.

"Yeah? What do you want, Mrs. Tuttle?" My mouth tasted foul. I felt the sweat and oil underneath my beard. My whole face itched like hell. I'd subtracted personal hygiene as the latest part of my process. Phase Two, I called it. They might have ditched me, but I still loved my parents, even Papa. Phase Two was my proof. Despite his own mudroom experiments, I could tell Agustin just didn't have the same level of commitment. The closest he got to Phase Two was that tattered bathrobe he wore around his house.

"May I come in?" Rhonda asked, one hand propping open the screen door.

"I'm on my way out," I said, curtly. A few flies slipped through the opening and out into the parking lot. What was her problem? My green terrycloth robe was smeared with brownish stains, but it was tied tightly across my waist, despite the heat. It hung down past my knees. She couldn't even see the tomato-sauce-stained underwear I wore underneath. Some days I spent hours rearranging the contents of my bedroom. It was hot, disgusting work. I usually left the robe off.

"Mr. Rodriquez, here." She extended a sealed envelope down in my general direction as she tried to peer past me into the apartment. She was a good couple of feet taller, but the door itself got in the way. She couldn't see shit.

"Mrs. Tuttle." I leered up at her. "So forward. Guess you've heard what they say about little men ... Certain things on a woman fall at just the right height." I gave a little shudder and smacked my lips. I couldn't seem to stop myself. It probably didn't help that I could see the flush of distaste on Rhonda's face.

My entire body itched like hell. Even worse, I was about to see Agustin, the star expert, the golden boy, the inheritor of all our family's earthly possessions. I was a good person, a good son. Why did no one ever seem to notice?

"Enough, Jack. Your apartment." She stopped. "Your person," she tried again. "Well, there've been multiple complaints. Flies. Roaches." She looked directly at me, a grimace of disgust stuck somewhere beneath all that make-up. "We run a clean building, and we expect our tenants to do the same."

"You took my money."

"You signed our lease." She waved away a dive-bombing fly. A second one buzzed just out of reach.

"You know what? Forget the offer. I doubt even Bob Tuttle touches that wide ass of yours." I slammed the door on Rhonda Tuttle's face. I tossed the envelope and its contents onto my bedroom pile and reached for my wheelie cart. Perhaps I'd find something worth collecting on my walk over to Agustin's.

Names can hurt. I know that. Unkind words are the worst; they make you want to crumple up and hide. They make you want to disappear from this universe.

Rhonda was standing outside the office when I left a few minutes later. She seemed to be trying to get the key to work in the office door's lock. Her face was scrunched up. It almost seemed like she was going to cry, though maybe not. Maybe it was just the stink that wafted out as I slammed my front door, slipped on my sunglasses, and headed down the road.

Despite Agustin's two years of ownership, our old, family house looked exactly the same: a small flat-roofed ranch on a street of ranch houses that ran just north of Interstate 8. Fifties-era construction, it looked like a glorified trailer home covered in faded yellow siding. Inside the yard's chain-link fence nothing grew except for the two palm trees that towered above their enclosure. Agustin stood in the open doorway, his lips pressed tightly together. He must have been watching for me through the window.

"In your case, the life of a star has got to be an improvement," he said from the entryway. "The liquid plasma would burn off all the dirt. Even Mama wouldn't kiss you smelling like that."

"Just shut up, Agustin." If I could have reached that high, I would have smacked him in the face. He acted like I enjoyed this filthy existence. Romulus and Remus, Cain and Abel, Osiris and Set. Fascinating stories sure, but killing your brother hardly seemed enough material for immortality. Brother hate, it had to be as common as sheep shit, even in the ancient world.

"Just forget it, Jack," Agustin sighed. He looked tired suddenly. Not angry at all. "Why don't you come on in?" Agustin swung the door wide to let me pass.

We both knew what came next: the two-man parade from the living room to the kitchen. Agustin didn't breed flies and larvae. He never touched garbage and he barely skipped a bath. Instead, he'd added his own spin to Papa's mudroom collection of recyclables. Each week as I walked through the rooms of my childhood home there was one more constellation on the living room ceiling, one more NASA poster hanging from the wall. Two months ago he added a new picture of the Omega Nebula in the hallway. Today, when I stepped inside, it was a photograph above the living room sofa, framed.

"A composite image of the SN 1006 supernova remnant. From the European Southern Observatory," Agustin said, making sure to stop for a moment so that I could admire it. No choice really, he was in my goddamn way.

"Beautiful, isn't it?" he said, as though admiring a recently acquired archival replica of Van Gogh's "Starry Night" or, perhaps, a Frida Kahlo. He coughed. "Some friends and I are planning a trek this summer to all the radio telescopes in the VLB array, even Hawaii."

Agustin was acting as though his star obsession had nothing to do with our family travel plans. I knew better.

"Nice," I said, which seemed to be the magic word.

Agustin finally moved. We crossed through the hallway and into the kitchen. That's when I saw the glowing, greenish-yellow light, leaking out from under the mudroom door. There was even a faint scuffling noise.

Agustin remained silent. And why not. The glow said it all: soon. Soon Agustin would win. Again.

A couple of days later, Rhonda Tuttle left yet another letter. This one demanded that I clean up the "premises" for "health reasons." I believe she used the word hazard as well. More paper to toss on the bedroom pile.

The days continued forward. Another dinner with Agustin. Another chance to observe the mudroom glow. I thought I heard a crinkling, perhaps a faint meow. Agustin didn't seem to notice. "How are you feeling, Jack?" he asked instead. "When's the last time you saw Dr. Conz?"

At night I barely slept, stretched out on the couch, sweating. Even with rolled up towels pressed against the cracks, the heat leaked through the bedroom door and out into the apartment's tiny living room. This was more than the usual summer heat. I could feel the minute gravitational force of each object in the bedroom starting to bend toward one another. All those years watching Papa tend his own collection of cardboard and paper was paying off. No light emissions yet, but I knew my craft.

"Equality is an illusion," Papa used to say, as if that was some consolation for all the differences between Agustin and me. "Balance. Equilibrium. That's the important thing."

"Tricky, mijo," Mama would interrupt with a slight frown. "So tricky. Sometimes a runaway star is the best possible outcome. Separation."

Perhaps I stood a chance, despite Agustin and his goddamn glow. Charmed or not, Mama and Papa had left both of us behind.

Gila Bend was the only home Agustin and I knew: two thousand residents, two power plants, one one-thousand-year-old archeological site and a convenience store that doubled as the town's only grocery. In its own way, Gila Bend was a tiny dust cloud in the galaxy of Arizona. Even the petroglyphs people associated with our town were actually eighteen miles out.

I talked to the deputy sheriff for less than five minutes, but it was the deputy, not Agustin and his goddamn glow, that finally tipped my world over the edge.

After Tuttle's stealth inspection and her second letter, the deputy, some newcomer fresh from the academy, showed up at my front door. He wore aviator sunglasses and very little hair. His pink skin glowed, oily from the summer heat, as he stared down at me. I thought I saw his nose wrinkle as he bent down to give me the papers.

"I don't want them," I said, trying to wave him away. This was only partially true. Paper was always a useful addition to the collection. It was the words written on them that I didn't want.

"I drove all the way out here," the deputy said in slow, careful tones, as though he was sure I'd somehow never noticed the county sheriff's substation on my walks around town. As though my tiny stature indicated a tiny brain.

Stupid Arizona hick. I knew the titles of most works in the Phoenix Art Museum's Latin American collection, along with a handful more in the Heard. I spent my time with Vik Muniz, Mario Martinez, and Gabriel Orozco. When I looked at their works, I felt myself stretching high into their private universes. Breathing was easier inside those frames.

"Mr. Rodriquez?" The deputy repeated, frowning down at me. He'd shifted one hand to his gun belt.

"Yes, all right." I took the papers. The first one had a title, Summons of Forcible Entry and Detainer, and an official looking seal. I noticed the word eviction somewhere below in the mix of sentences and signatures.

"Court date's on the paper," the deputy said, and then turned and walked back to his air-conditioned cruiser.

I marked my calendar and tossed the papers on top of the bedroom pile. God, people were weird. The deputy and I both knew that if I failed to appear I'd automatically lose the case. And yet he'd made a point of mentioning the hearing.

The judge was not as ambiguous. In less than five minutes, he made his judgment of "guilty" and requested the keys to my apartment.

"I know my rights. God, damn it! I'm Title Eight housing. For Christ's sake, my SSI check isn't going to stretch to sticker-priced apartments. Ninety days. You have to give me ninety days' notice, not ten!"

"Mr. Rodriquez, you will quiet down here or in the Maricopa County Jail," was the Honorable Harold R. Cookman's only reply. "The ninety-day rule doesn't apply to health hazards."

I quieted down, but I didn't hand over the keys. Ten days and counting. The heat in my apartment might be spreading, but Agustin was the one who'd managed to conjure an actual glow. I was close but not close enough.

My brother, Agustin, and I only ever agreed on one thing: it's hard enough being human. Being human in Gila Bend is even worse, or at least it was for our parents. I think after a while all that desert heat was like a never-ending reminder of everything Papa and Mama missed from their before-time. I wonder if they speak English in their new home. I wonder if they speak at all.

A list of things I'll miss when my time comes: the Phoenix Museum of Art, strawberry ice cream, the sound of crying coyotes, *Ax Men* on the History Channel, and the Desert Shrimp Festival—well, at least the shrimp scampi they serve. I could do without all staring. There's not much in the way of good food here in Gila Bend. Not much in the way of little people either.

My biggest complaint about our parental separation, Agustin got to tell me the news. "They're gone?" I asked when he called me that July morning. "Where to?" I was standing in my apartment's kitchenette, digging through the refrigerator. Ten a.m. and the place was already broiling.

"The mudroom isn't hot anymore. Why don't you come over for dinner tonight and I'll show you?" he said. "The least I can do for my little brother. Maybe you can help me look for Mama's cat. She seems to be missing as well." And just like that, Agustin took possession of both the house and Sunday dinners. And why not? After all, he was the son who had returned home, despite his college degree, to care for our aging parents. He'd taken that degree of his and found a job at one of the solar companies scouting Gila Bend and its over-heated blue-sky days. He'd started an astronomy club, cleaned the windows of the old house. He'd even driven Papa and his frail human bones down near Tucson for a special night viewing at the Kitt Peak Observatory.

Didn't matter. I'd moved out that same week. Now I had my own home at the Oasis Estates along with all those art books Mama had given me.

Papa may have taught us astronomy, but it was Mama who taught me about the stars. Every year Mama drove me out to a specialist in Phoenix where I was weighed and measured and declared "perfectly fine." After the medical cataloging was complete, Mama and I headed to the Heard Museum of Native Cultures.

Our ritual was always the same. After taking in Mario Martinez's *Sonoran Desert: Yaqui People* mural, we'd walk the few blocks to the Phoenix Art Museum. The two of us, Mama and I, would stare for hours at the bright colors of Rufini Tamyo and the darker tones of José Chávez Morado. One Morado painting, *Carnaval en Huejotzingo* was dominated by a powerful dwarf on a hobbyhorse battling death itself. At least he looked like a dwarf to me. I knew the word dwarf was only acceptable when associated with a star: dwarf stars, hundreds and hundreds of times larger than our own massive earth. Somehow, I was only a "little person." Seemed to me, I could use whatever term I damn well pleased.

"Dwarf looks fucking fierce," I said, trying out the word. "Like he could actually win."

"Mm," Mama replied, ignoring the swear word. "The small ones always last longer. Even your Papa knows that." Her smile seemed to light up her entire face. "It's getting dark, Jack. Almost time to go home."

I knew exactly what she meant. This was my favorite moment, the reason we saved the Phoenix Art Museum for last. I held Mama's hand as we headed outside, not even worried about what other people might think. We walked to a spot on the southeast corner of the museum, and then Mama and I both tilted our heads up. On a second-floor wall, a couple walked across an LED display. The piece was entitled *Julian and Suzanne Walking*, but Mama called it *The Lite-Brite Family*. In the darkness, they looked like star people walking across the night sky.

"Solid matter," Mama said, glancing down at me, "is overrated."

"Do you think I'll battle death one day?" I asked, my mind still half on the José Chávez Morado painting and its unnamed dwarf, half on that recent visit to my doctor.

"Everybody does," she replied. "Dwarfs and stars alike."

Just a week after my court date, the deputy sheriff showed up for the last time. It was Sunday, my Agustin day. What was it with these people and their weekend hours? Tuttle and her cleaning crew were waiting behind the deputy, wearing rubber gloves and carrying a roll of garbage bags.

"Step right in," I said, as though unaware of the deputy's holster and handcuffs. I would not yell. I would not lose focus. Not now.

"Mr. Rodriquez," Tuttle called from her safe distance.

"Yes. Yes. I won't be a minute. I need my special gear, you know."

I pushed the wheelie cart out of the apartment just as the crew started to unroll the bags. The cart contained all the essentials: my grabber, my stool, my art books, including the José Chávez Morado and Tamayo books that Mama had bought me. I even had Mama's *Ladies of the Canyon* album by Joni Mitchell and the circle of polished pyrite. The album's cardboard sleeve had disintegrated in the bedroom pile, but the vinyl itself seemed unwarped.

That's when it hit me: that bitch Tuttle, Judge Cookman, and even the deputy sheriff had all done me a huge favor. It didn't matter who built the portal. The first one through won.

"You remember Mama's cat, Bonita?" Agustin asked as he pushed the bowl of prickly pears toward me. We were both sitting at the kitchen table. Agustin faced the stove while I watched the mudroom door. My eyes were on the greenish light. It was definitely brighter. Hotter too. Sweat ran down my neck and back. Soon. It was going to be soon.

"Mama's cat?" Agustin repeated.

"Always thought it was a dumb name," I said. "Who calls their cat Pretty?" I took a couple of pieces of prickly pear from the dish, licked the purple juice off of my fingers. "Mama's recipe, right?"

"Right," Agustin said. He smiled at me. "I've been trying out a few things. Even made some fresh nopales for the astronomy club. Did I tell you

Veronica joined? Drives down from Phoenix. She's going on the club's VLB array trip."

"Veronica Rosales, your old girlfriend?"

"You know, sometimes I hear Mama's cat meowing," Agustin said, ignoring my question.

"What?"

"Bonita. Mama's cat."

"Oh, right, Bonita." I waved my hand as though shooing a fly.

Meowwww.

"Did you?" I shifted off my chair and stood up. Along with the light, I could see a stream of smoke rising from the mudroom door. The glow was actually scorching the wood.

Meowwww.

"Jack."

Mrow. This time the sound was quieter. I could imagine Bonita's head tilted to one side, questioning.

"Jack, you're my brother. I—"

"Agustin, can you just shut up for a moment?" I started toward the mudroom, my slippers shuffling on the worn linoleum. Agustin, miraculously, remained silent.

Mrow.

The sound was so soft. Damn cat had probably already found its way back through the portal.

"Jack, life isn't really that bad," Agustin said. "Maybe we could—"

"Just this once, Agustin, let me go." I reached for the mudroom door. The knob was hot, but not painfully so.

"Anyway," Agustin said, his voice barely above a whisper. "You know, you should be the one to find Bonita. I know Mama would have wanted that."

I could hear the sliding of a chair somewhere behind me, the clink of plates. It seemed Agustin was cleaning the table. Maybe it was a trick, but I turned anyway. Agustin was my twin, my brother. "What about all the time you've spent?"

"Jack," Agustin said. "I'm busy." His voice seemed calm, but his face was all wrong. His lips were quivering. "At work we've just begun designing that new solar array. And Veronica is supposed to drive down from Phoenix next weekend. Guess I'm not quite up to chasing Mama's cat." Agustin took a slow breath and then looked down at the kitchen table, fussing with the dirty plates.

Through the sliding glass doors I could see night descending. Already the stars were filling up the sky. I turned back toward the greenish light, quickly twisted the mudroom knob, and stepped inside. Despite the glow flowing out from under the door, the room was darker than I expected.

The dinner plates crashed to the floor.

"No take backs," I whispered, pressing the pop-lock into place.

I could hear the beat of Agustin's footsteps rushing, and then the handle started to rattle.

"Jack. Jack." Agustin's voice sounded farther away than I'd expected, muffled. "Look. Why don't we both leave this for another day?"

"It's okay, Agustin," I said. Silence was Agustin's only reply. The handle, however, was shaking harder than before. Funny.

For some reason the mudroom's heat didn't even bother me. Dim starlight came through the far window along with the orange-yellow of a nearby house light. However, it was the greenish glow that held my attention. It spread out across the teetering stacks of paper piled across the floor and continued along the shelves that lined the length of the right wall.

The shelves were pure Agustin. Covered in overflowing stacks of screwdrivers and random lengths of pink string, I could see Agustin's order underneath the mess. Tools on the third shelf. Cleaners near the top.

Agustin. He wasn't that good a clarinet player, no matter what Mama had said as we sat through yet another band concert. Or was it swimming and a swim meet? Pole vaulting, perhaps? All of it so hard to remember. All those wasted hours watching Agustin. Agustin winning and smiling and holding his trophies aloft.

And now he'd managed to construct the portal ahead of me. If it were me, I wouldn't have let my scrawny ass anywhere near that mudroom door.

"Jack, Agustin has to try so hard, honey," Mama once tried to explain. "He's like a roaring fire made of nothing but paper. He just doesn't have much time. Do you see?"

But I didn't see at all.

On the other side of the door was silence. The handle was still. Agustin seemed to have stopped trying to convince me of anything. Inside the room, it felt like a starlit summer night. The heat, the smells, even the sounds.

A rough crinkling came from the far left corner where the newspapers and magazines were deepest. In the dimness, gleams, like campfire sparks, slipped out from beneath the moving papers. I could hear a faint whooshing noise.

Meow. Bonita cried from the stack, farther anyway than before. It was almost like the cat was guiding me through.

Agustin. It always came back to Agustin and his clarinet or oboe lessons. The long hours I had to sit listening as Agustin recited one constellation after another.

"Over there?" Papa would prompt him, using a red laser pen, pointing to something in the northwest quadrant of the star chart laid across the living room floor.

"What month?" Agustin would counter.

"July."

"Aries, then," Agustin said. His voice sounded confident.

"Jack, do you agree?" Mama called from the kitchen, trying to make it all sound fair.

"Sure." But my reply was as far from "sure" as I was capable of making it.

"Supernovas, mijos," Papa had responded to some question I never actually heard. Agustin, I was convinced, had made sure to ask it at the perfect moment.

Now that same grownup brother had sent me to collect Mama's cat.

Meow, Bonita said from inside the depths of the dusty mound of papers. A tuft of gray-black fur hung like a jaunty flag from the corner of an *Astronomy Now* magazine. More sparks. Below the sparks the ground seemed like a ring of fire leading toward the cat and all those super-charged, stardust particles.

Meow.

Mama wore starlight woven in her hair, her long black locks falling in waves, silver threads holding the gold in place. "Dust everywhere," she would say whenever Agustin complained about the latest mess. Rings in the tub. Tumbling weeds growing beneath our beds.

"Dust, Mama—my life is filled with dust."

"Yes," Mama would respond. "Of course it is." And then she would smile at him in that certain way and touch his hair, as though checking him for something. Whatever it was, Agustin must have passed. Because, after the smile, and the hair, always came the food, dusty clouds of flour rising up from the kitchen counter, spreading across the kitchen floor.

Mama didn't hide a thing, not really, not if you were really paying attention. She was always singing Joni Mitchell's "Woodstock."

"We are stardust. We are golden."

"How did she know?" Mama would say with a smile and a shake of her head.

Agustin must remember something entirely different. After all, he was going to Hawaii with Veronica and his astronomy club.

Meow, Bonita called again, and then came the music. "I Love the Night Life," The Pointer Sisters' "Fire," a whole litany of songs tumbling out from the papers, scattering across the mudroom floor.

I stepped forward, hands slipping beneath grease-stained fragments and crumbling clods of broken earth, slipping farther, my skin unable to hold me back. My wrists and elbows and thighs were sliding, all of me slipping through, following Bonita's meow.

Mama and Papa couldn't say I hadn't tried. After all my work, there was no way they were going to be disappointed Agustin hadn't come through...

No more Sunday dinners. No more posters. No more taller brother looming over me.

My arms and legs. I'd had arms and legs just moments ago. I remembered them just as I remembered those nights with Mama in Phoenix staring up at *The Light Brite Family*.

Memories are an animal thing, chemical connections in the brain. Somehow, I'd never considered that before. The taste of the sweet pear slices was long gone. I couldn't even smell the loamy scent of Agustin's papers. No cat's meow. Instead, my particles were filled with a pulsating light. Perhaps Mama and Papa wouldn't even notice I'd made it through.

And Agustin. I might not notice Agustin staring up from one of his earth-bound telescopes. I might not even care.

Such chemical worries.

Separat

FLORIDA MIRACLES

*E*STA, *IT'S EXTREMELY IMPORTANT that David and his razor-blade join us*, Mrs. Henry tells me. *Don't fret, child. He'll barely notice the blood.*

"Three days," I say. I grab a slice of pizza from the box on the coffee table, then glance at David and his blood-spattered paper towel. It's gotten to the point that David barely winces when he draws the blade across his skin.

Tonight's distraction, *The Perks of Being a Wallflower*, mutters in the background. The movie is all suicide and drugs. Considering David's dad, David's cutting, and worst of all, his mom—well, sometimes being human means being stupid—like right exactly now.

"Three nights?" David squints at me, confused. If I hadn't already guessed from the slowly expanding lines across his flesh, tonight is clearly one of his rough nights. David and I, along with Mrs. Henry, have been tracking the days until our trip for months now, performing our own private count-down.

"Three days," I say as I carefully roll the slice of pizza, trapping the melted cheese inside, "until our camping trip."

"Oh, right." David sets his double-edged blade on the coffee table next to the paper towels, the pizza box, and my sketchbook. "What do you think?" He holds out his arm, showing off the four equidistant cuts.

"You know what I fucking think." No matter what I try—threats, sympathy, even one interminable week of silence—nothing seems to help. At least he won't bleed to death with me around. That's the hope anyway.

Guilt, Esta, Mrs. Henry says from somewhere deep inside, *is a wasted emotion.*

Mrs. Henry has spent the last fifteen years nestled inside my brain. One of Florida's many hidden Maskers—at least that's what she tells me. Mrs. Henry, she tells me, is almost eight thousand years old. Despite her age and all that "flesh time," sometimes that old lady knows absolutely nothing.

Titusville used to be called Miracle City, USA. Our engineers built the space shuttle, the Apollo rockets, the Gemini series. But not anymore. These days, our town is flooded with unemployed aerospace engineers. I don't blame our moms for trying to escape. It's just that my mom used a corporate transfer to Maryland, while David's used a knife.

"Pretend this never happened," she said that last night as I stood in their kitchen. "Promise."

I wish I could.

Guilt and love. They put me in David's car each morning on the way to school, make me tell him another lame-ass anti-joke. They hold me against the couch as David bleeds, razor blades and pizza boxes stacked around us.

Cocooned deep inside my head, how could Mrs. Henry ever understand the necessity of letting the mess leak out? The human need for tears—or blood?

When I was little I thought the world must be full of Mrs. Henrys: a second voice safely encased inside each special child, watching everything through their bright young eyes.

Back then, David didn't care that he couldn't see or hear or even touch Mrs. Henry. After all, Mrs. Henry was funny. And I was more than happy to repeat everything she said.

"When I'm bigger..." David said. "When I'm bigger, I'll drive a car all the way to Alaska so I can see the polar bears and the igloos. Esta will come too because she's my friend."

"I was bigger once, little David Tissandier," Mrs. Henry replied in her

Mrs. Henry way, and already David was cracking up. "No. Really. Much bigger. With two extra rows of teeth, just like a dragon."

"Fat whopper, Mrs. Henry. Fat whopper. Everyone knows dragons have one row of teeth. It's sharks that are all jumbled." But David was laughing. And Mrs. Henry was laughing too, the sound like a deep hum or a rumbling purr.

Of course, I was the only one who could hear her.

I used to call Mrs. Henry a monster, a dragon, an alien visitor from outer space. Perhaps she's all of those things. Perhaps none. Masker seems closer to a calling than a species. Whoever or whatever she used to be, Mrs. Henry has rested inside my mind for my entire life, talking, always talking, over whatever I have to say.

Most nights, after the pizza, the movie, and the blanket thrown over David's passed-out dad, David drives me home while I stare at the lit-up houses and wonder. How many sad rocket-kids are sitting inside their air-conditioned homes right this very moment? How many are stuck waiting for their secret transformation?

It feels like we must be legion.

Just two days left.

Masker transformations can be—messy. You may have to guide David's hand. Be prepared. I wouldn't want to lose either of you.

"It'll be fine," I say. "Go back to sleep."

So you can ignore me? Mrs. Henry sounds almost imperious. I'm no longer a little kid. She doesn't have to be quite so nice.

It's my *goddamn mind.* I pull the pillow over my head. I'm tired.

Really? Is that what you tell yourself?

"Why did you even choose me?" I'm so irritated I actually speak the words out loud.

Maskers worship people, Mrs. Henry whispers, as though the words prove her love.

Mrs. Henry. More and more, she feels like the parasite nestled in the center of my brain: a helminth, a protozoan, a horsehair worm just waiting to burst out.

Fifteen isn't what it used to be, Mrs. Henry says.

Whatever.

Only two days left until the old dragon flies away and finds a new fleshy home. Only two days until I enact my own transformation. And David's.

At some point after Mrs. Henry announced her departure, she made me an offer I accepted. David may not know it yet, but the two of us are following her, burying ourselves inside someone else's neurochemical enclosure. After fifteen years with Mrs. Henry, I know exactly what to do. Imagine living life ensconced inside the safety of a Masker cocoon. It has to be better than this.

You'll try anything if you're desperate enough. Survive it too. The camping trip is more than Mrs. Henry's good-bye. "Camping trip" is my code for getting the hell out of here.

The final day.

On this trip, my sketchbook is staying put along with all those unwanted memories: the dim moonlight, the shadows that moved across Mrs. Tissandier's face, the knife she pulled from the kitchen drawer, how my fingers itched to hide behind my sketchbook as David's mom started to cry.

I carry a Moleskine everywhere: to school, to Sand Point Park, to David's house. It's one of those notebooks with the special elastic closures. Sometimes I draw David with that straight-edged scar bisecting his left brow, or my dad, or even the bright arch of rocket fire from yet another nighttime launch. Mostly, though, I draw my other self—old Mrs. Henry—hidden away inside.

Mrs. Henry tells me she has long straight hair, pure white. And that the skin is dark and ashy from lack of sunlight. My Mrs. Henry teeth are even. My eyes laser sharp. It's like those formal portraits hanging in the Orlando Museum of Fine Art: any scars erased.

Our last night, and still Mrs. Henry can't stop talking.

"Esta," Mrs. Henry says, "did I ever tell you about my fingers? Beautiful tapered things. Nails like shimmering pearls. You should draw them. Wouldn't that be nice?"

"No." I ignore Mrs. Henry and focus on my bedroom mirror. I bend my head to the paper, move my charcoal pencil across the page. The picture has to be just right. Dark hair, wavy. A frown line between my eyebrows. A dimple at the corner of my left cheek. I'm determined; the me I've been for fifteen years will be tacked to my bedroom door when I finally walk out, watching over Dad even after I'm gone.

There are no more days left to count.

Mrs. Henry and I pause outside Dad's study door.

Florida is in the full flower of spring. Five p.m. and the sun hasn't even started to set. Inside my house, though, the blinds in Dad's room are all the way down.

Hour after hour, Dad sits in front of his flickering computer screens. He claims the sunlight interferes with his work, though all I can see when I glance over his shoulder is the usual mess. A half-finished game of *Halo 2* takes up one screen, stock quotes and a steady stream of news blogs another. When Dad isn't vanquishing imaginary people, he likes to comment. Late into the night StarmanXtreme burns up the message boards.

"Dad? I'm heading out."

"Right. Okay."

"Camping with David," I clarify.

"Good."

I can see Dad's face reflected in the monitors. No matter which version I look at, his expression doesn't change: starman lost, starman lonely. That's my dad, all right. I lay my hand on his chair. There's a fold on the back of his neck, a deep crease like a heavy frown. Most days that's all he shows me: that fold of flesh and the graying stubble that runs just below his hairline.

"Bye, Dad." I try to put real meaning into those two words; after all this is our final father-daughter goodbye.

"Bye," he replies and turns his head in my direction, surprising us both.

I'd hug him with my two fleshy arms, but I know that would only make him uncomfortable—me too. We've never been a touching family.

He wasn't a bad parent, Mrs. Henry murmurs. Her own way of saying goodbye, I guess. And why not. She may not be human, but she's known him my entire life.

It's dusk. David and I crouch in the scrub next to Crawler Way, the road that used to carry the space shuttles from the Vehicle Assembly Building to Launch Pad 39B. NASA may be what this area is known for, but the Maskers' secret expeditions into our world started long before the missile ranges, the aerospace engineers, and NASA's Mercury program arrived.

David and I are both wearing our flame-resistant coveralls, long waders, and the class-four-rated insulating rubber gloves I ordered online. I should be more excited. I've waited fifteen years to really see Mrs. Henry. Fifteen years with only thought-words and pencil sketches. It's important to keep all traces hidden and not spook the flesh. That's what Mrs. Henry tells me. After eight thousand years of life, I guess she should know.

The land around the launch site is a mix of marsh grasses, empty paved roads, and drainage ditches. The NASA control center stands a quarter mile away. From our lookout it's easy to see the center's main parking lot and its dwindling collection of cars. David and I can't start anything until the last of the workers have left for the day.

"David."

"Yeah."

"You've always been a good friend—even when you were a baby."

David looks at me askance. "What's that supposed to mean? We're the same fucking age."

"Right." Despite my request for razorblades, I'm sure David's more than half-convinced this is just another one of my schemes. Like the time we went gator hunting in Moore Creek, or the time we built a transmitter to communicate with the dolphins that swim near the causeway: all half-assed kid-dreams with very little in the way of results.

"Getting a little old for this, don't you think?" David says into the silence.

"Worried you won't get to use that blade?"

For a moment David actually looks pissed. "I'm here to help you, yeah? The razor was your fucking idea."

Some secrets are best kept inside, that's what Mrs. Henry has always told me. A ritual cleansing, I called it. Freeing Mrs. Henry, I said. But tonight,

David's blade is going to do much more than set one Masker free. It's going to take all three of us to a whole new life.

One glance at our dads and you can see the truth: young bodies might be adept at adjusting and reapplying masks, but eventually everything gets old. Graying, slumped over a computer screen, their fleshy envelope doesn't even fit. And still guys like my dad aren't able to slide it off.

I think that's what David's mom was doing with the knife: trying to escape. She was just too old to get it right. Her hair was black when she died, not the tiniest bit of gray. Of course it was easy for her to miscalculate her available window of time.

I cried that night as I stood in David's kitchen—just me, Mrs. Henry, and David's mom. I cried as I repeated Mrs. Henry's words. "Shh. It's so late. Just let them sleep. Shh. It'll be all right." And those final Mrs. Henry words as David's mom lifted the knife: "Don't worry. David will always have me."

I hated Mrs. Henry and her promises. And all the blood, I hated that as well.

I miss David's mom. I miss old David and his crazy-happy smile even more. The way he opened his eyes extra-wide as he tilted his head to one side. Sometimes it feels like those pieces of David are lost forever. Mrs. Henry, she worries about things like that, missing pieces that "break the integrity of the whole." Me, I just worry about being left behind, the Florida heat and the birds a constant reminder of everyone who has flown away.

"David?"

"Huh?"

"Why does Mr. Emmanuel wear coveralls?"

When David turns his head toward me, his eyes have a knowing glint. "Okay, I give. Why?"

"Because it makes practical sense for an electrical worker to minimize the possibility of injury due to a high-energy arc-flash event."

"That has got to be your worst anti-joke ever," David says, but I swear to God, he almost looks like he's smiling.

And then the smile fades as he scans the drainage ditch and surrounding brush.

"Mrs. Henry is the worst kind of friend," David mutters. "Gators all over this place."

Don't worry, David. Alligators are actually quite timid around people, Mrs. Henry says. Despite my own worries, I feel compelled to translate.

Seven p.m. and the parking lot is finally empty. I can feel the heat building inside my chest.

"So how much longer are we gonna wait?" David looks tired.

Soon, Mrs. Henry says.

"Soon," I repeat, unzipping the top of my coverall and scratching at my skin.

It's about to get a lot hotter than this, Mrs. Henry says.

"I have no idea how old I really am," I whisper. I can feel the racing of something fiery and sharp inside my flesh.

"What the hell are you talking about?" David snorts. He remembers me coming over to his house for first-grade sleepovers. We used to take baths together—all that unlined scrubbed-clean skin. No way am I some old lady playing with a puppet life. I'm sure that's what he's thinking.

But it's getting harder and harder to untangle myself from Mrs. Henry. It's not just my skin. I can feel a blaze deep in my gut. I can feel a weight bashing against my skull.

I've always listened to Mrs. Henry. Mrs. Henry worshipping my bits of bone and flesh. Mrs. Henry reveling in my many moods. Mrs. Henry promising me, always promising me something more. Today, David and I are finally going to find our just-right home. That's the deal.

Just a little cut, she said. Another Mrs. Henry lie. My head feels like it should be nothing but blood and shards of bone. "My whole life, it's all been one long game of dress-up," I say with sudden anger. "No wonder you liked me better when I was little."

Esta, that's not—

"You loved it when I made a rocket pack out of soda bottles and painted Dragon on the straps," I say, barreling over her words. "You loved it when I never once asked you why." I pause, surprised by the tears in my eyes. "People aren't supposed to listen in to everything."

"I'm not people."

"You always knew you'd leave one day. That sounds like people to me."

———

Launch and separation.

Lightning pushes up through my ribcage, working to burn its way free. *It's time.*

"David, you're going to have to cut deep, really push down."

"What? No! That's not what I signed up for. A ritual you said. A kid thing."

"David, I need you to trust me." Overlaying my own pain-roughened voice, I can hear Mrs. Henry's repeated cry: *New flesh, new flesh.* Her words feel like choking smoke and rocket flame.

"David," I say as I step toward my friend. "Please." I keep my hands at my sides. My chest roars with flame. "Let's fly away. The two of us and Mrs. Henry. Just like before."

"Are you sure—"

"Do it!"

David pulls his razorblade from his coveralls. His face is scrunched in some ugly mixture of concentration and fear. He raises his arm, and then with a quick left-to-right motion, he drives the blade along the exposed flesh at the top of my coveralls.

For one gasping moment, the cut stings, nothing more, and then I'm ablaze, shaking with the power of that old worm as she pushes her way out.

Finally, Mrs. Henry roars.

I can feel my throat closing against the searing air trapped inside my lungs. If she doesn't find the opening soon, Mrs. Henry will incinerate me from the inside out.

"Esta. Jesus," David cries. He takes a step back. Stops. "This helps us fly like Mrs. Henry?"

"She promised me, your mom. She—"

"My mom? Esta, what about my mom?!"

I close my eyes. This is all wrong: Mrs. Henry, the pain, my own self. *Focus, Esta.* A sharp stabbing pain beats against my rib cage. *Let me out!* Drives itself against my breastbone and spine. And I'm sobbing, snot and tears falling across my face.

"Esta? I . . ." David starts, then says nothing more.

I open my eyes, meet David's stare, screaming, screaming, as the skin over my chest splits wide. I can feel Mrs. Henry filling my throat, pressing down against my lungs, and then finally she tumbles out. The part of me David only half-believed in is leaving.

"Fuck," David says and nothing more.

"A new life," Mrs. Henry hisses, exultant. Out here in the real world, Mrs. Henry's skin is puke-green. She has a snout and wide heavy jaws. Her claws are long and thick and flaking. There's no lovely white hair. Instead there are scales—and teeth. So many teeth. Mrs. Henry isn't beautiful. She's terrifying.

She writhes in the drainage ditch, letting my blood wash away, while David watches, still silent. The bloody razor hangs from his right hand.

It's not just David's razorblade. Blood runs down my own neck and chest. There's a weird gap above my heart. But I exist. I'm here, breathing, despite the fiery dragon.

I'm also still human. Masker free. "Mrs. Henry?" I have to speak actual words to talk to her. The silence inside my head is like a miracle. "What now?"

But Mrs. Henry says nothing. Instead, she rises up from the ditch, sways. "Hurry, David. Let's fly." She opens her mouth wide and shows her dragon teeth, all three rows. "Too slow."

"I don't get..." David replies. "My mom. Just explain."

"Finish or don't, little David Tissandier. It's time." Mrs. Henry stares at him, then snaps her teeth together with seeming irritation. I stare too, her meaning suddenly clear. Sometime in the last few minutes David made one small cut along the flesh of his left wrist and lower arm. Sometime in the last few minutes he stopped.

"But I still don't..." David isn't lifting the blade, but he isn't letting go of it either.

"Child, she doesn't matter. Neither of them ever did." Mrs. Henry unfurls her leathery wings and staggers toward the stand of marsh grasses on the other side of the road. "So weak, David Tissandier. Just like sad little Esta."

"Esta?" Dave is looking at me as he speaks, not her.

This David isn't close to the kid he was when we were five. He isn't even the same as he was last summer before his mom died. But he's my living David.

"Esta?" He watches me, seemingly willing to wait as long as it takes. "Is this really what you want?" He waves the razorblade in my direction.

"Your mom. She asked me not to tell." I actually say the words out loud.

There's a screech and a leathery flap of wings as Mrs. Henry rises up from the marsh and starts her flight, escaping from the launch site, the blood, and us.

Escaping. Shedding our human skins. I can't imagine anything less appealing. "David. No." I grab David's hand, take the blade, toss it into the nearby scrub. I can still see Mrs. Henry heading east. Her wings move in clumsy arcs. Her body is low to the ground. She looks like she's hiding from the sky.

God, I missed so many things. Despite her fifteen, or fifty, or eight thousand years, Mrs. Henry is no miracle. This entire time, it's our lives, David's and mine, that have been miraculous.

"Esta." David pauses, sweat streaming down his face. "I don't want to be all alone." His words are like an echo of my entire childhood, so afraid to let Mrs. Henry and her Masker promises go.

There are things I could say, like how sad his mom was to leave him, like how she didn't mean to hurt either of us, like how I've got his hand in mine and I'm never letting go. "I'm here," I say instead. I squeeze his hand, firm and so very fleshy.

Mrs. Henry was right; it was a miracle, a burning painful miracle that David and I needed all along.

Maskers may be an ancient tribe, but they are not my people. They have no real children. No friends. They can't feel pain like us true Florida dragons.

Real Florida dragons scar when you cut them. We bleed. Sometimes we even break. But it is the one true miracle that I almost didn't figure out: Real Florida dragons don't remain entombed and protected forever more. They don't run. True Florida dragons try to take to the sky. True Florida dragons want to soar.

MOURNING FOOD: RECIPES INCLUDED

DEATH IS DELICIOUS, but it demands guidance to get those dishes right.

Even before the Ratajkowski sisters left their father's house, they were excellent cooks. They understood the true pleasure of food: its slivers and flecks. Its droplets. They accepted that feelings were a necessity. Most importantly, they recognized that recipes are a human right.

In their seventies, the sisters are older than Millinocket dirt. Older than all their dead anyway: Their father, the handful of Kempf cousins, and all three of their husbands have passed. Their mother too, though she's a special case.

Now the winter of their life has finally arrived. Veronica, Bertha, and Helen Ann sit for hours at the kitchen table, the kettle slowly cooling on the stove. Helen Ann, the youngest sister, prefers blackberry tea with honey and those special ashes she sprinkles on top. Helen Ann can be a little gauche. The other two no longer mind. With crooked fingers and wrinkled, age-spotted skin, they flip through their yellowed book, careful to hide their pleasure in a job well done.

The Ratajkowski recipe book is thick. Pressed between its pages are loose cards and scraps of paper attached with yellowing tape. On almost every page are dots and splashes that could be either chocolate or age-darkened blood. Most of the recipes are handwritten. Many annotated by a later hand. Veronica, Bertha, and Helen Ann are much more than sisters. They are lifelong neighbors—and enemies. Most importantly, they are old friends.

Let the feast begin.

As the oldest sister, Veronica married before the other two. From that first dance with Hubert, her silver-ringed finger was a promise: When Hubert's belly pressed against his belt and his hair had wintered to a sparse patch of gray, Veronica would mourn him as a widow should.

Recipe for a Husband Once Loved and Then Endured

1. Start with a twelve-hour brine soak. The ratio of salt to water is critical. Tears of rage are different than tears of pain. Both will be necessary. Plan accordingly. Pictures may not be enough to draw the necessary salts. Consider hand-crocheted hats, never worn. A birthday card with only a signature. A medical bill. Contemplate the round watermarks on Grandmother's coffee table, the broken light at the bottom of the basement stairs. Stretch your body across the bed where, by the end, you preferred to sleep alone. Make sure you have a glass vial or a small bowl ready to collect the tears. Ingredients for this particular dish are always hard won.
2. Smoke will sting your eyes when you check the grill, lift the hood. Be careful. Don't despair. Save that for the penultimate step when you touch the heated meat, remembering that some acts can never been undone.
3. Apply the glazing at the very end, sealing in everything that has come before. The most effective glaze consists of honey, vinegar, cloves, and the coarsest ground salt. Don't skimp. The honey must be collected from a hive by your uncovered hands. Make sure the sweetness is in no way worth the still-reddening welts.

This dish is best served on a china platter kept in a darkened sideboard.

A gift from your wedding day. The platter should be covered in a floral pattern and edged in gold.

Make sure to approach each of your guests as they partake of the funeral meats. Make sure to hold their gaze. Note their discomfort. Their uncertainty concerning the source of their tears. Bask in a job well or badly done. Bask in a dish finally and unalterably complete.

The Ratajkowski sisters had no time for self-delusion, *Babe*, or *Charlotte's Web*. Axe in hand, they spent long hours helping their father with the hogs, the slops, and later the knife slash across the hogs' pink freckled throats. Blood sprays easy if your cut is right.

But a lost baby not even grown is a different thing. A loss Bertha didn't expect. It pressed against her womb, so small she could go for months or years without even noticing the ache. And then she would think of her second child, whom everyone called her first, growing, growing and then fully grown. For Bertha, her first pregnancy was something undone, rather than something expelled. An unguarded wound that never left her.

Recipe for a Miscarried Fetus
Most recipes require hours not days. Fruit cake, sauerkraut, hákarl, the Icelandic dish, are exceptions. Such dishes require months and years to evolve. Babies are like that as well. It takes nine months to grow even a mediocre, average newborn.

Failure to Thrive.

Failure to Finish.

Failure to Grow.

A seven-week recipe is an act of transformation. Expert instruction is required.

1. Sadness is a single note. Folded with a wooden spoon, mixed for fifteen minutes, whipped into stiffened peaks—no matter your preferred technique, to be successful, this recipe requires that you also pull forth your bitterness, your isolation, and your rage.
2. For proper fermentation, the base mixture must be kept at a continuous

fifty-one degrees Fahrenheit, the same temperature as an underground cave. Burial of the crock is a necessity. Hard, ice-covered ground is preferred. Make sure you surround the crock with a stuffed animal purchased far too early, a miniscule cradle to rock the broth. Make sure the burial of the dish is unseen and unnoticed. Make sure no one even considers the empty patch of ground.

3. Remember, at its heart, the dish demands interment, periodic tasting, but to be successful, it must never be entirely exhumed.

A rank beginner's mistake: The hospital people erupted en masse from the birthing room. All that blue cotton and those squeaky white shoes. The supposed professionals: two doctors and two nurses, a balanced set. One of the women gave the news. The younger man couldn't even look the two older Ratajkowski sisters in the eye. When Veronica and Bertha followed him back inside, they watched as he tried and failed to avoid looking at the new mother's—the new mourner's—sweat-soaked hair, the metal scales and waiting bassinette, trying to avoid thinking about someone who, it turns out, would never arrive.

That doctor's silly-looking blue cotton gown. Blue cotton hadn't changed the outcome.

Recipe for a Stillborn Child

1. For this recipe weeping is required. Dissociation is no excuse. Copious quantities of salts must flow.
2. Remember to feed your husband. Comfort food is best. Liver and onions. Boiled potatoes. Turnip mash.
3. Remember to thank him when he tells you perhaps it's time to move on.
4. Remember to have sex.
5. Remember that children are like pennies or mewling kittens. Work hard enough and you can always find more.
6. Remember you've never considered specific dates important before.

Cancers are hard. The fat gone before the cooking can even begin. And then there are all those chemicals—cyclophosphamide, doxorubicin, paclitaxel—suffusing the meat. How is a family to properly mourn?

Veronica carries a pair of sharp silver scissors and a long skein of yellow twine in her purse, along with a collection of stained recipe cards. Twine is versatile, useful for both binding a roast and a game of cat's cradle when her sister's children wander too close, interrupting her work. Show enough interest and most children will eventually walk away. Cat's cradle and patience are all that is needed. And then it's back to the careful measurements, the slicing, and the herb ball wrapped tightly in cheesecloth. Finally, the dish is complete.

Recipe for a Mother Lost Too Soon

1. The key to this recipe is intent.
2. Ingredients: chocolate, dark and unsweetened, the bitter taste a surprise to most; minced chilies that burn your fingertips and stop you reaching out with injured hands.
3. This is a layered dish, some sweetness is required. A dull slug of rice poached in cows' milk should suffice. Something that makes it hard to create a solid form.
4. Fresh and hot and ice cold all would help the flavor. Don't get the final step wrong. Tepid suits this dish best. Burning bitterness and the flavor of burnt milk should do the rest, forcing the mourners to gulp it down.

Sometimes avoiding memories, not savoring them, is best.

All good cookbooks contain recipes for unexpected events, unplanned for except by the expert cook: the anniversary of a broken promise never forgiven, the arrival of an unsettled stranger, the slow unraveling of memory along with the self. The Ratajkowski sisters place their book at your disposal, along with their final recipe.

———

Recipe for Three Missing Women Whom Nobody Cares to Name.

Already the stained recipe card, though it was pulled from the book, seems wrong. This isn't really a recipe at all. It's a lack; the last of the sisters has died. The card contains the text of multiple hands, but there is no one left who can say which sister wrote the blue-inked words, or why additional ingredients were added by a soft-leaded pencil almost too faint to read. There is no one who was actually present at the creation of the dark stains.

But a true cook knows how to improvise, scratch out the title at the top of the card, write eight words on a new line. Three Mourned Sisters: Veronica, Bertha, and Helen Ann.

Three separate loses. Three separate deaths. Three makes it harder. It isn't the number. It's the timing. The sisters had long hair for the most part, though not always, and a sense of unease in their smile. One had a son who lived, Braiden. Two had boyfriends in late middle age. Their homes were less than a quarter mile from each other. Town was only ten miles away, but the drive became tricky after the husbands and boyfriends and various children had gone.

You are an expert now. You know the mix of flavors has to be just right. It's imperative that the sisters don't get separate plates. For some, such a thought would carry a whiff of skimping or second best. But while mourning food requires overabundance, you also know it requires the correct effect: the layers that seep, the groaning tables and plates full of years-long simmered broth. You know that, in this case, the flavors of the three sisters must flow together on a single plate. The dish, along with the standard condiments and edible table display, will be more than enough.

To remember Veronica, Bertha, and Helen Ann, it will be exactly right.

The Faces Between Us

DRIVE LONG ENOUGH and you can find anything. Copper-eyed goddesses. Gilded August afternoons. That arid stretch of Oregonian high desert in the southeastern corner of the state. Keep driving and you might catch something even more precious—a path through. Perhaps even a fairytale ending. That's what Amber promised me during that long ago summer.

Didn't matter. Back then the girl could have said almost anything and I wouldn't have listened.

Each Saturday morning I drove while Amber sat beside me, watching the miles slide by. Unwanted photographs and half-finished journals, scratched and dusty vinyl, Amber knew exactly what she wanted. Bessie Smith's "Baby Won't You Please Come Home" or, better yet, early Helen Hume and Anita O'Day before the heroin slide. "Oregon's true spirit" was Amber's term for all that transformed darkness. As though I had the slightest idea what she meant.

That particular Saturday morning, Amber was already waiting on the front step when I pulled up in my truck. She stood pressed against the handrail, as far from her mother as physically possible. Amber's mom sat hunched in the sunshine, picking at the scabs that ran along her too-thin arms.

It was just Amber and Mrs. Destros. Amber's dad, Mr. Destros, had disappeared months ago, just before Amber and I had started going out. "Didn't even bother to show me the way" was all Amber's mom would say on the subject. Somehow, I had the sense Amber knew exactly where her dad had landed.

"Hey, babe," I called from the open passenger window. Amber bolted down the stairs and across the weed-strewn yard while Amber's mom stopped picking at her scabs long enough to grab a nearby metal can opener.

"Let's go," Amber said as she opened the passenger door. "You're fucking late," she added.

"Sunstone?" Amber's mom had started waving the can opener in our direction. "Sunstone? I'm only trying to help. No one else gives a shit if you ever find the way. Not like me. Not like Dad pretended to."

"Brilliant parenting, Mom," Amber said through the open passenger window. "Stellar, in fact." Turning in my direction, she repeated, "I said let's go."

"You look hot, you know? Combustible," I clarified as I put the truck into drive. And she really did. Back then Amber smoldered with some strange amalgam of rage and pain: flushed skin, scorched honey-dust eyes—and those breasts.

Amber glared at me. "What the hell are you smiling at?"

"Nice try, but I'm not even close to angry," I said, steering the Ford away from the curb and her mom's strange obsession. Hopefully, the gas would last.

Amber's house was littered with can openers: easy-grip double-wheels, standard butterflies, and those old-fashioned church keys that you punch down against the can. "The same old parent shit—just with spirits and crumbly bits," Amber told me the one time I bothered to ask.

"What?"

"They like to snort it. Or she does, I guess. Dad did too, before he cut out."

"Snort what? Tuna fish and cling peaches?" I ignored the dig about her missing dad.

"All sorts of stuff. Basically whatever might push them through."

"Huh." After that I left the topic well enough alone. Asking Amber too many questions was exactly the wrong sort of hassle. Like why she called me her "little catalyst." Like why her mom kept talking about "Oregon's Golden Realm."

"So where the fuck were you?" Amber leaned forward and turned on the radio. "I've been waiting for almost half an hour out there with *her* and her kitchen utensils."

"Still not angry." I rolled down my window and turned onto Highway 206 and the empty miles between central Oregon's fade-away towns. "You get as mad as you want. Doesn't matter to me. No Feelings Larry, right? I'm your 'no demands, no expectations' guy."

Amber laughed, flecks of smoke-tinged gold shining from her eyes. "God, I really love you."

"I'm glad," I said, refusing to parrot back her words. Girls and their feelings were dangerous—this girl anyway, busily tracing her secret path.

Home for both of us was on the wrong side of the Cascade Mountains. Our stretch of Oregon was full of barely-there towns, faded aluminum siding, and old men in lawn chairs, waiting for the reappearance of something even they suspected would never return.

According to Amber, towns like Wasco weren't just small-town Oregon. They were entry points into the true Oregon—Oregon's spirit realm.

Maybe, and maybe not, but back then I could drive my truck forever if it meant I'd get laid.

"Amber?" I tried, slipping one hand between her thighs.

"Shh, Larry. I'm concentrating." Amber swatted me away. The wind came through the open windows, whipping her dark hair into a shroud that covered her eyes and mouth.

"Come on, babe," I said. "Sing me one of your old-timey songs."

That got her attention.

Some days, Amber was just a girl with faded bruises and stories she didn't share. Other days she sang. Those hot-and-crumbly ghosts, she claimed, required her music before they'd reveal the path's next turn.

God, Amber could sing. Billie Holiday and Etta James took me that way, but Amber was the real thing: an "old soul" carrier, all ashy with second-hand shame.

It took two songs and thirty minutes to flush out our prey.

"This is it," Amber said, pointing to a trailer home set in a patch of hemlock and pine. There were no other people in sight, just a woman with stiff, salt-and-pepper hair and a rough slash of lipstick.

"Hey," I said as I stepped down from the cab. The old lady nodded but remained silent. The two of us watched Amber pick through the tables of stuff: a box of Nancy Drew novels covered in tattered dust jackets, a crockpot with a brittle-looking cord, a broken wicker basket filled with buttons.

"Larry." Amber held up a dented metal cylinder about ten inches tall. Inside, I could see red-and-white drinking straws.

"You sure?"

"Definitely."

"Eighteen dollars." The old lady frowned, daring either of us to argue.

"Give the lady her money, Larry," Amber said with a grin.

"Okay," I said, pretending to reach for my wallet.

Then we were both sprinting for the truck, Amber still wrestling with the cab door as I pulled away—fast.

That's what I remember about that Saturday in August: red-and-white straws and the two of us laughing as we traveled west along Highway 206. Blue skies all the way.

Forget souls or emotional vibrations; truth is ghosts are closer to ambered flies trapped in their own past. How much do they even notice the needs of the living? That's the question neither of us thought to ask. Amber assumed the ghosts were trying to help, and perhaps they were, but there are only so many ways to use those red-and-white drinking straws.

No more Saturday morning drives. No more flushed cheeks while my hands slid down Amber's naked belly. Those first few weeks of August were all the same: me standing in the gloom of Amber's basement, waiting impatiently as she worked on her homemade pixie sticks.

A single light bulb hung overhead. A can opener rested on the edge of the table, ignored, at least for now. Amber had never explained its presence. She didn't need to. Even then I knew it was Amber's metaphorical cyanide pill, her option of last resort.

"Get this right and it'll be even better than my 'old-timey' songs," Amber promised yet again. Her voice sounded grim. There were dark circles under her eyes and a tightness to her lips. The pink streaks in her dark hair, though, still made me think of melt-in-your-mouth spun sugar.

"Maybe the old lady's straws weren't the key after all."

Amber grunted but otherwise ignored my comment.

I'd been sampling Amber's pixie sticks every night for the last week. No snorting; that was one of Amber's few rules. We swallowed it all down: the powdered nutmeg and straight-up sugar, the pulverized shrooms and crushed Neco wafers, we even cooked up a homemade extract of weed, plastic-bottle vodka, and honey.

Kids' stuff. The two of us searching for that path through to our fairytale ending.

I shifted restlessly, watching from a spot just behind Amber's chair as she taped shut the end of yet another straw, added the Ritalin I'd scored, and then poured in my favorite version of her sugar chasers: Sour Patch Kids remnants she'd saved from a grocery store candy-run the week before.

"The kick at the end" was my name for that sweet, acidic tingle. A taste like cotton-candy rage coating the back of my throat as we fucked.

I reached out and touched the nape of Amber's neck, frowning as her shoulders stiffened. This basement stuff was getting old.

"Just five more minutes," Amber muttered.

"Right." I turned away from Amber and her latest soon-to-fail experiment, kicking a can opener left at the bottom of the basement stairs. It made a satisfying clatter as it skidded across the floor. My sneakers scuffled out my progress as I followed the can opener toward the dimness of the far wall.

"No going back there. You promised, Larry," Amber said, still not looking at me.

"Okay," I said. But I didn't stop. Amber's game was going nowhere. It was my turn at spirit guide.

I pulled the cord of a nearby light and leaned in for a closer look. All I could see were metal shelves set across the length of the cinder block wall. Each shelf was filled with rows of dusty cans the size and shape of canned tomatoes but copper colored with thick lead seams. Some of the cans had mineral bleeds of blue and turquoise. A few still had partial labels, more than half worn off.

I grabbed a can. Already its coppery weight felt so much better than any candy-coated pixie stick. On the ragged bit of label, I could make out the word "Hospital" in bold black letters. And higher up, typed in fainter print, was a name: "Maisel."

"Amber, check this out."

"You fucking promised." For once Amber was looking straight at me.

"Explain why again," I said, striding back with the "Maisel" can in my hand.

"Dad left them here. When they closed the hospital, they didn't even bury their ghosts. Just left behind all that ash. He was the only one who cared. Well—knew how to use them," she amended.

The light bulb above Amber drew strange shadows across her face. Still, there was something funny about her expression. Sadness maybe? Anger? Euphoria as well. The girl was ready to burst with it.

"Looks like he already opened some of them." I grabbed Amber's can opener and gave the "Maisel" can a quick shake. Even before I cracked it open, I could feel the ashes inside, just waiting for the two of us to say hello. "What's the worst that could happen?" I said, grinning.

Amber stared at me, but didn't answer.

Despite Amber's rules, turns out swallowing ashes works just fine, no snorting necessary. Ghosts really aren't all that fussy.

That first time I had no idea what I was getting myself into. Amber, though, her hand trembled as she held the red-and-white straw to her lips.

"Old souls take me away," she mumbled, and then tilted her head back, swallowing the contents down in one long slide. She didn't even bother with a sugar chaser. Almost immediately her face seemed to harden, her skin flushed a bloody red, her lips pinched and cracking. When she spoke, her eyes looked far too dark. "Your turn, dearest." The laugh that followed was a gritty rough sound, nothing like my Amber.

I sucked in my own strawful. It was like being rinsed clean, my own thoughts tossed aside as I slipped into someone else's groove. Forget indulging in her sad-sack games. Maisel and I had another agenda.

Amber didn't look angry anymore, and she didn't look scared. Her entire torso trembled, as though under the thrall of some kind of palsy. She stood in the middle of that damp basement, the musty scent of mold filling her nostrils as her eyes rolled and her cracked lips bled. Meanwhile, my own body was getting warmer, burning up. No shakes, though. No spirit visions either. Just heat, as though the energy from Amber's shaking body was combusting me from the inside out. My hands reached for her, tearing at her T-shirt, her jeans, at that thin piece of cotton between her legs.

"Don't worry, baby," Maisel said, using Amber's voice. "I still like to fuck."

Maisel, it turned out, was good at transporting things—one piece at a time. He wasn't the only one. But Maisel was the first. A fragment of Amber traveled through to the other side with our very first hit of ash. Fairytale transformation, ragged piece by ragged piece.

"Amber..." I leaned toward her, brushing the hair away from her face. Even in the dim morning light, I could see the bruises along her neck. My own body was no better: nail gouges across my lower back crusted and stiff, across my cheeks as well.

"Don't," Amber said, wiping a thin coating of ash from her lips.

"Sunstone?" a voiced called from the top of the stairs. "Are you down there?"

Footsteps followed and then the click of an overhead light.

Amber's mom kept her eyes on the desk and the three open cans, rather than our own blood-and-bruised selves. "I told you they could help."

"Sometimes. They haven't taken *you* anywhere," Amber managed to shoot back.

"They will. Of course they will. It was your dad's fault. He's the one who told them to keep me out." Mrs. Destros glanced our way, not quite catching our eyes, then turned and headed back toward the stairs.

"She always was a burnout," Amber whispered.

And then, just like that, Amber and I started laughing—Maisel too, his voice ice-cold as it exited my throat and lungs. The other ghosts joined in: Josephina with her blood-red scream—and little Wallace. Only a boy,

Wallace stayed mostly silent, just wanting to draw more of those black cartoon elephants on the basement floor.

It was a matter of moments and a two-dollar can opener, and then Amber was taping another paper straw, shaking out another bit of ash onto the water-stained desk.

"Maybe this time they'll take me all the way through," she said, always the true believer. Her magic, fairytale ending just one ashy line away.

Me? I was too busy reaching for her naked and bruised body to even notice.

Outsiders think of Portland or maybe Salem as the heart of Oregon, but the truth is it's the empty stretches that hold our state's deepest secrets. Oregon's fairytales are dry and brutal, scattered with dust.

I wasn't the only one. Most people miss the important things. Few have even heard of Oregon's sunstone. One of those seemingly worthless gems that people think are best left below the ground. Amber's mom wasn't entirely wrong. Shine them up just right and the copper platelets in those sunstones look just exactly like the sunset flecks in Amber's eyes.

Don't know how I missed it. The girl was a goddess even before she finished traveling through.

And me, I've lived in Oregon long enough to finally learn some of her secret truths. Drive those vacant, mid-state miles and eventually you'll find her. You'll find them all: Josephina, Maisel, even sweet little Wallace. Amber's copper eyes are shining out from each of those unwanted Oregon rocks.

Waiting.

Perhaps one day, if I drive long enough, I'll find the way through. Perhaps Amber is trying even now, trying to show me the way to her secret path.

Idle Hands

Sylvia: 1971

GOD OR NO GOD, Sylvia Vieira's special day was all wrong. No mother helped Sylvia fasten her dress for her First Communion. No little sister burst into her bedroom, upending her collection of pressed flowers and carefully preserved damselfly wings, then looking falsely outraged when Sylvia complained.

Grandma Vovó couldn't make it all right, no matter how many fresh flowers she wove into Sylvia's hair.

"They're so stupid. I hate them both." Sylvia's tone was fierce.

"Shh, Sylvia. You need to stop."

Over the last few weeks Sylvia had heard Vovó's explanation so often she could recite the words herself. It was Sylvia's choice to stay behind on Flores Island, just as it was her sister Olivia's and their mother's choice to leave. But Sylvia knew Vovó was lying. Mother and Olivia hadn't just left behind their home in the Azores. They'd left Sylvia as well.

"You'll see them soon enough." Vovó fastened the last flower, an Azorean bellflower, in place. "That man, the one with the long gray hair?" She attempted a smile as she adjusted the collar of Sylvia's white dress. "You're a Vieira. He'll find you when the time is right."

"You didn't travel with him. And now you're really old."

"Old enough for him to leave me alone," Vovó agreed.

Olivia and Mother were selfish. That was the real truth.

"Trying out my wings," Sylvia's mother used to laugh whenever someone asked why the three of them, Mother, Sylvia, and little Olivia, had moved from Flores Island across the archipelago to the city of Ponta Delgada. Most Azoreans either stayed put or flew west to the Americas. For her first journey, Sylvia's mother had traveled just three hundred miles east on the Atlânticoline ferry with baby Olivia and four-year-old Sylvia firmly in tow.

Years later Sylvia still remembered fragments of the journey. The brilliant blue of the sky. The breeze that pushed against her hair. And the heated messages that leaked through her eyelids as she tilted her face up toward the sun.

Sylvia remembered the gray-haired man as well, the one Mother talked to while Sylvia practiced sun-speaking and baby Olivia slept in her pram.

"Beautiful day," he said, or perhaps, "Beautiful woman."

"Como?" Mother's voice sounded uncertain, but in that way she had. Even with her eyes closed, Sylvia could sense her mother's smile.

"Beautiful," the man said again, or perhaps, "Beautiful world."

"One of many," her mother replied.

Sylvia felt her body begin to melt, puddly and soft, as the sunlight found its way beneath her skin. Why was Mother even talking to this person? The talking made it hard for Sylvia to hear the sunshine's words.

"A good luck charm for you," the man continued, interrupting the sunshine yet again. "From one traveler to another."

"Obrigada."

"Obrigado, Miss Vieira."

How did he know Mother's name? Sylvia opened her eyes, curious, but the man was already walking away. Even from the back, she could tell he didn't fit. He was tall, too tall, his long gray hair tied in a knot at the base of his neck, and even though it was summer, he wore a high-collared shirt.

"O que um homem estranho," Mother said. What an odd man. But she smiled as she looked down at the metal pendant in her hand, an insect with two sets of wings. One of Vovó's special damselflies.

Sometimes men were friendly in the wrong sort of way; that's what Vovó had explained before four-year-old Sylvia got on the ferry. No talking to strangers. And yet here was Mother, accepting presents.

"No fair," Sylvia cried, reaching for the pendant.

"Sylvia, no!"

As she finished fastening the buckles on her First Communion shoes, Sylvia remembered Mother holding her hand and the metal damselfly just out of reach, wearing her usual Mother frown. Sylvia felt the anger rising up. That's what had made Mother look so wrong. Her mother's happiness while she talked to that man.

"No and no again," Sylvia had said when Mother suggested the flight to America, as though any parent would accept their nine-year-old daughter's decision to stay behind. But both Mother and Vovó took her at her word. Vovó and Sylvia had accompanied the travelers to the airport, no suitcases in hand.

"Goodbye, sweetheart," Mother said. She bent down to kiss Sylvia's cheek. "Try and talk to the man, hmm? We Vieiras are meant to travel."

"Talk to a stranger?" Mother's face was only inches from Sylvia. Despite the carefully placed scarf, Sylvia could see the green marks pressing out from the base of her neck. To Sylvia they looked like the first ugly shoot of a sprouting plant.

"The man's name is José, Joseph," Mother said. "So now he's not a stranger, yes?"

"Yes," Sylvia replied. She could feel herself scowling.

"Final boarding call for flight 486 to Boston," a voice declared over the airport's intercom.

Olivia was the one who Sylvia felt sorry for. She looked so sad as she clutched her Raggedy Ann doll.

"Stay with me," Sylvia whispered as she wrapped her arms around her little sister. "You can share my room and Vovó's damselfly collection."

Olivia cried, but she walked onto the plane. Of course she did. At five, Livvy was still a baby. Sylvia watched the airplane launch itself into the sky, and then she and Vovó caught the ferry back to Flores Island and Vovó's little house. For most of the trip, the two remaining Vieira women stood on the ferry's top deck, ignoring the pounding wind and the incoming storm. Sylvia didn't meet a single gray-haired man trying to offer her presents. For this one moment, the man with the gray hair had enough sense to keep away.

Vovó's cottage had red, tiled floors and thick stone walls. It sat halfway up the hill with a view of both Lajes das Flores harbor and the old whale-processing factory. One of Flores Island's eight sister islands, Corvo Island, was visible from the harbor, smaller even than Flores itself.

Sylvia started confirmation lessons with Father Corvas. She attended services at the parish church. And twice a day Sylvia shared a bench on the school bus with Lucia Almedia, the only other nine-year-old in the village.

By the second month of school, Lucia and Sylvia were tired of the same old topics, and of each other.

"You must have met your father," Lucia pressed. "Or at least know his name?"

"No."

"But how can you be sure you weren't born from an unconfessed mortal sin?" Lucia glanced around the bus before whispering the last three words: unconfessed mortal sin. For whatever reason, Father Corvas spent most confirmation classes focused on the three mortal sins: adultery, idolatry, and sorcery. "How can you not have a single photograph of him or your *grandfather*?"

There was a something about the way Lucia emphasized the word *grandfather* that Sylvia didn't like. "Shut up, Lucia. Vovó's name is Mrs. Vieira. Misses. Of course she was married," Sylvia said, ignoring the strangeness of her mother's name also being Mrs. Vieira.

"There's no need to be so mean, Sylvia Vieira. Your whole family's going to be denied entrance into God's kingdom. That's what my mother says. She says you Vieras aren't fooling anyone."

Sylvia looked out the window. At the far end of a field, a woman stood in a cottage doorway. A few meters from the bus, a man, gray-haired, walked alongside the road. He glanced up in Sylvia's direction. There was something familiar about his face. All that long hair and that funny smile, like he was laughing at her. Then the bus moved ahead, leaving behind the man and his unsettling lips.

Neither Lucia nor Sylvia spoke for the rest of the twenty-minute bus ride to school. And for the first time, they didn't sit together on the bus ride home.

"Vovó, what's my father's name?"

"Hmm. I'm not exactly sure." Vovó didn't sound embarrassed. She almost seemed to be holding in a small smile.

"Vovó, it's not funny. Father Corvas—mortal sin."

"Ah." Vovó paused. "Sylvia, you are island born. One day you'll fly away—just like your mamãe and sister and all your aunties and cousins. Till then, pouco libélula, try and let things be."

"You know I don't like the gray-haired man." There was something terribly wrong with that old man, leaving her grandmother to live all alone. "I'm not traveling anywhere with him."

"I pray that is true." Vovó kissed Sylvia on the forehead with a loud smack. "You can stay with me then, yes? Just as long as there are no more island babies," Vovó added, which made completely no sense.

Sylvia wasn't so sure about sticking around. The rest of the Vieira women were onto something, flying away from this tiny island and Lucia Almedia and all the stupid neighbors. But Sylvia was onto something too. She didn't need some old man's permission to leave. She just needed money. That's how everyone else did it.

Sylvia Vieira's Rules of Silence by Sylvia Vieira
1. No talking to Lucia Almedia on the bus.
2. No talking to Lucia Almedia at school (unless Mrs. Enos makes us work on a school project together).
If working on a school project together, no smiling at Lucia Almedia.
3. No talking to Lucia Almedia on the walk to or from Father Corvas's rectory.
4. While in confirmation class, no smiling at Lucia.
5. While in confirmation class, no hateful thoughts about Lucia Almedia. God wouldn't like it.

Instead of walking toward the village center when she and Lucia got off the afternoon bus, Sylvia took to wandering in the opposite direction, down to the harbor.

The village harbor was bounded on one side by a cliff and on the other by a narrow spit of concrete and rocks. There was no marina. When the wind blew, the boats that did bother to drop anchor rocked back and forth as though they were being tossed by a blue-skied storm. Travelers. It was the perfect place to find the gray-haired man. Sylvia was going to corner that Joseph and make him fix all of it.

Sylvia knew her plan had one huge problem: Her body felt weird, different, when Joseph was around. As Vovo kept explaining, Sylvia was an island-born Vieira, which really, when you thought about it, was no explanation at all.

The gray-haired man was always wandering about Flores Island, his back to Sylvia. Sometimes Sylvia caught a glimpse of him hiking inland to the old crater lakes. She could tell it was him from his long hair and that strange tingly feeling that rose up in her throat whenever he was near.

It made Sylvia furious. He'd visited with all those cousins and aunts, convincing them to fly. He'd talked to Mother not once but twice. If Sylvia didn't know better, she'd almost believe he was biding his time, convinced she would talk with him. Green-marks-and-needles talk with him.

The day of the Divino Espirito Sáoto festival a short, gray-haired woman with one gold tooth led a nine-year-old girl in white lace up to the Nossa Senhora do Rosário Church. Child and woman were clearly related: both had the same dark-brown eyes and firm chin, not that there was ever any doubt. As everyone on Flores Island knew, all Vieira women looked the same and none came with fathers.

After First Communion at the church and all that standing in front of the altar, the crown was placed on Lucia Almedia's head. Of the four girls who took communion, Lucia was the one who sat down on the altar steps, unworried, while Father Corvas droned on for too long. Sylvia didn't care. Not one little bit. Once she'd saved enough money, she would fly away from Flores Island and head west, never to see Lucia Almedia again. Never mind Joseph and his ink-stained fingers. Somehow, she would fix it all.

OLIVIA: 1985

Ever since Mother disappeared, Sylvia's raged-filled phone calls from California were on the upswing.

"Brane-travel is just a fancy term for suicide, Livvy. People aren't meant to travel across parallel universes. You know that, right?"

"Viera women aren't just people, Sylvia. Joseph helps us the only way he knows how. We're meant to be travelers."

"Oh, Jesus. Let *me* help you, Livvy. You're not a little kid anymore. You need to break free of that gray-haired bastard and his Vieira groupies."

"Sylvia, just because you're afraid to face him in person, doesn't mean he's—"

"Yes, Livvy, it does. Do you think I can't feel it when he's near? At least I'm in this universe. I'm alive. Come here, Livvy. Come stay with me. Please, honey."

Livvy's sister actually sounded tired.

But in the end it wasn't her big sister's phone calls that drove nineteen-year-old Olivia out of Boston. The thing that finally caused Olivia Vieira to flee the family apartment was a noise.

At first Olivia barely noticed it. The sound was like the ticking of the kitchen clock or the water moving through the building's pipes, constant but easily ignored. And Olivia was busy. There was work and school and nights with Joseph in the apartment that Olivia used to share with her mother, Regina. Joseph had been Mother's friend for as long as Olivia could remember, at least until Mother had disappeared on that cloudless day and never returned.

"She's traveled" was how Joseph put it. And somehow Olivia could never find the courage to ask him where. Olivia, like Mother, had always loved Joseph. And she could feel the Vieira need welling up inside, demanding her attention. Like Mother, she needed to fly. Somehow, Joseph was the key.

Joseph worked construction. After Olivia's classes were over or, more and more often, before they were done, Olivia would track Joseph down. On his working days, she'd find him walking along some length of plywood or pushing a wheelbarrow full of broken sheetrock and bits of lumber.

Charged ions, humidity, or perhaps the concentration of carbon monoxide lingering in the city: whatever the reason, some days were non-work days for Joseph. On those days, Joseph disappeared to his other unknown universes.

Joseph, Olivia's mother liked to say, was both good and solid, just not in this particular world. He had other qualities, though. All that long gray hair and the strange mix of features that everyone, all the Vieira aunties and cousins in Fall River anyway, seemed to find so fascinating. He understood the truth about being a Vieira in this universe. He offered them a path.

"What if she comes home?" Olivia had asked that first night Mother didn't return.

"She won't." Joseph's smile had been soft, his fingers gentle as they stroked Olivia's collarbone, moved up along her neck. "Skin just like your mother's," he'd murmured, making Olivia frown.

At least someone was touching Olivia. At least someone was holding her as she fell asleep at night. These were the truths Olivia was afraid to tell Sylvia when she called and demanded Olivia move out. How did you tell the sister you left behind about your own loneliness? About all the nights and years no one noticed if you cried at night?

You didn't.

"Do you hear that noise?" Despite the belt Joseph was tightening around her arm, Olivia was distracted. The sound combined the dull pressure of a heartbeat with a rasp like air escaping from a constricted windpipe. Worse, it seemed to be coming from inside her own body. Each time the hiss crescendoed, Olivia swallowed, making sure she still could.

"Joseph?"

"Shh."

Olivia and Joseph sat in the middle of her mother's double bed. Joseph was bent over Olivia's arm, busy with his kit, while Olivia stared at the blue-flowered sheets. Olivia could remember the day Mother had bought the sheets.

"They remind me of home," she'd said. Mother's smile and the thick tendrils of green rising up her neck had made her face look so damn haggard.

The vines looked thicker, stiffer, darker somehow, though perhaps Olivia had just stopped noticing the change.

Her name was Regina Vieira, Olivia thought. She was a real person, not just another dead traveler. Lost traveler, Olivia tried to correct herself, but the phrase seemed wrong even in her own head. Despite the family stories of parallel worlds and Joseph-mediated travel, she'd never met a Vieira from another universe. Brane-travel went in both directions, but in this universe, it seemed brane-travel was a one-way journey for everyone except Joseph.

Some things Olivia had known for what felt like her whole life. Despite his outward appearance, Joseph wasn't human, at least not in the normal non-Vieira way. And Joseph managed to do something not even a Vieira could do. He carried himself in two universes at once. Strung across the multiverse, Joseph was what made flight, real Vieira flight, possible.

Other brane-travel facts. Aunt Izabel said that if Joseph ever traveled all the way through, he'd break the connection and wouldn't be able to come back. More than that, she'd whispered, he'd likely break apart. And Viera women would never again be able to step across. Aunt Izabel had acted like that would be the worst possible outcome. Vieiras, no matter what Vovó and Sylvia might say, were born to travel.

"Joseph..." Olivia turned toward the older man just as he slipped the needle into her vein. God, she hated the stab of pain and the stomach churn that followed.

As Joseph pulled out the needle, Olivia felt the noise cut against her teeth. *Thrum, hiss.* The sound burrowed into the flesh of her gums. And then the wave of H flowed out from the crook of her arm—a chemical calm that crushed all other feelings.

"Damn it, Olivia! You need to pay attention." Joseph reached over and undid the belt buckle, then patted her arm. The sensation barely registered.

The noise was following her tongue muscle, undulating down her throat, past the beating heart in her chest. A bass-driven frenzy, it shook loose all of Olivia's pain.

And then, somehow, Olivia was lying on the flower-covered sheets, while Joseph sat nearby, watching.

The Dead Kennedys. Social Distortion. Black Flag. Olivia used to play their cassettes, headphones over her ears like some enraged airline pilot. It was the 1980s. The record album had disappeared, but its ghost lingered in the words it left behind, like tracks.

Tracks of all kinds kept finding their way into her head: the needles Joseph brought home; the strange green tracks traveling up Mother's neck; and now the music hissing its way through her own blood.

"Tracks?" Joseph asked. She must have said the word out loud.

Tracks also meant traveling.

"Yes, making tracks," Joseph replied, the fingers of his left hand pinching her bare nipple. Mother had made tracks, leaving first Sylvia and then little Olivia behind.

Branes: universes piled one atop the other. Once you wandered you could never come back, unless, of course, you were Joseph. No more Mother, in this world at least. Probably not in any other. Even Joseph knew brane travel was dangerous.

"Yes," Joseph said. "Yes, I know. But you Vieiras don't give me any choice." And then his hair fell across her belly, the thick green branch at the base of his neck clearly visible. The strange green growth carrying each brane traveler, even Joseph, across.

"Fucking Vieiras." Joseph's lips pulled hard against Olivia's erect nipple, cupping her breast with one calloused hand.

Olivia avoided the apartment's few mirrors. Dark-red scabs had spread across her arms and toes, while the growth embedded with the needles in Joseph's second kit had made its way up Olivia's neck. She looked more and more like Mother. Just another Vieira getting ready for flight.

These days the noise never stopped.

"Cell integrity," Joseph repeated as he plunged a needle under her big toenail. He gripped Olivia's foot with one hand while the tremors shook her arms and hands. "The trick to traveling is to maintain your cell integrity while falling through."

And then Olivia was floating away on another hit of Liquid Sky.

The aunties had stopped coming round. Olivia's mind stuttered over the specifics. *Hiss* went the something inside her head and then came the choking sound. Joseph might have kicked the aunties out. Might have told them to "toss it" and "leave us the hell alone." Then again the aunties might have disappeared just like Mother.

"Sundays are supposed to be with the aunties," Olivia murmured from the tangle of graying sheets. Even Sylvia hadn't called. Olivia could hear Saint Anthony's church bells ringing out the end of Easter Sunday Mass. "Thirsty."

"Your aunts talk too much," Joseph said, offering her his cup of coffee. "Anyway Easter is overrated. The resurrection of God's tortured son? What kind of parent plans out his own child's suffering?"

Olivia considered sitting up and taking the cup, but decided against it. "I thought you liked the aunts."

"Yeah, well, I've got you to worry about right now. And me. Carrying a traveler—how do you think I started this journey?"

It was a non-working day. Joseph was out.

"What do you mean you didn't go to Tia's for Easter?" Sylvia said. "Of course, I called, but your phone just kept ringing. I bet it was turned off." And then as though she couldn't help herself, "Fucking Joseph."

"It's so loud, Sylvia," Olivia whispered into the phone's receiver.

"What are you—"

"The song in my head," Olivia cut in, then started to cough. Tears streamed down her face. Her chest felt like petrified stone, refusing to let her lungs expand.

"Olivia? Livvy, get a glass of water. Now." Sylvia didn't sound angry anymore. She sounded scared.

Olivia pressed her lips together, holding both the cough and her last gasp of air inside. Then she followed Sylvia's instructions: She put the phone down, stumbled to the kitchen, and drank from a half-empty glass sitting on the counter.

Air. And tremors. She needed to lie down. Olivia wandered back to the bedroom.

"Olivia? Olivia?!"

The phone lay in the middle of the sheets. Olivia picked it up, leaned back against the headboard, and closed her eyes. Now that the coughing had stopped, the sound was even louder than before. *Thrum. Hiss.* A storm of snake words and drums pummeling her brain. "Sylvia, the noise. It won't stop." Olivia swallowed, then regretted it. Her throat felt sandpaper-raw.

"Jesus, Livvy. You need to leave. I'm coming to get you."

"You can't. You know you can't. When he's near—and if I come to California, he'll just follow. My neck is covered in green."

"Livvy." Sylvia paused and seemed to hold in a whole slew of words. "Okay. How about this? How about a visit to grandma Vovó?"

"Maybe." Then Olivia was floating away. Sylvia's words became a blur of "infected," "useless aunts and cousins," and "Vovó."

"Olivia, do you hear me? Vovó will know what to do. She's seen plenty of Vieiras travel."

"What?" Vieiras were born on Flores Island, but no one ever returned once they flew west. And no one in their family ever left Joseph once the green needles began.

"Let me book the ticket." Sylvia's voice sounded desperate. "Look, this is what I think: Back on the island that fucking gray-haired man never talked to you, right? Just to Mother. You weren't supposed to leave, Livvy. That's why he has to keep all the aunties out. He knows you're not ready to even try. Please, Livvy."

"Okay." Somehow, Sylvia's anger made the danger so much easier to see. Made it easier to feel Sylvia's love as well. Mother had never been this bad. Mother who had surely never crossed over, no matter what Joseph said. Vieiras travel came like a storm. That's what everyone said. There hadn't even been a breeze that day. "Just make sure the flight's on a Friday. Joseph likes to disappear on a Friday." In a multiverse full of Olivias and Reginas and Aunt Izabels, he had a lot of people to visit.

Joseph could promise she would make it across the void all he wanted; the cacophony in her head told her a different story. It was time to go back to the island where all Vieiras were born.

A Friday morning in October. Olivia climbed onto a Green Line train. At Government Center she switched to the Blue Line and headed out to Logan

Airport. It was as simple as that. She wasn't even shaking. Joseph had set her up before he'd headed out for his Friday wander.

The airport was full of all sorts of people, not just older men with tanned skin and lips like ripe berries. A coffee vendor smiled at Olivia. Olivia avoided his eyes as she stepped onto the electric walkway and headed out to Terminal E. Of course Joseph was nowhere near. He was hanging with all those alternate-universe Vieiras. He was fucking some girl in a brane Olivia had never seen. She was getting as paranoid as Sylvia. The gray-haired, creased-and-sloping bodies that surrounded her were just men, human men, catching the SATA direct flight to the Azores.

Someone knocked Olivia from behind, her legs tangled together as she fell onto the walkway's ribbed metal.

"Excuse me," one of the Not-Josephs said, before speeding ahead. Or perhaps he said "Eu sou pesaroso." I'm sorry. Either way, he didn't help her up.

The crush of people felt suffocating. Shoes and boots on both sides of her. Suitcases and her own backpack hemming her in. Olivia yearned for her bed's graying sheets, for the coffee Joseph brought her each afternoon. *Thrum, hiss* went the sound, followed by the choking gasp. Surrounded by all the airport travelers, Olivia almost couldn't find enough air.

Eventually, Olivia stood up. Eventually, she reached the departure gate. A gray-haired steward smiled as he handed Olivia her boarding pass. He didn't remind Olivia of Joseph, not one little bit.

Olivia stepped through the airport doors and into the midday glare of Ponta Delgada, clutching a Raggedy Ann doll. The doll contained a carefully sealed package of powder while the contents of Olivia's backpack included a lighter and a small roll of tinfoil. Chasing the dragon, people called it. She might not use needles, but if she was lucky, Olivia would be able to maintain her "cell integrity." No shakes until her "Joseph problem" as Sylvia termed it, was solved. That was the goal.

"Taxi?" a man asked, reaching for her elbow. He wore a windbreaker and aviator sunglasses. His short gray hair was nothing like Joseph's. But his hands. The curve of his nails. Joseph's hands were the most honest part of his body; the nicked and wrinkled skin revealed exactly how long he'd been traveling.

"Sim. Yes, to the Ponta Delgada harbor," Olivia replied.

The Not-Joseph held the cab door open for her. "You need a boat?" he asked as he climbed into the driver's seat and started the car.

"I'm catching the ferry to Flores Island."

"Flores is beautiful, but so quiet. Pretty girl like yourself. You must be visiting family. Yes?"

"Yes."

Help, thought Olivia as she stared out the taxi window at the passing city streets. Help, help, help.

Olivia set the doll and her backpack by her feet and knocked on the wooden door.

The door was attached to a single-story cottage with a red-tiled roof. It rested halfway up the curving road that led to the village square and the twin domes of Nossa Senhora do Rosário church.

Lajes das Flores should have been a fairytale town, a subtropical Brigadoon, frozen in time. That's what Olivia had expected. Not the overhead streetlights and the trash truck. Men in overalls and gloves were busy picking up the yellow and green plastic garbage cans waiting by the side of the road. One of the men glanced back at Olivia and then quickly looked away.

Scared hue mans. Hue. Hew. Hiss.

Olivia knocked a second time on Vovó's door, and then slipped her foot against the doll, trying to still the tremors. She could feel the hard-packed stuffing of the Raggedy Ann.

From inside the cottage came shuffling footsteps and then the click of a latch. A wrinkled hand with long fingers and paper-thin skin slipped into view. A head followed, peering around the half-open door.

"Olá?" the old woman said.

"Como está, Vovó?" Olivia said. She pressed her right foot down onto her left, holding it still.

The older woman tilted her head to one side. "Your name?" she prompted.

Despite her grandmother's confusion, her expression was welcoming. Olivia had the same features and long dark hair as all Vieira women.

"Olivia, Vovó."

"Ah." She pushed the door open all the way. "The last time…" Vovó held one hand below chest level and smiled, revealing whitish, uneven teeth along with a single gold one.

"Yes, I was much smaller." Olivia smiled back.

The older woman guided Olivia off the step and into a house filled with lace doilies, dark wood furniture, and photographs of baby Vieira women, middle-aged Vieira women, angry and laughing and irritated Vieira women. A room full of faces just like Olivia's stared back from the walls.

"You are all right, yes?" Vovó reached up with one frail hand and stroked Olivia's cheek.

"Sim, I'm fine." Olivia could feel her lips beginning to tremble. "Sylvia sent me." *Thrum, hiss, thrum, hiss* went the tide inside her mind, and then came the choking death rattle.

"Sylvia was wrong to leave, but I was wrong too. Not enough babies in this world." Vovó patted Olivia's shoulder. "It is good you should stay here for a tiny while."

At twenty-two, Olivia certainly didn't feel like a baby, but she nodded all the same. *Hiss* went the voice in her head. *Hiss.*

After two weeks of wandering, the island no longer felt quite so easy to quantify. Cattle shared the roadways with buses and cars. Away from the harbor, moss-covered walls and hidden stone water spigots were everywhere. Almost daily Olivia came across mist roiling through yet another tiny valley.

The noise had changed as well. Like late-night static on the radio, it was easily ignored. Most nights, as she lay in her sister Sylvia's old bed, Olivia tumbled straight into sleep and dreamed: Not-Joseph the sailor wandered up from the harbor in a yellow slicker and boots. Not-Joseph stood next to a windmill, one foot on a low stone wall, older this time with sparse white hair. For some reason, the actual Joseph, with his own vine-like tracks and long braid, never once visited her dreams. Olivia didn't need that Joseph, not as long as she had her Raggedy Ann. Managing the tremors just involved a bit of cooking with foil packets and a bubbling, warm brownish liquid.

Every morning before breakfast Olivia hiked just past the edge of town to the cliff-side park. Once the lighter had done its work, Olivia sucked up the vapor with a thin roll of tinfoil and then leaned against one of the park's trees. From her perch at the top of the cliff, she could see old men sitting on the benches down in Lajes harbor. Sometimes, one of them glanced her way. In the other direction, she often caught sight of a hiker in a cloth cap heading inland across the rolling hills. All of these men had gray hair.

Joseph, Olivia thought, or perhaps said out loud. She closed her eyes, letting Joseph's roughened hands stroke the nape of her neck. Soon his hands moved lower, finding their way between her thighs, and Olivia forgot about the sky, the nearby Not-men, and the look in Vovó's eyes as they sat together at night.

Come home, Joseph, her Joseph, murmured in Olivia's ear.

Olivia shivered against the heat of his breath as his voice replaced the thrum-hiss and the death rattle that always followed. And then a horn from one of the fishing boats called out. And just like that, Joseph was gone, jolted back across the ocean.

After two weeks of morning walks, the Raggedy Ann stash was almost gone.

"The gray-haired man, Vovó." Olivia paused, trying to keep the frustration out of her voice. "Sylvia said I needed to talk to him."

"Sylvia thinks in straight lines," Vovó said, "hiding or not hiding. As though those are the only choices."

It was dark. Olivia and Vovó sat at the table next to the wood-burning stove. An oversized wooden hutch loomed from the stone-and-plaster wall surrounded by all those Vieira faces.

"Tomorrow you try a new trail." Vovó handed Olivia a piece of paper with a hand-drawn map of the southern half of Flores. A wavery line led from the village inland to the north and west. On the path walked a little stick-person. Stick-Olivia was heading toward two small ponds. Waiting little stick-insects with double wings were inked along the water's edge.

"Maybe," Olivia said, irritated by Vovó's refusal to help her with Joseph. "Obrigada."

Vovó grabbed Olivia's hand, removed the map, and spread it flat on the table. Her index finger tapped the smaller of the two blue circles. "Caldeira Rasa. You go, yes?"

"Ummm."

"You go," Vovó said, her index finger still tap, tap, tapping against the small blue circle.

"Sure. Okay, I'll go." Olivia took another sip of her coffee.

Tap, tap went Vovó's index finger. *Tap. Tap. Tap.*

And then Olivia's foot moved—*tap, tap, tap*—as grandmother and granddaughter stared at the lake outlined on the coffee-stained piece of paper.

Olivia's Only Question
1. In a family without men, where do babies come from?

"No men," Vovó had said the night before, pointing to the damselfly sketches on her map, "just like us."

"What?"

"The women damselflies. They make their babies without the men," Vovó had said, smiling.

Of course there were Vieira men, fathers. They just didn't stick around, Olivia thought, though she didn't say it out loud.

Olivia had followed Vovó's map west along ER1-2, before veering north and west: away from the road, through farmland, and up toward the two lakes Vovó had marked on the map. She didn't see a single person. After less than an hour, Olivia reached the crater lake. Up close, Caldeira Rasa seemed like a drop of inlaid blue sky covered by a single cloud. A dark swarm swirled and banked above the pond, a mass of circling damselflies.

One damselfly slipped from the mass and settled on a blade of grass next to Olivia. It looked just like the ones in Vovó's collection. It held its double-set of wings upright above its body as though waiting for the next command.

A gust of wind rippled across the water. Olivia heard the rustle of nearby grasses. But it was another sound that held her attention: a lone bass note pushed inward against her body. Somehow, without making any conscious decision, she contracted the muscles deep in her abdomen, let go, then repeated the movement. Above the lake, the cloud of damselflies banked and swerved in a frenzied mass.

The nearby forktail launched itself from the blade of grass and out across the lake. Follow me, it cried. Follow me.

Olivia took a step forward.

The damselfly cloud had shifted, drawing stuttering figure eights above the volcanic basin.

Meanwhile, with each step toward the water, Olivia's pelvis tightened and released. Tightened and released. Sex with Joseph had been such a passive affair. Naked and stretched out on the bed seemed to be enough.

Up close Olivia could see that the Citrine Forktails weren't quite identical. Some were yellow and green, others orange. But all had the same dark eyes.

"Time to fly without Joseph," Olivia murmured. She kicked off her shoes and shrugged quickly out of her clothes. Standing naked next to a volcanic lake on the westernmost tip of Europe felt good. Standing naked alone with those dark insectile eyes felt even better. Olivia's pelvis tightened, as though trying to pull the air or the water or the *thrum-hiss* sound back inside.

And then she let her body sink into the water.

Why had no one told her? Her lips parted. Her nipples hardened. The sex between her legs dripped.

Nearby, two female damselflies settled on a half-submerged reed. One arched into a C-shape as though in the throes of extreme pleasure or pain. The second damselfly hovered above, holding the breeding female's neck. Shiny, translucent spheres slipped from the lower female's abdomen. Olivia watched as the eggs floated for a moment before sinking beneath the lake.

No males.

The sun's one burning eye forced its way beneath Olivia's skin. The forktails no longer spiraled in figure eights. A haze of wings and twig-like bodies surrounded her. Legs settled on Olivia's hair and ears, along the narrow ledge of her shoulders.

Sun, Olivia thought. *Sun. Son, Song. Thrum. Hissssss.* Only her head remained above the water, while a swarm of forktails clung to her body, making sure she sank no further.

The water flowed upward. Olivia's pelvic muscles contracted. Her teeth came down against her lips. She bit hard. Gasping. And then it was done.

Olivia heard a noise from the nearby grasses. She turned, but the man was already walking away, his long gray hair flowing behind him. Damselflies flew above the lake, far less of them than before. Meanwhile, the sky was filling with gray-weather clouds. It was time to get out.

Inside Olivia felt different. No thrum. No hiss. For this one moment all was beautiful silence. Only her heartbeat remained.

Vovó should have given Sylvia a map instead of letting her run off to California to try and fail. No one deserved how lonely this fucked-up world could make you feel.

Olivia sprinted down the road, shivering despite the rising heat in her pelvis. The noise, a hard electric snapping, had started somewhere west of Caldeira Rasa. Now it speeded south, and despite Olivia's running feet, it was getting louder. Joseph's choking traveler static wanted back in.

"Just try it!" Olivia screamed, gasping, and then, unexpectedly, laughing as well. It was glorious. No thrum. No hiss. Just burning lungs pushing too hard as she tried to outrun the storm.

Heel. Toe. Gasping breath. A Vieira baby was growing inside her, formed in the same way as all Vieira girls. Her baby had sent all those damselflies out across the brane into an entirely different universe. Her baby had stopped the hissing call. And Joseph hadn't done a thing.

From somewhere behind came a new sound: *skreeet.* And then the wind started in earnest, whip-edge sharp against her skin. Whatever power charged through Flores Island's volcanic lakes and insect eyes, whatever charged through a multiverse of Flores Islands, it was way too close.

Olivia could see the village up ahead: the church with its two rounded domes and the smaller, plaster-white houses.

Push forward. Heel. Toe. Heel. Run.

Skreet.

A gust of wind struck Olivia to the ground. Grit stung her eyes. And still that steady, molten heat pressed up from deep inside. Babies without the men, Vovó had said.

Plastic garbage cans tumbled down the hill. A handful of tiles flew off a nearby roof and shattered on the street.

Olivia's feet no longer needed instructions. They ran.

Olivia hands left bloody tracks on the doorknob when she finally tumbled into her grandmother's cottage.

Vovó sat next to the stove. Despite the battering wind, her expression was calm.

"Vovó—the lake."

"Filhinha." The older woman stood and placed a frail hand over Olivia's own blooded fingers, then pressed her hand against Olivia's midriff. "So it is time for you to leave." She smiled a tight little smile. "The man will get over his anger. Babies are good."

The rattling wind quieted. There was a knock at the door.

"Ah," Vovó said, looking past Olivia to the window next to the front door. "Two of them, even."

There was a second knock on the door, sharper this time. Impatient.

Olivia felt a strange jolt along her spine. The vines on her neck bit into her flesh like a chemical burn. The worst part: just like the warmth between her legs, it felt good. She turned and looked through the window. Two men stood outside: the hiker from the lake and a shorthaired man, the taxi driver from Ponta Delgada. Not-Josephs

"Babies are welcome by everyone," Vovó repeated, patting Olivia's hand. "I will miss seeing her born. Still," she continued in a no-nonsense voice, "time for you to go. The Josés will get you back to Ponta Delgada and the airport. I want no more babies born here." For a moment, Vovó's dark eyes held Olivia's gaze. "Don't forget, meu amorzinho: a Vieira is more than some José's plaything."

Vovó, it suddenly occurred to Olivia, had lived alone on Flores Island all these years with just her damselflies and her Not-Josephs. And now Vovó would be alone again.

Joseph had a lot to answer for. And, one day, someone would force him to pay.

A baby.

Better than Mother, that would be Olivia's mantra. Far, far better than Mother.

Olivia might have already fallen with her the thickening tendrils on her neck, that vibration of Joseph flesh calling Vieira flesh that she felt even now, but her baby would be different. Not island born. Not Joseph thralled. Her baby girl would decide in which direction she would fly.

Laurinda: 2005

Laurinda Vieira's Relationship Requirements
1. No drugs. No heroin, no X, no meth, nothing you can only purchase with cash.
2. I like coffee.
3. And sleep.
4. Sex isn't a question. It's a necessity.
5. I get to play with needles too.

Laurinda closed her eyes, soaking in the scraps of sunlight as the chill of the concrete stoop seeped through her jeans. Brainerd Road always felt like a wind tunnel, something about the air currents in this part of Boston.

"Help her," Evie had shrieked two days ago as the two of them stood at the ER's intake counter, cousin Evie trying to hold Laurinda upright.

The ER doctors had run CAT scans and MRIs. They'd pricked her flesh with needles. Finally after two days, they'd let her go. Psychosomatic, they suggested. Perhaps stress or grief? "Perhaps bullshit," Laurinda had snapped before she had a chance to rein in her words. What the fuck did she care what these doctors thought? She didn't. Not really.

The emergency room visit hadn't changed a thing. Laurinda's body still stuttered and trembled its way through their second-floor apartment. Garbled words still kept Laurinda awake. Night and day, Joseph's expectant eyes followed her from room to room.

Only person Laurinda really wanted was her mother. But in spite of her clear-and-present love, green-veined Olivia had eventually gone the way of all island-born Vieiras. And now Laurinda was stuck with Evie and Joseph: one island-born cousin not-so-secretly swooning over one gray-haired asshole of a man.

Laurinda heard the building's front door creak open, followed by the metallic click of Joseph's lighter and a quick intake of breath.

"Soon," Joseph murmured, settling next to her on the concrete step. His callused fingers slipped the freshly lit cigarette between Laurinda's lips.

"Sssoon,' Laurinda repeated, her eyes resolutely closed. All she needed was one single push through. Mother had loved Laurinda so much. She would never have left Laurinda behind, not if she'd had any choice.

If universes were soap bubble–shaped membranes stacked one atop the other, Laurinda had never ventured beyond her own fragile film. Joseph assumed he knew exactly what all Vieras wanted: to move with him between worlds, extruding across the multiverse forever and ever, amen. Fucker couldn't be more wrong. This Vieira just wanted her mother back. Not that Joseph gave a damn.

"Laurinda, you need anything?" A voice called from the apartment window above.

"E-E-Evie should go home," Laurinda stuttered. Her tongue felt too heavy, as though the many Laurinda tongues from all those many Laurinda worlds were condensing together.

"Not yet, baby doll. We need the help. At least for a little while longer."

Laurinda could feel Joseph's demin-clad thigh pressing against her own trembling flesh. "N-N-Not trying to fuck her too, are you?" Laurinda asked, already knowing the answer. He really was a shitty old man. One even she was not entirely immune to. Vieira blood would tell.

No heroin, Laurinda had proclaimed that first night. No powders or smoke. As though words could shield her from the feel of his dick inside her and the heat after his needle sliced down into her neck. All so good.

Just like Mainland-born Vieiras, universe-traveling devils played by their own rules.

Fucking her, Joseph said her first night back from the hospital, was like wrapping his flesh inside a barely covered skeleton. Each time he pressed, he could feel the bones a little more. Didn't seem to bother him. He'd even smiled as he came. Afterward, they'd each had a turn with his needles and vials, coloring each other's necks with thick vines of Azorean, damselfly green.

Out on the stoop, Laurinda tried to push away the memory of her mother stretched out on this same step, jaundiced and skinny. Joseph's needles were supposed to help with cell integrity, Mother and Joseph had explained one too many times.

And retaining your cell integrity was crucial if you were going to attempt inter-brane travel. Laurinda wasn't opening a connection to the Azores. She wasn't creating a path west to Sacramento and Tia Sylvia. Laurinda was smashing a hole in this universe and through to the next. Or, like Mother, she was dying in the attempt.

Despite the woody stalks twining up her mother's neck, it had been a blue-sky day when Olivia Vieira finally disappeared. Not a damselfly in sight.

"Laurinda?" Cousin Evie called down again.

"She's fine," Joseph replied. "I'm keeping an eye out."

"'Course you are." No matter what Laurinda said, cousin Evie remained in her Aunt's old bedroom, terrified but resolute. She'd promised Aunt Olivia. Evie wasn't about to let her cousin wander away with "Mr. Neither-Here-Nor-There." *Island. Illness. Illicit. E-E-Evie.*

Laurinda opened her eyes and took a deep drag from her Newport Menthol Gold. The smoke's warmth scratched against the back of her throat, pushing down all those hissing voices. She held in the smoke for as long as her faltering body would allow.

"Used to be people hardly ever smoked," Joseph said as Laurinda eventually exhaled. "Shamans and priestesses wrapped ghee or dried snake skins round incense cones, smoking up their temples. That's about as far as it went."

"Huh." Laurinda took another careful drag. Her fingers were having trouble finding her lips. "B-B-Bet they hadn't th-th-th of menthol." Even with the shakes, her voice had that gravelly, Vieira quality that Joseph loved. Last night he'd grabbed her hair as they'd fucked, tracing the thick green vines that ran in a sinewy line from her collarbone up along her neck.

"The throat is a sacred object," he said now as he stroked her exposed neck.

Laurinda allowed herself a small smile. Her own vines lined Joseph's neck as well. "Viera rule number seven, remember?" she'd said all those months ago as she'd reached for his kit. And Joseph had laughed and acquiesced, as though indulging a lisping child. Careless old man.

"Done," Joseph had whispered last night as he zipped closed his kit. "Just one final step," he'd added, touching her trembling limbs.

Joseph's own quotient of vines, just a few lines shy of complete, hadn't even come up. After all, Joseph's limbs weren't shaking.

Joseph pushed himself up from the stoop and smiled down at Laurinda. "Time for me to head back to work."

Laurinda knew exactly what he was thinking: tonight, he would finish his latest Vieira transformation. And there was little Evie Vieira already waiting in the bedroom next door.

Joseph and Laurinda lay sprawled across the bed.

"My turn." Laurinda reached for Joseph's inoculation kit sitting on the bedside table, knocked it to the floor, and then spent long minutes aiming and re-aiming her hands until they were able to pick it back up. The noise inside her head felt like a countdown clock: a cycling rhythm of *thrum, hiss* followed by that asthmatic choking sound.

"At least let me do it," Joseph grumbled. "All that shaking. You could end up stabbing my face."

As though the shaking was Laurinda's fault. As though he would actually turn her down with her ripened and traveler-ready body. Stupid fucker.

"Don't h-h-have to draw straight." Laurinda's hands shook, but she managed to dip the needle tip into the vial. The thick liquid inside the glass container was an iridescent yellowish green. Joseph's own cultured bit of damselfly. Laurinda leaned toward Joseph, using both hands to try and control the tremors as he lay on his side facing her.

"I don't think this is—"

"Rrru," Laurinda cut him off. She might not be able to get the "ule" sound out, but her shaking head emphasized her meaning.

"Right. Rule number seven."

Thrum. Hissss.

Laurinda's eyes didn't stray from the vine trailing up the living trellis of

Joseph's neck. Mother must have trembled in this exact same way on her last night. So many Vieras lost. And yet here Joseph lay with his old-man paunch and weathered flesh. No worry lines though. As far as Joseph was concerned, Vieira-traveler was just another word for fool, all those women helping him remain the conduit between worlds. Mr. Neither-Here-Nor-There.

Perhaps some even made it through.

"I-I-I. Knowwww you," Laurinda said as she formed the final tendril. Joseph's neck was fully inoculated with a mix of iridescent green and his own red blood. For the first time, the vine reached along the entire length of Joseph's neck, then curved around his ear. His head was tilted back slightly, so that he could watch her hands and her trembling lips. Such greedy eyes, waiting to hear that choking sound. Fuck him. Breathe. Finish the damn vine.

And then his smile was gone. "Hey!" Joseph reached for her waist as though considering pushing her away.

Laurinda continued to hold the needle aloft with both hands. "Joseph? You all right?" She saw what might be a tremor travel along his grasping arms. Her own *thrum, hiss* made it hard to separate need from fact.

"Fine," Joseph grunted, a look of confusion on his face that was quickly replaced by a smile. Laurinda had started to cough.

Thrum, hiss. Her throat squeezed against the noise, blocking out the air. Laurinda was gasping, flop sweat rising up across her body. She swayed for a moment as a chill of goosebumps rose along her skin. Then a trickle of air, sucked in despite the barrage. Mother had gone through this. Mother who had loved Laurinda more than anything and yet still couldn't stay.

Joseph meanwhile was still lying on his side, the bed sheet tangled around his waist. But it was the expression on his face that gave Laurinda hope. He was staring down at his hands, his trembling damselfly-infected hands.

Not even bothering to aim, Laurinda plunged the needle down into the tender flesh at the base of Joseph's neck. There was no time left. Laurinda's peripheral vision was nothing but darkness. The bedroom was filled with the scent of ozone, and beyond the walls, Laurinda could hear the rumble of thunder.

"My mother is dead, old man. Dead," Laurinda whispered near Joseph's vine-encircled ear. Her hands shook, but differently than before. Rage. Such rage. Like nothing she'd felt before. Not even when she was fifteen and Mother and Joseph closed their bedroom door, Mother's laughter and Joseph's chuckle echoing through the thin apartment walls. Laurinda hadn't been nearly angry enough back then.

This morning Evie's gaze had followed Joseph's movements about the apartment, as though unable to keep away. Her expression reminded Laurinda of her own just before Mother disappeared: already half-enraptured.

And Laurinda had loved her mother. Hell, Evie loved Laurinda.

Laurinda lifted the needle with both shaking hands and plunged it once again into Joseph's neck, ignoring the choking sound of her own breath. More than Joseph's hands, which were trembling. His entire body seemed to shimmer and pulse.

"Stop L. L. L. Laurindaaaa. Stop!"

One moment Joseph's left hand was pressing against her hip as her hand worked the needle, the next Laurinda was screaming, her head thrown back. Burning, acid-hot pain. The first tear had appeared in the universe's membrane. The pathway had its own needs. Energy, Joseph and Vieira energy. So much pressure. Any moment now it would combust her into particulate matter. Laurinda raised the needle again. After all her careful planning she was slow. Too slow.

And then over the *thrum, hiss* and Joseph's cry of "Llllaurinda," Laurinda heard another sound. *Skrreet.* Followed by a plasma-hot storm that shook the windows, tore against the walls. She could no longer feel Joseph's hands on her waist.

"Lllaurinda," Joseph repeated, followed by, "Plllea…" and then nothing.

The mattress shifted along with the sheets. Only one body remained. Joseph.

Laurinda felt a burning, savage grin rising across her face. It was Joseph who had traveled. Laurinda and the damselfly vine had done their job. Joseph, Joseph not Laurinda, had fallen through that hungry tear. She had managed to push him all the way through.

The storm seemed to be calming. There was a crashing sound like giant, rootless trees, and then silence. The tear had closed.

Traveler lost.

Laurinda took a long slow breath and found only the scent of ozone and her tears remained.

For at least one Vieira family in one universe, the devil had disappeared and he was never coming back.

FINDING YOUR WAY TO THE COAST

TRAVELERS

PETER'S HAND MOVES SLOWLY, hovering above Delia's bare forearm, as little as an eighth of an inch between her flesh and his trembling fingers. The ghosts feel safest that way. That's what Peter had told her as he swallowed the last of his beer and set the glass aside, his eyes intent, lingering first on her lips, and then falling from her breasts to her right arm.

Peter doesn't look away, despite the sideways glances of their companions and the uncomfortable clatter of their silverware. A lone waiter watches from across the terrace. Delia bends her head, ignoring them all. She is focused on Peter's open palm as it creeps above her bare arm.

"Concentrate," Peter whispers. His hot breath envelopes the outer curve of her ear.

What do the ghosts feel? Delia wonders but does not ask. Instead, she closes her eyes. For a moment nothing changes. The night air still feels dark and cool on her bare shoulders. She can hear the cars on the nearby Boulevard Saint-Michel as the taxis bring their loads of tourists to the Left Bank. A cab parks just beyond the terrace's back stairs. A group of women erupts from the open door, speaking in English.

"Do these guys even get tips?" one of the women wonders. Her voice is pitched high, querulous with this unexpected cultural burden.

Delia shifts in her seat. Anxious. It's dark behind her closed eyes. And Peter's ghosts have such sharp edges. She can already feel her skin loosening as they tug at her flesh, ghost barbs finding their way to the viscera underneath: the heart, the lungs, the looping passages of her intestine.

This is what I came for, Delia tells herself. This is why I stopped the mail and packed all those cases. This is why I traveled through the night on that high-speed rail.

Let everyone else wander the Seine and the Louvre, or join those bodies crushing their way up the Eiffel Tower. For Delia, Paris in summer means a different sort of journey. Peter's ghosts seem to agree. The ghosts don't even notice the city: not the moped speeding along the cobblestones, not the women now running south toward the Boulevard Saint-Germaine, not the darkened sky. The ghosts are intent, burrowing, finding their rhythm as Peter's hand continues to travel above Delia's arm. Slowly. So slowly. Until, finally, the moment arrives. She is floating, freed, her flesh, temporarily, left behind.

Behind her closed eyes, Delia can feel the scorching sun. She can hear the soft *Shh* of something flying overhead. A breeze follows. The creature hovers for a moment before it moves on.

An arm presses against her side. Mark. Please, God, let it be him. This is better than any memory, better than any stories told to a therapist for $120 an hour. Peter and his ghosts have carried Delia entirely away. She hesitates, eyes still closed, the arm still pressed against her. Surely, it will be . . .

Delia can feel Peter's piercing ghosts settled beneath her skin. Their barbs are distant pricks, not even worthy of her attention. Delia opens her eyes. She turns her head. She looks.

Of course it's Mark, resting next to her on a thin cotton towel. The sky is a uniform gray. No sign of flying creatures. Before Delia is an ocean, slick and glassy and still. It shimmers, oily smudges like thumbprints scattered across its surface. The beach towel is all that separates Mark and Delia from the sand. Or the non-sand, gray-white and ashy. Scattered as far as Delia can see bodies lie, hands entwined. Strewn between the couples are twisted rocks and charred lumps of wood that remind Delia of late night campfires at Race Point, though it's doubtful any campfires ever spark along this stretch of beach. This place, Peter the cultural attaché's non-Paris place, is where people come after the fires.

Delia's gaze returns to her companion. Mark the silent. Mark the carefully brave. Despite the thready-white of his skin, she can see his chest rise and fall. He knows I'm here, Delia thinks. He must.

The air smells of salt and half-rotten seaweed. Car exhaust and candle wax—it smells of that too. Mark and Delia may be resting against the sand. But Peter and his ghosts—Peter with his electric hands and pale gray eyes——and the Parisian terrace are no more than an eyelash away.

TOUR GUIDE

"A cultural attaché," Wendy explained earlier as she'd dragged Delia from the hostel and through the labyrinth of cobbled streets. Dinner, it seemed, was a requirement of this Paris trip, dinner with Delia's three new friends and Peter.

"Peter," Wendy continued as she eyed Delia's pale pink tank top, "remembers you from the metro this morning." As though this was a special honor. Certainly, ribbons and a small brass band weren't far behind.

Delia remembered nothing but the gray tiles of the underground and Wendy talking, at last, to someone else. And now this person wanted to meet her again?

"Sure. Of course." Traveling was hard enough without arguments. In the end, it was so much easier just to agree.

Peter waited for them at an iron lamppost set just beyond the Luxembourg stop. He was taller than Delia had expected and his arms and legs seemed to bend at unexpected angles. Delia could imagine this strange human crouched forward, looking down at the city from some ledge or high-up window, motionless for hours at a time. His light-brown hair frizzed out from his head like an untidy halo, but there was no softness in his body. His skin was sandstone-rough, thick pores connecting the sallow membrane that was his skin. When Peter caught Delia's gaze, he smiled, completely ignoring the blonde-and-ponytailed Wendy. Meanwhile behind them, the metro entrance kept pouring people onto the street, bodies streaming in and out of the restaurants and cafés, everyone so hungry.

149

"Peter," the stranger said as his dry hand gripped her softened skin. It was then that Delia noticed Peter's tidy, little teeth. Delia couldn't quite place his accent. Like her, he was a visitor to this city.

Kurtis and Alex, Delia's other friends from the hostel, arrived soon after. A flush rose along Kurtis's pale cheeks as he clasped Peter's hand. And then Peter was leading the group north. All the while, he was talking, talking, talking, giving his tour of the Left Bank. It seemed he was an expert. Kurtis, Wendy, and Alex couldn't believe their good luck. Peter pointed out the palm trees in the Jardin du Luxembourg, the red neon of the tobacconist, La Favorite, on the Boulevard Saint-Michel, and farther along, in the center of the Latin Quarter, the Church of Saint-Severin with its own collection of ancient gargoyles.

Gargoyles covered the rooftops of the city. Paris was filled with crumbling and broken stone. Did no one else notice how hard Peter's back and shoulders looked as he guided them through the crowded streets? Did no one else notice the way his legs and arms bent as he walked? Their cultural attaché. Their ash-and-stone grotesquery.

"Hungry?" Peter asked, reaching for Delia's hand and enclosing it with his stone fingers.

"Yes." Finally, it was time to eat.

Peter, to everyone else's delight, chose the restaurant. The waiter dropped the menus on the table, while Peter, of course, sat next to Delia. And then Peter was turning his chair, his hard knees pressed against the side of Delia's right thigh. His flesh felt so cold, his flaking skin, revealing more ashy layers underneath. It was the first time anyone had touched Delia in days or weeks or months. That hand Mark's mother placed on her shoulder, surely, that hand didn't count?

"I can do it," Peter said without a hint of a smile. "I can show you the coast."

"Oh, come on," Alex replied, his dark brows pressing together as he frowned. "Without moving from this table? She's not that drunk."

At that moment, Delia almost liked Alex. Not that it mattered. Delia still agreed to everything, including Peter's hand creeping its way across her skin.

"Of course, I'll try it," Delia said.

"Only the ghosts will touch you," Peter said, looking straight at her. "The ghosts," he explained as he leaned even closer, "generate the heat."

And then Peter's hand hovered above Delia's arm, and the little hairs on her bare flesh rose up, connecting with his palm. Despite the thin blue veins that lined his skin, his hand doesn't feel cold anymore. That is Delia's first thought. And then there is the beach. And Mark. And the vast and shiny ocean, brittle, hiding an infinite number of waiting eyes. Finally. Delia wants nothing more than to slide her hand up along Mark's inner thigh. Her breasts are soft against Mark's stone chest as her mouth searches for some sign of warmth.

"Delia," a voice murmurs.

It isn't Mark's voice. His lips haven't moved even once. And the other couples lying on the beach are just as unmoving. Delia can feel ash swirling up, battering her face, stinging as it finds its way into her eyes.

Shuush. Shuffle. Shuush. Shuffle. Something steps across the sand. Someone's shadow covers both Delia and Mark.

Delia wipes her face. Forces herself to look. There's a glimpse of stone talons rising up from the ashen sand, each arched claw the same thickness as Delia's own fragile wrists. And then there is no more time. Her skin has tightened back around her body, the ghost's hooks undone.

Blood floods Delia's cheeks as she opens her eyes. How long was she gone? The tables on the restaurant terrace are almost empty, the space lit by dim orange bulbs. Alex—or is it Kurtis?—has pulled a small pocket calculator from his fanny pack.

"How many should I divide by?" Alex asks.

Alex, Kurtis, and Wendy are all careful to avoid Delia's eyes.

"We can go to my place," Peter murmurs in Delia's ear. His hard knees are still pressed against her legs. His lips too close for anyone else to hear. Delia knows she should pull her arm away, but the warmth of his hand reminds her of a time before torn white undershirts and unwashed bedding, before sleepless nights spent on molded plastic chairs. His hand reminds her of a time before she even considered this trip to Paris.

Delia doesn't reply. To the west she can see Notre Dame's towers, just beyond the River Seine, rising above the surrounding buildings. Underneath the night sounds, she can hear the lapping water of the ancient river. The old stone walls that press up against the distant bank are not that far away. The top of the wall, as she follows the curve of the river west, seems covered in fairy lights.

"In the folktales," Peter says, noticing the direction of her gaze, "it's always a mistake to follow the lights."

His breath smells faintly of cigarette smoke and smoldering ash.

"I'm not afraid," Delia replies. And she means it.

Wendy is frowning, two lines appearing along the bridge of her nose, more cracks across her forehead.

Paris is for lovers? Who says? Delia came here alone. And despite Alex and Wendy and Kurtis sharing her train compartment from Amsterdam, she's remained alone. Earlier in the day she visited the city of the dead, the Père Lachaise Cemetery, alone, leaving Wendy and the others to find their own way through the city. Later she stared at the gargoyles and marmosets carved into Notre Dame Cathedral. One in particular, with his folded wings and a rough scar that seemed to cut across his forehead, held her attention. His mouth half-parted and stone still. Was he angry or afraid? He should be able to tell her, right? It doesn't seem fair to spend an eternity trying and failing to speak.

Now Delia is sitting with people who speak but who don't seem to understand what questions should be asked. Alex was Kurtis's teacher. That's what they are telling her as they explain their mathematical formula for dividing the check, but the words make less and less sense.

"Let's go" is all Delia hears as Peter whispers to her alone. A curl of his hair actually touches Delia's cheek. Her arm is electric with ghosts. All of them waiting. Does no one else notice? She is caught at the wrought-iron table with Peter, the thirty-five-year-old cultural attaché, and her three traveling companions. But only Peter, Peter and his ghosts, matter.

Peter's left hand has, somehow, found its way under the table. His fingers have settled on her thigh. When did that happen?

Peter's hard knees press insistently. He knows what she wants; he's the only one at the table who does. More than that, Peter is the only one who can show Delia the way back to the coast. The beer is buzzing in Delia's brain, and after two months, her body still craves sleep, white-sheeted sleep.

"Leave them," Peter repeats, nodding toward the darkness.

Kurtis waves his fingers toward the waiter. "Another Coke, please."

Ignorance is happiness's shield. Her sweet Mark knew that. He was the one who told Delia not to climb into the ambulance. He was the one who told her to go back to bed. And later, as he lay in that hospital bed, he was the one who told Delia to go home. As though that would have changed anything. Almost two months. Has it really been almost two months?

Peter's hand still hovers above Delia's goose-bumped flesh, though his lips have tightened in seeming frustration. He's the cultural attaché, not me, Delia thinks. Isn't it his job to convince me? Isn't he supposed to be the one with the plan?

And then she lets it all go. "Okay," she replies.

They rise together from the table, Peter's fingers locking with Delia's as they run across the terrace and out toward the river of fairy lights. His hand is dry and cool. Delia pretends she doesn't notice the heat in her arm is spreading. The ghosts are burrowing even faster than before.

A SPECIAL EXCURSION

On the Boulevard Saint-Michel behind a plate-glass window, Delia notices mannequins wearing belted, houndstooth dresses and capped sleeves. Suddenly, she is tumbling back into memory-land, shopping with Mark for her first work suit. Three doors down, the spotlight in a gourmet shop shines on barrels of brine and dark olives while Mark stands in their old kitchen stirring his special tomato sauce and discussing the perfect ratio of salt to oregano. With each step forward, the cracks spread along the storefronts of the Parisian street. More memories are en route.

Peter's grip tightens, driving Delia's fingernails against the palm of her hand, and then he is pulling her in, tilting Delia's head, his lips grinding against her lips. The pressure of his hands and arms are not comforting. When Peter finally pulls away he leaves his arm draped across her shoulders. Meanwhile, the ghosts continue to burrow, cutting their way through.

Delia notices her reflection in a clothing store window, Peter's lanky frame hovering over her. The top of Delia's head barely reaches his chest. Her face seems to waver, a pale and uncertain reflection. Remembering.

It is then that she hears the siren, an ambulance. The red and white flashing lights follow soon after. She watches as the lights dive along the street from window to window. Terror reflected back from the plate-glass storefronts. Help. Someone is failing. Someone is dying. Someone is dead, they say. Ghost lights. Grounded stars lost amid all those shattered memories.

Delia remembers the *uh uh uh* sound of shuddering breaths. She remembers pulse rates and sweat-soaked sheets. Despite the price tags on the Parisian window displays, it is the reflected ambulance lights that demand her attention: wounds of all types for sale on this summer night. Delia stands with Peter on the sidewalk, his arm still across her shoulder. Both of them are still as the ambulance moves farther and farther away. Delia is traveling back on final time, getting ready for her final excursion.

Funerals are all the same: tears and music you never want to hear again. Prayers. Delia wore tights even though it was ninety degrees outside. Mark's mother leaned into Delia's shoulder as they carried Mark's casket inside the old stone church. His mother's smell was all wrong: floral and powdery. Delia wanted sour. She wanted sweaty. She wanted three days of forgotten showers and a night on the river with the mud sliding between both of their feet. She wanted Mark. She comforted Mark's mother as she cried. No one asked Delia if she wanted to cry. Why should they? She wasn't even there, too busy floating, ashes against the sky.

THE COAST

The door to Peter's door sits in the middle of an alley: dark, old wood, and peeling paint, a stone lintel hanging above. The house faces the river. The wall and the fairy lights are all that separates the two of them from the water. Delia can smell the boat fuel and a sweetish rot, like flesh, wafting up from the water. The door's brass doorknob is like an open hand waiting to be taken. Delia wants to reach out and grasp it. Darkness is waiting. Cold and heat. The coast and Mark and the hard and staring water. But Peter's arm is like a crushing stone. Delia can feel bruises rising up along her shoulders. She hears a cough from a nearby window and the slow putter of a boat moving on the other side of the wall. In the end, it is someone, someone on the other side of Peter's wooden door, who finally turns the handle.

Not Mark.

Delia steps forward as Peter follows, his hands now on her hips. Delia can feel his breath against her neck. His body is like molten rock: hot and hard and blazing.

Delia shudders, her body racked by a sudden coughing fit. Ghosts are everywhere: sharp jabs to her lungs, a twisting in her gut. But it is Peter's house that attacks her stillness. Delia expected the crouching gargoyles and damp stone walls. She expected the dimness and the smell of charred remains: wood ash, the acrid stench of scorched hair, the oily, cloying sweetness of charred meat. Even the cot, set in a far corner of the room, seems familiar, the sheets hospital-thin and hospital-white. It is the girl who takes Delia by surprise, the girl who opened the door. She is watching Delia with those silver, ash-coast eyes that shimmer but do not blink.

It is Peter who shuts the door then his hands tighten on Delia's waist, pressing the cloth of her cotton skirt hard against her hips. All the while the girl reaches out, her face as untroubled as a Christmas ornament, something red and fleshy in her outstretched hand. Each of the girl's thin little fingers ends in a black nail, sharp and pointed. Each nail is at least half the length of the finger itself. The girl's fingers cradle the red contents of her palm. There is red on her cheeks as well, blonde curls under her velvet cap, hot ashes escaping her nostrils and perfect lips. The girl opens her mouth wide, and a cloud engulfs Delia. The cinders make Delia cry. Nothing makes me cry anymore, Delia thinks as ashes and water stream down her cheeks. Delia can feel Peter behind, inhaling deeply.

The stone creatures watch the trio from the corners of the room. Meanwhile, Peter's hands slide upward, cupping Delia's breasts. His hard tongue runs from her collarbone upward against the base of her skull. Cold and then hot. Burning. Delia can feel her skin pulling back in protest. A whimper escapes her lips as Peter's tongue traces lines along Delia's flesh, his hands like crushing stones as they grab at breast and hip and thigh.

The gargoyles are not the ones to worry about, Delia realizes. The stone statues with their long ears and sharp teeth have such gentle eyes. It is only Peter, Peter with his halo of brown hair and electric hands, who wants to touch her. The rest just want to return home, to fly to the coast once Peter opens the door. The closest gargoyle, a female to Delia's left, stretches her legs, her back a concave length of stone that curves toward the ground, then she settles once more against her back legs, content, it seems, to wait.

The lights on the boulevard were nothing. The memories are tumbling now, pressing hard. Delia gasps for breath as the cinders fill her lungs. Peter's dry fingers like an abrasion against her thighs, the small of her back, and Delia is falling back against the bed, hospital-white sheets covering the backs of her legs, her waist, her bruised and shaking arms. Inside, she is untethered. The ghosts are rising up, carrying everything with them as they rush back through Delia's skin.

It is almost time to open the final door. It must be. Delia can hear the girl breathing somewhere nearby. She can feel the heat of her cinders. She can see the girl's eyes, the flashing silver light that doesn't look away.

Mark lay in that hospital bed for ten days while Delia sat on the molded plastic chair, willing him to stay asleep.

"Just sleep," she murmured as she stroked his sweat-stained hair, but it did no good. The vomiting would start: his legs curling up against his chest, his skin covered in a pattern of splotches and welts Delia couldn't begin to translate.

"He needs to rest," the attendant said as she added another ingredient to the bag of fluids that hung near Mark's head.

Delia noticed the woman's kind brown eyes. Then Mark's own eyes closed, and Delia started to breathe again. She timed her inhalations with the movement of his chest: the rising and lowering of the hospital sheets telling her Mark was still alive, the air in Delia's lungs telling her there was enough for both of them.

Toward the end, Mark mostly slept.

"Just go and get some rest," Mark said that last time. But Delia didn't go home. She couldn't. Home was where the bed was empty and the cat expected Mark to feed her at 6:00 a.m. Home was the pile of clean laundry heaped and unfolded in a corner of the room, the trash rank after too many days left untended. Home was a place that didn't exist anymore.

Delia wanted to climb onto that narrow hospital bed. She wanted to wrap her arms around Mark's chest and smell that sour male scent. She really did. But his skin looked so drained, and the smell when Delia hovered over him was closer to chemical antiseptics and veterinary visits than the salt of living flesh. The scent closer to death.

Instead of leaving, Delia pulled that molded plastic chair close, held Mark's hand.

He is sleeping, Delia thought as she watched the sheets rise and then fall again, breathing.

When Delia opened her eyes, it was dark. Women were hovering around the bed, two or three of them, and someone was pushing Delia back with hard stone hands. Mark's fingers were no longer in hers.

The heat in the room, was Delia the only one who felt it? And now they were pulling in a cart. It was like a TV episode, a movie-of-the-week special. Wasn't Delia supposed to start weeping? But she didn't. And she didn't. And even when they left Delia with Mark, or Mark's body, for "a few moments" still she didn't. Mark and the Hospital. This wasn't a story. This was pretending to float while you crashed and broke across the rock-strewn ground. This was the Great Blackout of 2010, and Delia locked inside the elevator listening to the cable unravel. Devastation doesn't have a script. Shattering and then smaller still. Pulverized. A cloud of floating debris.

It was easy to get on that plane. Easy to float across the ocean, landing with Wendy and Alex and Kurtis, the metro and the tourists' maps. And finally night fell, Peter's hand holding hers as they headed across the city.

Of course Delia went with Peter. She was like a box of ashes, carefully contained, just waiting to be released.

"To ghosts," Peter had said, tossing back that last beer while they sat on the terrace. But Peter's ghosts all seemed so small under his hands, more like a child's toy or dangling charms rather than actual people. Nothing but a palmful of energy. Delia needed more than that.

They are almost done.

Delia is lying on the bed, face up. The sweat drips from Peter's neck and chest hairs onto her naked body. Peter's hands are cradling Delia's breasts, heavy, pressing inward. Delia can feel the bones of his hips grinding, his thighs leaning into hers for a moment before she is forced to bend her knees. Peter's face flushes as he finally slips inside, eyes now closed. Delia's body rocks with Peter's while her hands reach outward, wrapping themselves in those hospital-white sheets. She can smell the sweat of their bodies and the candy-sweet scent of her crackling flesh. Underneath it all is the scent of linoleum hallways and that white-tiled hospital room.

The creatures lining Peter's room do not roar, they bellow. A wave of rage and grief that crashes through the open door.

Delia's hands have stopped moving. Her arms and legs no longer shudder as her mouth gasps for breath. Meanwhile, Peter is sliding off, stretching his legs. He stoops down to the floor and then sits, his hands now holding a pack of cigarettes and a book of matches.

Delia remains wrapped in the sheets. The bed feels worn, threadbare, overused. The room is empty of stone creatures, empty of girls who watch her with ocean-silver eyes.

Peter watches Delia from his seat by the bed. The cigarette smoke lingers above his nascent horns. His hips and clavicle press outward, their outline clear beneath the skin. He's skeletal now. Only a thin layer of gray skin keeps Delia from seeing his organs: his kidneys, his heart, his ash-filled lungs.

The bed feels prickly and far too warm.

Why didn't Delia notice Peter's chair when she first stepped through the door? It's made of the same molded plastic as the chair in Mark's hospital room. The metal legs are attached with those too-small screws that make it tip slightly whenever you sit down. It is not a chair anyone should trust. But Peter slouches in it all the same, the cultural attaché. His face, despite the slouch and the curling lines of smoke, is more petulant than tired. His part is done.

The scratching warmth of the bed is drawing Delia inward. Her body curves against the other body that now rests next to hers. The sheet covers them both. She can feel an arm against her naked shoulder, feel a chest under her hand. Delia's feet wrap themselves around his calves.

Mark.

I am sure we will arrive at the coast soon, Delia thinks. Her eyes have closed, but she knows the pallor of Mark's skin matches the thready-white of her uncovered breasts, both of them white as sheets, as she sinks beneath.

Finally, Peter and his gray smoke are lost on the other side of the broken windows.

LEVEL UP

LEVEL 1: MARGERY'S RODENTIZING SHRINK RAY

MARGERY KEPT HER LOVER in a hamster cage atop her cluttered and dusty desk. Every day she poured pellets into the ceramic food dish and refilled the plastic water bottle. Hamsters have long curving teeth—sharp. Some days Margery forgot and reached in too close, and then that hamster did what he needed to: he bit, drawing one tear-shaped drop of blood.

Margery's hamster lover fit into the palm of her hand. His fur was warm and soft, seemingly begging to be touched. Even with those brown beady eyes, he was hard to resist.

The hamster lover and Margery had what people called "history." Margery knew precautions were necessary. When that particular feeling overcame her and she just *needed, needed* to touch him, she held a strawberry or peeled grape just out of range. Hamster lovers understood rewards.

Before he was a hamster, her lover used to have tufts of fuzzy belly hair that she liked to run her fingers through. The hair on his head was silky, even as a man. But his hamster fur was soft in a way her human lover had never been.

Some weeks she could barely hold off petting him. Other weeks she barely noticed him beneath his nest of wood shavings and newspaper, her mind wandering to other things as she rehung his water bottle and relocked his cage.

And then there were the dark weekends when Margery paid the neighbor's boy to take care of her lover, pretending she would be out of town. On those days, she wandered for hours through the library stacks, pausing always in the same two sections: 573.688 2 animal husbandry and 152.434 5 the psychology of love. If she was feeling particularly brave, she might make her way up to the mezzanine where 619.457 3, the section concerned with lacerations, vivisection, and forgiveness, was housed. And then, eventually, breath trapped in her throat and clawing to get out, she would force herself to move on.

LEVEL 2: STEPHANIE'S POCKET UNIVERSE

Stephanie could hear the voices the moment she pinched an opening into her pocket universe.

"Nokia? Really? Man, where *did* you get that phone?"

"Fuck off, fucktard. I bought it last week."

"No signal whatever the brand, right?" That third voice was Stephanie's latest lover, trying for a conciliatory tone. He was good at that.

Stephanie's universe was a bit dusty with a scattering of dead leaves and abandoned spider webs. Grandma Steverin had given Stephanie the universe when she turned sixteen. "Every girl needs something special on her sweet sixteen," Grandma had said, though Stephanie hadn't felt sweet, even then.

The workings of the pocket universe were no different from any other. It had its own shape, its own lifespan, and its very own movement of time. From their pocket-universe perspective, the three residents—Horace, Luis, and David—had arrived over the course of a single weekend. For Stephanie it had been almost ten years

Just like every other time Stephanie visited, all three boys, men, ex-loves-of-her-life, sat on the circle of blue-and-green plaid armchairs, their feet settled against the oily, pocket-universe ground. A plastic bin stood in the center of the chairs. It doubled as a table, laden with a half-finished lasagna, bread sticks, and a twelve-pack of microbrew. The beer was a moment of weakness Stephanie tried not to regret, even when Horace held up his half-empty bottle and saluted her with a bleary, "Great brew, my friend."

Horace had been Stephanie's first boyfriend. After they fucked, he carefully explained how it was better if they remained "just friends." Stephanie, being eighteen and so recently unfucked, hadn't understood. The things he said when they made love. The way his mouth and tongue slipped between her thighs. Of course he felt something more. Then came the night he stood next to her closed dorm door, waiting for the people outside to walk on by. "Don't want to give the wrong impression," he'd whispered. Winked. Smiled.

Horace was two firsts in one: Stephanie had never dropped a lover through a portal before.

It was five years before Stephanie opened the portal again. Stephanie and Luis lived together in a fourth-floor apartment: no elevator, a shower that required Luis to open the skylight whenever he got in, a barely-there bedroom closet. So what if Luis stayed late at the library with Sheila. So what if Stephanie had put on all that weight. She was still beautiful. That was what all those Dove commercials said.

And then came Luis's graduation party and the black peasant blouse and swirling skirt Stephanie bought especially. Stephanie realized her mistake as soon as Luis pulled her out onto the fire escape "to talk in private." The dark colors hid more than Stephanie's fat. Her curves were all lost in a tsunami of dark linen and matching boots. Despite the close quarters and the way Luis's left side pressed up against her right knee, leg, shoulder, all Luis wanted to do was "be clear." He droned on and on, explaining the difference between love and being-in-love, which he most definitely was not. "I just don't want to be with you anymore."

"What do you mean?" Stephanie could feel the nearby heat of her pocket universe despite the cool night air. Her entire left side, the side not pressed against Luis, tingled.

Luis didn't seem to notice a thing. He shrugged. "Really, mine was always a more rational kind of love. I was never as into it as you were."

Stephanie's pocket universe never drifted far, but now it was almost cleaved to Stephanie, a pool of heat radiating from a spot next to her left hip. Stephanie reached down and twisted her thumb and forefingers against the patch of air. The tear was barely the width of her pinky finger but spreading quickly. The temperature on the fire escape had spiked into almost-uncomfortably-hot, and still Luis noticed nothing. Instead, Luis contemplated the night sky with its spring constellations of Hercules and Ursa Major. A sky made just for lovers. That was what he used to say already oh-so-long ago.

"Too bad we won't be together to watch the Perseid meteor shower. Actually, that part of our friendship has always been pleasant. Great, even."

"Pleasant? What the hell? Is it Sheila?" Stephanie's fingers were frantically tearing the opening now, the edges of the portal tangling around her thumb and middle finger, the edges both sticky and slightly moist.

"Jesus, Steph. It's nothing to do with Sheila. It's you. We've lived together how long now? At this point I know you so damn well. Truth is, you're always going to make me miserable."

"Okay, then." All it took was a tilt of her upper body back through the open window and a quick tug of Luis's stupid skinny tie. Stephanie still remembered the look of surprise on his face as she heaved him through.

David was the last one: the friend, the confidante, the never-endingly aroused lover—until he wasn't.

Even as she coaxed him through the portal with that promise of one last fuck, Stephanie was sure David would figure it out. But as the three armchairs emerged, David didn't question her choice. Instead, he smiled down at her with just the right degree of forbearance. "You know, whatever happens it's nice to see you. Not talking to you these last few months felt weird, but also fine. I thought I would miss you more."

"Ah."

"Hello," Horace bellowed from the depths of his armchair. His beer bottle was almost empty.

"Hello?" David replied, turning to greet the other two.

And then Stephanie did what needed to be done; she pinched the portal's hole closed.

Pocket universes run by their own rules. Rule number one: pocket universes always trail behind their owners. Even after the tears were over and Stephanie no longer looked for texts from David, some nights she found herself pinching open a small hole and listening in.

So many carefully crafted solutions to global warming. So many hours spent discussing the texture of the plaid chairs and whether sitting on them made them complicit in the sweat-shop-factory culture where they'd been built. So many long drawn out silences when all three exes seemed spent of words. And still, no matter how long Stephanie listened, her name never came up. In that way things were exactly the same as before.

LEVEL 3: MARY'S TOXIN ERADICATION

Mary placed the sample box in a shopping bag and drove to the Charlemont post office. Mary was a teacher and a planner, or as Dominic liked to joke, "a failed academic." The hardest part of this enterprise hadn't been the money, or even tracking down the mail-order lab. The hardest part had been the collection of the sample itself. In the end sample collection had involved asking Dominic to blow up the balloons for his own birthday party.

"I like surprises so much better," Dominic had said, exhaling into the last piece of green latex.

Mary couldn't have been more thrilled by his statement. Back turned, she had carefully marked the Dominic-filled balloon before tying on its string.

When the lab report on the balloon's contents came back via Priority Mail, not a single toxin was listed. Instead, the report findings included 78.04 percent nitrogen, 15.66 percent oxygen, 5.30 percent carbon dioxide, plus 1 percent of other "harmless gases." Mary didn't despair. She was used to failure and trying again. Plus the symptoms couldn't be anymore goddamn obvious.

Her throat burned, cheese-grater raw. Her heart felt weirdly heavy, like it was skipping beats. At night her limbs twitched. She couldn't sleep. She couldn't focus. She couldn't even pace the house. Mary's body knew the truth. Dominic and his toxins had burrowed deep.

For her second analysis attempt, Mary tried a more precise selection of Dominic words. She placed her cell phone in the largest of the LabGen containers and replayed his Monday morning message, the one that had greeted her at work. "Mary, you know I'm no good at this phone stuff. Yeah, I guess I knew you'd be really upset about the extra week away, but I'm not sure what you expect me to do about it. You know I'm not a feelings guy." Despite Dominic's testy tone, the lab's stance was unwavering: the second sample was as clean as the first.

For some, this would have been the crisis-of-faith moment. But not Mary. She smiled. She grinned. She twisted her face into an ironic expression that almost looked like happiness. Finally, she had him figured: It wasn't sounds alone. Touching flesh and leaking fluids were the catalysts. His toxins required her flesh.

When he returned from his too-long conference, Mary writhed on the bed, carefully inhaling while Dominic's fingers unhooked her bra, pulled at her pants, wandered down to settle into the wetness between her legs. "I missed this," he whispered looking directly into her eyes. His face was only inches from her own. "This," he said, not "you." Just like every other time they fucked.

Dominic bent to pull off the last of his clothes and Mary took advantage of her moment. She exhaled "this" into a vial and licked the plastic interior, before sealing both air and moisture inside. Quickly, she slipped the vial into her bedside drawer. Easy peasy.

Third time's a charm—that's what the lab's cover letter should have said. The first page of the LabGen report was full of chemical names that began with terms like *chloro* and *poly* and *hexa*. Next to the words the report listed the detected percentage of that particular compound. On their own, the results of LabGen Corporation's analysis told Mary nothing. She taught Eastern European history with a specific concentration in the Baltic region. She played the djembe hand drum. She did not do chemistry. But it was the report's second page that Mary had paid all that money for. The second page was titled Recommendations in bold, fourteen point font. Only four words were printed below the heading: "evacuation or immediate containment."

Finally, irrefutable proof.

YouTube and DIYers took care of the rest. In less than forty-eight hours Mary had both the step-by-step instructions for Dominic's environmentally secure containment area along with all the necessary supplies, including her own breathing apparatus and goggles.

The following Tuesday, right on schedule, Dominic left for yet another conference. "After this trip I'll stick closer to home." He kissed her cheek. "I promise."

"Sounds good."

He slipped his arms around her waist for the obligatory hug, their two bodies pressed briefly together. "You should take advantage of all this free time to hit the gym."

No more words. Mary had all the information she needed. And like most homeowners in New England, she also had the necessary basement. With Britney Spears's "Toxic" blasting on repeat, Mary began to frame out the necessary eight-by-eight area, taking her time, measuring three and even four times just to be sure. Containment meant airtight and soundproof. Containment meant never inhaling her man's toxins again. Containment meant finally being able to count on Dominic's silence.

MASTERY: TARA'S BLACK HOLE

Tara stands over Richard's chair adjusting his helmet and checking the oxygen-level readout. Tara is so sorry. If only faster-than-light travel were possible, she would take the time, build the necessary rocket engine. But in this universe, physics doesn't work that way.

"Don't worry, Richard," she says, patting his manacled, suit-covered hand. "Eventually, you'll get there."

This is the point of no return. All she has to do is close the rocket's door and press the big red button.

"But I . . ." Richard begins, starts again. "You have to look at it from my perspective." His panicked look probably isn't even for show.

"Why?" Tara doesn't even hesitate. Instead, she locks his helmet in place, latches the metal door, and initiates the launch sequence. The flame as the rocket rises up beyond the atmosphere is an unwavering orange-yellow. Tara watches the rocket's final push away from earth's gravitational pull and the eradication of the last drop of fuel, followed by invisibility, darkness. Now Richard is just another meteor, a distancing star making his way to the nearest event horizon.

Richard promised her forever. He pledged to love her flaws and fears. He pledged to love her when she was frail and her skin was paper-thin. Richard spent hours and days and years braiding his life with hers.

Just fifteen hundred light years: that's the time his rocket ship will take to enter the Orion Nebula and reach the unnamed black hole's event horizon. Just fifteen hundred light years until Richard's promise will finally hold true, or close enough. Time dilation: from Tara's perspective, Richard will look like a constant in her night sky.

Richard promised her forever, and thanks to one black hole and Tara's little rocket ship, he is going to deliver. Meanwhile, Tara has things to do down here on earth.

It's only later that Tara considers her final words. It would have been a nice touch if she could have remembered to say goodbye.

Still, mission finally complete.

Pretty Little Boxes

BOXES SURROUND US.

Every night Barry builds more walls, fastens more lids. Sometimes, when I can't sleep, I slip down the hall to his workroom and watch. His eyes remain focused on the contents of his bench: the wood, the pulped flowers and all those dying insects—the grasshoppers, the damsel flies, the hissing cockroaches—that will eventually make up the lining of each petal-and-limb box. Little pools of haemolymph, the fluid he collects from his crushed arthropods, rest in jars, waiting to be mixed into the glue.

Most Gray Witches know only two things about Barry. They know he is one of the best craftsmen in the city. They also know he's the child of a Gray Witch, one of the few children they didn't manage to train.

"It won't be easy," his mother said after Barry introduced me as his fiancée. We stood in a workroom somewhere deep inside the Gray Witch Union's granite walls. The room was filled with benches and scurrying creatures. No windows. It was when she stared at our intertwined hands that I finally noticed her eyes. They were exactly the same shade of gray as Barry's. "A Sadness Carrier and my son," she continued, turning those gray eyes in my direction. "Well, I hope you didn't traipse down here expecting a Witch's blessing."

Barry's fingers tightened against mine.

"We know Gray Witches only bless each other," he replied.

"Of course you do," she said. "You've always been a clever boy."

Blessing or not, Barry and I married the next day.

The photographer Barry hired snapped picture after picture as our few guests moved through the receiving line. These were our neighbors and co-workers: students still in their first apartments, urban gardeners with calloused hands, women from the alley off of Market Square, where I ran my stall.

"Congratulations," they said. "Best wishes." They even toasted our happiness.

The wedding photos, however, are focused on something else entirely. My hair, in frame after frame, is long and glossy. My cheeks are glowing with foundation and rouge. In some of the pictures, Barry's hand rests on my waist, heavy against the stiff silk gown. I still remember the feeling of heat as the side of his body leaned into mine. Yet each picture shows the same thing. My face is strained. My lips turned downward.

Just two days into my vacation and already I was falling apart. I'll be lucky to last another day; that was what I was thinking as the photographer snapped his shots. Along with the photographer, officiant, and cake, Barry had also booked a honeymoon. I'd be away from work for over a week.

I didn't love my job, but I damn well needed it.

"Barry?" I wiped the tears away with the back of one hand as I stared into Barry's workshop, careful not to get in the way.

Barry was scrubbing one of the large mesh screens with a stiff metal brush, readying the tray for the next sheet of paper. He'd been making a lot of paper lately, spending long hours in the studio. Perhaps the Gray Witches had given him an extra commission. I glanced at the carefully stacked rectangles. Not worth getting distracted about. "We paid them all that money, Barry, so my sadness wouldn't grow back."

"At least we can make up the money now that you're working again," Barry replied, his back still turned to me as he scrubbed the screens.

"That's not the point."

"I'll make you some more boxes." Barry's brush made a scuff-scuffing noise as it moved across the fine mesh screen.

"No," I said. "I don't want..." I grabbed the workshop's door, rattling its loose metal handle.

Barry was silent as he dipped the wire brush into a pot of boiling water. He shook the brush off and poured the contents of the pot across the screen, sluicing off the cellulose and chitin. He didn't even glance in my direction.

Sadness Carrier is the only job I've ever held.

We Sadness Carriers are licensed for only one thing: sadness. The most important tool is the box. Too little space inside and the feelings might morph, condense into the heavier moods. A dangerous thing, carrying a box like that. Most likely thing in the world that it'll be tagged as a Gray Witch offense. And then the boxes can go entirely the other way, the size just too big, the walls meant to hold more than you can offer. With a box like that, the mood might escape entirely, leaving nothing but emptiness and air.

When business is good, it feels like an honorable service. You never know who your next client is going to be: perhaps it'll be a West End climber with his new money and not much else, making sure he has some backup during *Madam Butterfly*. I get clients like that all the time. What if they can't wait to check the game scores until the end of the performance? What would people think then? One of my little boxes gets rid of all that anxiety. I get other types of clients too. One afternoon that nice waitress from over on Ninth Street might stop by my stall, looking for a bit of sincerity while she breaks up with her summer fling.

But the box has to be exactly right. There's nothing worse than listening to a neighbor describe how she's seen that Eaton's waitress laughing hysterically while her boyfriend wept or overhearing the story of a man who committed suicide at the opera. Those pretty little boxes are important. And, before Barry, they were tough to find, tough to afford anyway. Anyone who's any good sells to the Gray Witches.

Barry changed everything. That's why I married him.

"Honey," he said on that first night. "Let me help you."

And God forgive me, I did. I let him help me. In the end, I did much more than just open that apartment door.

Everyone has a "how we met" story. Barry and I are no exception.

I was holed up in some corner apartment on Fifth Street. Barry had just moved in next door. Even on that very first night, he found me hard to ignore.

"Tears equal money," I kept muttering as I kicked the small pile of misshapen containers against the wall. Some of the boxes broke apart on impact. Not surprising. The entire batch was nothing but cheap balsa wood and a couple of staples. Cheap balsa wood I'd dropped my entire month's rent on. I had no more cash and now, with these rip-offs filling up the room, I couldn't even work. I lifted my foot, crushing another of the misshapen rectangles. Meanwhile, my tears kept flowing.

That bastard box-builder, Francoise, had stiffed me. No liner paper and, even with the stapled edges, the joins were so bad the contents poured right out. Now, not only did I have nothing to sell at tomorrow's market; I also had nowhere for my tears to go.

I slammed into a pile of boxes with both feet and then screamed. That's when I heard someone pounding on my apartment door.

Of course I didn't answer. I had no idea who it was. Still, Barry must have known I was standing nearby. He must have heard the snuffling as I tried to stifle my sobs.

The pounding eventually stopped. That was good. But I could still hear him breathing. Eventually, that first sheet of paper slid under the door. I watched as it wafted above the floorboards and then settled against my feet: thick, textured fibers twisted across the page, an almost unbroken wing like a translucent rainbow in one corner. I'd seen paper like this before in the glassed-in display cases at Gray Witch Union. I'd even seen this paper once in my own childhood home, wallpaper tight against the sides of that pretty little box my mother had emptied her savings to obtain after Daddy left us. Not once had I ever seen it written on.

I stumbled back a few steps, but the notes just kept on coming. Fern fronds and grasshopper antennae flying from beneath my door. Three pages had fluttered through.

"Go on. Pick them up," Barry said. "Don't be afraid." His voice was quiet now. I could almost feel his hands press against the other side of the door, his breath warm against the fading paint.

I bent down, glancing over the papers.

It's all right, the first note said. *I'll just listen,* said the second. *Trust and faith are fine,* said the third. *You should try them. I dreamt about you last night, not even knowing your name.*

A fourth sheet of paper followed. I caught it before it even had a chance to settle. *Perhaps, I can tell you my name,* it said. *Would that help?*

In the end, I opened the door, just an inch or two, and peered into the hallway. Tears were still leaking from my eyes. I think I even hiccupped a time or two.

"Barry," he said. He held a wooden box in one outstretched hand. "My name is Barry." I noticed his gray eyes even then, stormy-ocean gray. I noticed the box as well: a pattern of beetles with half-open wings burned across its surface, a musky smell rising from the wood. Beautiful. Yet, Barry's box was sized all wrong. It was the kind of box that would sit empty by morning, the contents dissipated instead of contained. It was the kind of box a Gray Witch might carry if she was so inclined, a personal disposal unit, a place to stop the drowning. No way could I afford a box like that.

"Barry," he said again. He continued to hold out the box. "Consider it an early birthday present."

I kept my own hands at my sides. "But you don't even know when I was born."

"That's okay."

"What about—"

"Go ahead. Open it."

The edge of my right hand grazed his palm as I lifted the box toward me.

That's when he smiled. Turns out he's the kind of man who likes to see his boxes used.

Turns out, in the end, I'm no different.

———

Earlier this evening we sat across from each other at the dining table. My eyes were fixed on Barry and his computer, the way his fingers flew across the keyboard.

"Barry, we paid all that money."

Barry stayed quiet, reading the contents of the screen.

"We should ask for it back or maybe ask for a new spell. The first one didn't even last half a year." I fiddled with my untouched pasta. It was already cold.

"Barry, I just think—"

"Gray Witches, Celia," he snapped. "I may not be a goddamn Witch, but Mom didn't raise an idiot. I'm not going to ask for our money back just before they cast my spell."

"Look, what if it happens to you?" I dug into my jeans pocket, fishing for a Kleenex. "Barry?" I blotted the water from my cheeks. "What if it doesn't stick?"

"That's not gonna happen," he muttered. Then, finally, he looked up from his screen. His face was like a rain cloud, almost full to bursting with feelings. Despite his best efforts, I knew it wouldn't last. Barry never felt anything in the least bit heavy for more than a minute or two.

"Barry—"

"You probably did something to break it anyway," he said. "Gray Witches don't make mistakes." And then he stood up and headed for the hallway. After a moment, I heard the workshop door slam.

"But you don't care what the Gray Witches think of you. That's what you said," I screamed at the closed door. "Right, Barry? Right?" All I got was silence.

My own permanent Gray Witch Vacation cost $2,200 and the death of one mid-level executive. It lasted only three months.

The decision to purchase the spell was easily made. I had just finished sprinting up all three flights of stairs, newspaper in hand, only to stumble into the gloom of our apartment. Barry stood in our living room, holding his cup of coffee.

"Barry..." I started.

I held up the newspaper, pointing to a photograph of a man in midair, falling from the South End Bridge. "Third Jumper This Year" the headline read. Inside the picture was a small inset, a portrait of a smiling thirty-something-year-old man in a suit and tie. He had very even teeth.

"Barry, I know him," I said.

"So?"

It was early evening. I'd been working the stall all day. By the looks of things, Barry had just got up. His fine brown hair was mussed, his face still creased and bleary.

"He came by my stall yesterday," I said. I set the paper on our dining table and inspected the picture one more time. The image of the bridge was too grainy to make out the man's expression. It must have been shot at a distance. "He bought two boxes. Bought two the week before as well."

"Did you tell him—" Barry started as he wandered closer.

"Of course," I cut him off. "I told him the boxes wouldn't keep. I always tell my customers."

"Well, it sure looks like you messed something up." He reached over and turned the newspaper in his direction. My hands shook. I placed my palms on the tabletop, as my stomach roiled and twisted. Barry's expression, as he watched me, held the same slightly puzzled look I used to love so much. Right then, I couldn't stand it.

After that, there wasn't much Barry could do. Despite all his cajoling, I refused to return to my stall. In the end, despite my job and the money, he agreed to hand over our savings to the Gray Witch Union and purchase my permanent Gray Witch Vacation. He even came with me, though he wasn't happy about any of it: the trip, the box, the loss of income that this "whim" of mine was going to engender. Still, the two of us, the Witch's son and the Sadness Carrier, walked across the Market and up the Union steps together for the second time.

I don't think either of us expected any favors, and we didn't get any.

We stood in line on those gray granite steps. We politely waited our turn, and then, after I explained to the assigned Witch exactly how I wanted to feel, we received my very own petal-and-limb box. Barry, like always, watched while I opened the lid. That box was supposed to fix everything. And, for a few months, it did.

Every year on my birthday Barry gives me exactly the same gift: his own handcrafted Gray Witch box. Even this year, just weeks after we'd spent all that money on my Gray Witch happiness, he presented me with my usual birthday present. The box was etched all over with carapaces. Spiders' eyes watched me as I opened the lid. Spiders' eyes and Barry.

I didn't suspect a thing. Despite Barry's grumbling, I trusted him. Trust is something, it seems, I give out for free. Like love. And tenderness. I could never be a Gray Witch.

Boxes all work the same way. First there is the initial spell. The carrier or Witch, whoever it is, has to fill the interior. Then it's all on the new owner. They decide when to open the lid. For me, though, it's the limb-and-petal paper that is the true magic.

With the paper, there's always that moment when the glue melts and the limbs, the haemolymph, and the dead leaves and petals coalesce, the mosaic inhaled by the recipient like a cloud creature settling into their lungs. Sometimes, after opening one of Barry's boxes, my eyes would burn with iridescent mist for minutes afterward.

This year on my birthday, innocent me, I laughed as the black-and-yellow striped insect rose from the remains of Barry's box. Its wings were bluish-violet and fringed like the petals of an Aster. I leaned in to get a closer look. I'd never seen an actual fully formed creature emerge before.

"A hover fly," Barry said. "Mixed with a few flowers. It just looks like it can jab you."

I must have given him an odd look, because he kept on talking—either that or he was nervous.

"Hover flies don't sting. They eat aphids and other plant suckers," he explained as though that made all the sense in the world. And somehow, in that moment, it did.

I laughed again and even opened the window, letting the striped insect with the flower wings find its way out of our apartment. The two of us, Barry and I, stood by the window and watched the almost-wasp disappear into the city.

"How?" I asked. I turned to Barry, amazed all over again by the magic.
"Happy birthday," was his only reply.

That man has more of a sense of humor than he lets on.

It took two lines on a receipt, a dollar amount and a date, for me recognize
Barry's betrayal.

After all the screaming and the slamming doors and the breakfast nobody
ate, Barry took off for the Union. I headed straight to our bedroom. That's
where I found the receipt: on top of one of my cardboard boxes, the box
that holds the only two Gray Witch receipts I've ever owned—Mother's and
mine. *Gray Witch Ltd.* was printed right on the top along with the price and
a detailed description. It was the cost that caught my eye first: "$2,200." It
was printed next to the word "Total." The same amount Barry was
supposedly about to spend on his own Gray Witch Vacation. The same
amount we had spent on my original spell.

Why had Barry taken out my receipt? That was my first thought. Then I
looked more closely. The date on the receipt was all wrong. It was from last
year, sure, but weeks after my own procedure. In fact, the date was exactly
two days before my birthday, September 12th.

My Barry went down to the Gray Witch Union just two days before my
birthday and spent $2,200. My Barry bought me a present I didn't even
know I had. That black-and-yellow striped insect with the petal wings? The
item's description made everything clear. That supposed hover fly was a wasp
after all. "Unbinding Spell," the receipt said. Break me apart spell. Take away
my happiness spell. It seemed Barry had spent his own Gray Witch money
months ago to undo everything the Gray Witches had just fixed. He'd turned
my happiness into a wasp and watched as it flew away.

And, now, Barry had left the receipt out where I was sure to find it. He'd
set me up. Tears weren't even close to an adequate response.

After three years, Barry had trained me well. I knew everything I needed
was in his workshop. And Barry? Well, Barry was out. He'd run down to
the Hall to buy his own Gray Witch Vacation. At least that's what he
said. Couldn't imagine anything less likely. All that talk of purchasing a
little "joy" was just a ruse. We both knew joy was never going to be enough.

Barry was waiting until I built my own pretty little box, one made just for him.

I'm standing in the workshop entrance, clutching the receipt in my right hand. The room is a cacophony of hisses, whirs and scrambling legs. In the middle of the room stands a long bench, though the majority of the floor space is reserved for the papermaking: the presses and sieves. Overhead, long stems full of drying leaves and petals hang from a wooden rack.

The long cedar boards sit in the far right corner. Expensive wood. Barry must have been certain they'd be used.

I set the receipt on Barry's bench and pull out the first board. Already, I can tell there is just enough cedar to frame the box I have in mind. I have one human-sized box to build. One body box to line with all of Barry's limb-and-petal paper. Of course, the paper isn't the only thing I need. Glue. I'll have to make more glue.

I close my eyes for a moment, then open the cricket cage and drop a handful into one of Barry's presses. After the crickets come the brown wood spiders. When I'm sure the press's interior can hold no more, I push down on the handle, putting all my weight against the metal, then I add the clear, greenish contents of the collecting jar to the glue pot and start all over again. Not even Barry has ever lined a box this large.

I thought the liquid would smell, but there is barely any scent at all. It is the press's screen that nearly does me in. Carapaces and leg joints shudder as I flick the contents of the screen onto the floor. Barry's tidy workshop is littered with dead insect debris.

I push on as the tears finally start. I'm not sure if it's sadness or rage. My eyes stream either way. Meanwhile my mouth mutters nonsense words that I only half-hear. Words about cracked and broken and making him feel *something*.

I've collected enough haemolymph. I cut swaths of elder blossom and honeysuckle from the overhead racks, drop them into the metal brazier along with a match. When the fire has banked, I scoop up the still-hot ashes. My fingertips are red. I can feel them throbbing. It's as though all my blood wants to push its way outward.

Not yet.

I tip the ashes into the pot of haemolymph and stir. The greenish liquid turns a putty-gray.

Finally, it's time to construct the box. I know that, after the glue, the box itself will be no problem. Pretty interlocking joints may mark a good craftsman, but a staple gun can work just as well. The magic is in the contents. And if you are very lucky, if you have someone like Barry, someone, it turns out, like me to press the paper into place, someone to sketch her own ashen face and "happy birthday" across the top when she's done with a burning-hot coal, then all the better.

First, though, I have to take care of the blood. It's the last step—the glue requires it.

Barry has a special block plane for finish work. The glue jar rests nearby along with the receipt. I hold my left arm above the glass. My veins look so small, blue lines that quickly disappear below the surface. I raise the metal plane, jab down, test the angle. Even that small cut stings. I raise my right hand higher, and bring the blade down again, a straight line up my arm, starting at my wrist. I can't help myself; I close my eyes long before the blade finishes its cutting.

I'm tired.

The slash along my arm has been dripping for almost an hour. The box is completely lined. All that's left is to climb inside and press the receipt against the lid. My legs feel somehow disconnected from the rest of my body. I slump rather than step inside the narrow enclosure, banging my bleeding arm against the box as I sit down. Despite all the glue I've brushed onto the paper, I can see that a few of the corners are already curling up. I run my trembling left arm along the edges, smoothing the paper with my blood, making sure the seams stay in place, then I curl my body into the shape of a question mark. The tears have stopped; all that is left is a strange, buzzing nausea. I glance around the workshop. Finally, I reach up and pull the lid down, sealing that final square of paper just above my head.

It's dim inside Barry's box but not entirely black; light creeps in from the edges between the boards. Even with the light, it's hard to separate my limbs from the paper they press against. It's almost as though I am dissolving into the paper itself.

Doesn't matter.

The buzzing feels louder now, the paper like half-tattered wings. All I have to do is wait. Wait for Barry to finally return, wait for that lid to finally rise and for my reborn self to crawl, all petal-softened chitin and twitching antennae, to the window ledge and fly. If I know nothing else, I know that before the magic ends, Barry's Gray Witch eyes will be the ones that finally cry.

The Re'em Song

Save me from the lion's mouth; for thou hast heard me from the horns of the re'em.

Psalms 22:21

O F COURSE, LEAVING WAS EASY.
"The same damned people, the same damn trees, even the same damn work, all our God-fearing lives. Do you really think we would have married if there'd been even a handful to choose from?"

Jawbones and sections of vertebrae hung from the rafters of their house. Ribs and phalanges contained in carefully sewn skins were piled outside, waiting to be shipped off. And always there were the horns calling from somewhere deep in the woods.

Harvesting unicorn bones wasn't easy work. With death, re'em bones condensed God's blessing inside their hollows, little bone-trapped bolts of His holy spirit just waiting for an opportunity to jab through a digger's flesh and find the living bone underneath. The entire Kerill Valley was charged with ghosts.

Sunnifa stood in the kitchen while her husband, Orri, remained by the hearth in the second room of their small home. "Vulture." Sunnifa glared at her Orri's back. "Orri the bone picker," Sunnifa tried again. Orri didn't respond. He almost seemed not to hear her. Sunnifa reached up and grabbed the jar of honey from a nearby shelf, rubbing some across both hands. The honey helped hold off the scar-bent fingers, at least for a time.

Centuries ago Sunnifa's ancestors had crossed the Athlant Ocean in their longboats, carrying their Bibles and their shiny new faith, determined to track down Daniel's iron-toothed monster and the rest of God's magical beasts. Fools, every single one of them.

Sunnifa reached for a second bottle then grimaced. They were out of lavender oil. Again. "Who'd you lend the oil to this time?"

"One of Dora's crew hit an old cache while he was still ungloved."

"Who the hell trenches ungloved?" Sunnifa pressed her thumb deep into her left palm, trying to ease the aching burn. "How bad was it?"

"Cut marks reached as far as his chest." Orri finally turned and looked at Sunnifa. The dark skin of his arms and face was splattered with mud from the day's excavations. "It was one of those Sturluson kids. Dora only took him on because of what happened last winter."

"Orri." The word was almost a sigh.

"I'll track some oil down tomorrow, all right?"

Sunnifa felt her anger spiking. "God's earthly paradise, my scarred ass."

Orri took two steps toward Sunnifa and the kitchen then stopped. He looked sad—and angry. "What do you want me to say? I like it here? I don't want to leave?"

"I don't care what you say." The words were out almost before she realized she'd thought them.

"I know." And then Orri was walking to the hearth, pulling on his now-warmed boots. A few steps later and he stood next to the door.

It wasn't just Sunnifa. Orri was leaving as well. Leaving Sunnifa anyway, if not the Kerill Valley.

The people might call it God's magic, but re'em skeletons were also central to the nation of Norumbega's economy. New farmland, stone bridges, and walls did best with a few skeletal remains buried beneath them. Man-formed items, like bricks and clay pots, preferred actual blood.

More than fifty years ago, the knifemen of the northern Kerill Valley had culled the wild re'em herds into oblivion. Farmers further south now provided the necessary bone-and-blood wares. Didn't matter. Valley children still learned "The Knifeman's Song," along with their first nursery rhymes.

The Re'em Song

Nine screaming horns cry out beneath the hunter's moon,
Calling for our devil blood.
Nine to call the live ones home.
We'll drain them dry. Render the flesh.
We'll cover the world in magic.

The city of Burne was a good two-week's journey. Sunnifa paid the wagon driver an entire basketful of ribs. No horns, though. Sunnifa didn't want her sprint to freedom accompanied by the wail of a Valley ghost, following its disinterred horn south.

"Don't find too many of your kind heading south," the driver said, nodding toward the bone burns that ran along Sunnifa's hands and arms. Similar scars on Sunnifa's neck were hidden by her high-collared shirt, the result of a childhood dare gone wrong and a tumble into an open grave.

"Aren't that many of us left," Sunnifa said noncommittally as she clambered up onto the running board. More than the man, it was the two horses that held her interest. The valley's remaining re'em—the dead ones—didn't take to their unhorned brethren. Horses weren't allowed in Kerill. Instead, valley families carried their goods in shoulder baskets over the South Lancing Trail and into the nearby town of Gherl.

Sunnifa paid the driver enough bone money to take her all the way to Burne. Beyond that, she had no idea. A city near the sea sounded like the opposite of everything she had left behind. It sounded like Heaven.

Tapestries hung on either side of the city's open gates. Embroidered unicorns, ghost-white, sat inside carefully sewn corals. Their heads rested on the laps of golden-haired girls wearing long blue-green dresses.

"You ain't that different, eh?" the wagon driver called back, nodding toward the embroidery. It was the first thing he'd said to Sunnifa in hours. Almost two weeks travel hadn't made them friends.

Sunnifa knew the wagon driver wasn't comparing her to the girls. Sunnifa's hair was imaginary-unicorn white, not blonde. Her pale skin was sliced by bone-burns. Even if that hadn't been true, her winter-sky eyes were nothing like those of the untroubled, tapestry virgins.

"Your people live in the Warrens, up toward the knackeryards," the driver said, tossing Sunnifa's carpetbag to the ground. He'd stopped his horses at the edge of a large square not far from the city gates.

"Knackeryards?"

"The slaughterhouses where they slice up all that magic flesh."

"Ah."

The noise of the market was like nothing Sunnifa had ever heard before. There were more people in this one square than in the entire Kerill Valley. Stalls were piled high with carrots and turnips, grown in bone-laced soil, of course. Hooks hung with legs of mutton and half-carcasses of pig. Really, the square wasn't that different from smaller town markets. If you didn't look too closely. Brickmakers' apprentices stood next to stacks of red-tinged bricks while potters' boys hovered nearby, ready to sell their own reddish-clay jugs and bowls. Fresh unicorn blood. Burne's crowded market was soaked in it.

"You need to head back to the Warrens," the driver repeated, more slowly, as though unsure Sunnifa had understood him the first time. He had brown hair and brown eyes, no smile. He nodded toward a cobbled street that led off the square, one of the few not made of those reddish bricks. "Oreste Street."

Sunnifa could see fresh bones hanging from the street's archway. Some of the bones still had dried bits of cartilage clinging to them.

"Right," Sunnifa said. "The Warrens."

"Welcome to Burne," the driver said, already turning back to his horses.

Sunnifa held tight to her bag as the shoppers and the stall workers swirled around her. Honey-blond hair. Brown hair. Reddish-ginger hair. Freckles. She'd seen freckles before, but never in such profusion. Hair kinked like Orri's but longer, braided down the back. People tall and short and everything in between. Broad-chested men with oversized bellies. Little women with honey-colored skin.

So many of them. And there seemed to be a pattern to their groupings. That she hadn't expected. The petite, honey women wore wrapped head cloths that covered all their hair. They stirred steaming kettles, their faces flushed from the heat as they offered "laced tea" to passersby. Blood-laced tea.

Orri's granny used to talk about the strange infections that could spread across un-blooded land. The dead were always trying to claim back a world over-filled with humanity. God's bones and blood protected both the land and the people of Norumbega. And the city's domesticated re'em were at the center of all that commerce.

Sunnifa took a slow breath and started toward a handful of men standing at the edge of Oreste Street. Her people. Was that who these pale strangers were?

One of the men nodded in Sunnifa's direction. "Little sister," he called out.

"Hello." The knackerman smiled as he bent his head to look Sunnifa in the eyes. He reminded Sunnifa of her father: tall, with the same pale eyes and fish-belly skin Mama used to joke about. But it was the tilt of the man's lips, something about the line of his jaw and those creases along his eyelids that did it. No bone burns of course. That was one difference.

Sunnifa's unicorn-white hair and the smiling man were enough to get her an apprenticeship in one of Burne's slaughterhouses. The man was like Sunnifa's father in that way as well, sharing the family trade.

When Sunnifa and Orri were still too young to work the crews, Orri's granny placated them with stories.

"A wild re'em is a vengeful creature," she would start, settling back into her wooden chair. "That's what the knifemen counted on."

Like most children back then, Orri's granny had been a Beater. During the hunt, her stick smashed through the forest undergrowth, driving the re'em herds toward the nine singing horns.

"Nine threaded trees and nine dead re'em horns," Granny explained, stroking Sunnifa's white-blonde hair. "It's important to get these things right."

A re'em hunt was a valley-wide affair. The Blooded Lure, a knifeman with at least one kill, ran just ahead of the herd, making sure the re'em knew their killers were close at hand.

"I'd hate to be that guy," Orri said, his dark eyes solemn.

"But he was the most important person of all. He kept the re'em focused."

The unicorns all looked the same as they thundered forward: red eyes and dun-colored hair. Their black cloven hooves matched the darkness of their spiraling horns. Their rage—they were the same in that way as well, each one of them just about bursting with it.

Once the herd of wild re'em reached the clearing, the trip lines brought them down and the knifemen descended.

Change takes time. Her husband's name, Orri, was no more than a ghost breath, a whisper Sunnifa chose to ignore.

For six seasons, Sunnifa lived far from the Kerill Valley's white pines and hemlocks, far from the bone-notes that rose from beneath its tamped-down earth. In that sixth season, though, the city's silence finally drove her home. Burne had not a single ghost.

Sunnifa rode a wagon north to Gherl, walking the last few miles along the South Lancing Trail. A chill wind seemed to follow her to the clearing where their little house still stood, the door closed, smoke rising from the chimney.

"Orri?" Sunnifa called.

"What..." Orri opened the door, but got no further.

The broad curve of his lips hadn't changed, though his hair was much shorter than Sunnifa remembered; she could see the contours of his skull beneath the thin layer of fuzz. Dark lashes so unlike Sunnifa's own.

"Hi. Orri...I..."

He stood aside, silently gesturing her into the house.

Their table still rested next to the stove. Jars of honey and lavender oil sat on the kitchen shelf. There were new things as well: open bottles and a collection of yellowed teeth, artifacts of some dig, strewn across the table's surface. Beer and not much else seemed to be on the menu.

"Don't worry," Orri said. He stood a little closer than Sunnifa would have liked. "You can stay."

And that seemed to be it.

When Sunnifa left, Orri had held tight to his silence, hurt, it seemed to her, but nothing more. Now the silence felt more like its own creature, sharp and feral.

Three weeks of close-to-silence.

"Why don't you come out and say hello to Robert and Isibel?" Orri said.

"It's dark in here. Can't you at least keep the fire going?" Orri said.

"Varr is looking for some help down at the mill," Orri said.

While Orri and the crew worked yet another re'em grave, Sunnifa sat in their house and worked on not moving. Eventually some other plan would occur to her.

Each night, Sunnifa slept in their old loft bed, while Orri sat at the kitchen table with his bits of dead re'em. Touching—that tangle of legs and glide of sweat against flesh—wasn't part of this new world. Other night-sounds emerged instead.

A clatter of teeth scattering across a table, a quick scuffing of enamel on wood. Instead of sleep, Orri spent his nights tossing re'em teeth. From the loft, Sunnifa could hear the chink of glass as yet another empty beer bottle was set against the floor.

The memory of their old life was like a ghost, haunting both of them into silence.

Just a finger of moonlight slipped through the living room's eastern window. Sunnifa could hear the clatter of the gate opening, followed by the sound of voices.

"Make sure you check the stitching on that one."

"Haul's about ready to go over the mountain. Can we at least get Sunnifa to help carry the baskets?"

"What the hell does she do all day anyway?" That last voice was Cousin Isibel. Isibel might be only five years older than Sunnifa, but with that spider web of bone-burns across both cheeks and her shock of coarse white hair, it seemed more like decades.

"Gone over a year and now she just sits in that house eating your food," Isibel continued in her low, gravelly tones. "Bet you're not even fucking her."

"Enough!" Orri snapped.

"Isibel, just leave it," someone else said.

After that there were minutes of blessed silence before the yard filled with the sounds of the crew calling their goodbyes.

Now came the moment when Orri would open the door and find her still sitting in the wooden chair.

"I need your help," shadow Orri said from the doorway.

"Help?" Sunnifa pressed her back more firmly into the wooden chair.

"Robert forgot the horns. We just finished the inventory. They aren't here."

"Ah."

"I told him the two of us would take care of it." Orri started across the room toward Sunnifa.

"Why? Tell him you changed your mind."

"Too late. He's already left." Orri's voice seemed calm, but then there was that set of his eyes, his lips—something.

"Can't we just go to bed and deal with it tomorrow?" Sunnifa said, wishing almost immediately she'd left the words unspoken. The smile on Orri's face wasn't pretty.

"I didn't think we did that anymore."

The world outside is a strange and unbalanced place; that's what Sunnifa should have told Orri when she walked back over the mountain, bone-weary from the hike home. Instead, she and Orri barely spoke. Sure she'd flown away, but she'd also returned to Orri and the valley and all those burial mounds. Returned to their valley of ghosts. Somehow, that felt like it should count for something.

"I'm not going," Sunnifa said while Orri slipped on the pack he'd set near the door.

"I mean it, Orri," she said as he filled one of the smaller lanterns with kerosene.

"No choice. Hunter's moon tonight." Orri stood over Sunnifa, hands at her elbows, pulling her up and out of the chair. "The crew and I have been working the area near the Eslot River."

"An old horn site? Goddamn it, Orri." Older remains were the worst, overflowing with holy magic. They also paid the most cash.

"I needed the money." Orri turned and opened the blanket chest next to Granny's chair, pulling the top blanket aside. A leather sheath, hand-sewn with rough stitches. A handle worn smooth with use. A knifeman's blade. Orri's great grandfather had used that knife during the last of the re'em hunts—Orri was bringing it with him.

"Orri."

"Horns and moonlight, dearest. We might actually get lucky. You'll have to carry this," he added, handing Sunnifa the knife. "Not exactly my skill."

Sunnifa wasn't sure how it happened, but she somehow found herself following Orri through the front door and out into the night, the weight of the knifeman's blade hanging from her waist.

Buried, the forest's horns sounded like a muted prayer. Tonight though, the horns left out by Orri's crew laid bare the lie. Loud, frenzied cries filled the wood.

"Exactly how many horns are we talking about?" Sunnifa asked as she ducked under yet another tree branch.

"Nine."

"Nine—"

"Nine screaming horns cry out beneath the hunter's moon," Orri recited. He tilted his head up to toward the sky and laughed. "Don't worry, Sunnifa. You know there's not many wild re'em left, none in this valley. We'll probably just prick ourselves with the sewing needles."

Sunnifa trusted Orri. At least she'd trusted him enough to come back home after more than a year in the city. Maybe Orri hadn't meant to mix the horns with moonlight. The last few weeks had been—difficult.

Still, she didn't quite dare reach for Orri's hand. "I'm cold," she said instead.

Orri paused, pulled a woolen scarf from one of his pockets, and reached for Sunnifa.

She couldn't help herself. She flinched.

"Since when don't you like to be touched?" Orri muttered, tightening the edges of the scarf so that no gaps remained. "Sunnifa." He paused. "I want you to stay."

Orri's dark skin and hair stood out against an even darker sky. His face, though, was still hidden in shadow. Didn't matter. Sunnifa knew exactly what he looked like. She used to get high on the smell of him. The tang of salt she'd find along his collarbone. The bitter green that filled the space between his thumb and palm.

Sometimes she'd drag him atop one of those rough-grassed mounds with its hidden bones.

"I like the feel of all those eyes watching," she'd whisper as he slipped his hands beneath the band of her skirt, fingers searching lower. Of course, she was already wet.

The clothes didn't last long. Neither did the standing, at least on Sunnifa's part. Her lips ran along the inner muscles of his thighs, biting just enough to make him flinch. Her tongue moved as well, waiting for that long inhalation before she lowered herself into the dark hairs between his legs. Untainted and earthy, that was another scent she remembered. The taste that followed was just the same.

"The city was warmer," Sunnifa said, feeling the rough wool against her neck, the heat of Orri's body. "Something about those ocean currents." She paused. "It's dark, Orri."

"Don't really need much light to see what I've got to show you."

Did he really want to screw while those nine horns listened in?

Orri sighed. "I brought the lamp, Sunnifa. It was a joke."

"Orri?"

"Um."

"Light the damn lantern."

"Fine. Right." He pulled the pack off, unearthed the lantern, carefully lit the wick.

"We had to hack through one of the old overgrown trails to find this site. Robert's idea," Orri said as he started forward, holding the lantern in one hand.

"Robert is full of stupid ideas. You know that."

"He's not the only one."

Orri took the lead. Somewhere close by, Sunnifa heard a splash as a rock or stick fell into a puddle. Then another cascade of dirt and rocks as she and Orri stumbled down a slight incline. It almost felt like something was following them.

Up ahead, Sunnifa could see Orri's hand gripping the lantern. Those hands used to raise Sunnifa up and onto him, hold her still, his eyes daring her to move first.

The dig site. Star chips clung overhead along with that orange-yellow hunter's moon, while the shadows of wild grasses wavered atop the old burial mound. None of it unexpected. Still, the re'em bones lying open to the air made Sunnifa shiver. She hadn't seen earth-cleansed skeletons in over a year.

The lantern sat on a flat stretch of ground next to the discarded backpack. Orri's hands held a coil of rope. He'd brought trip lines. Of course he had. The sound that had followed them all the way to the site was like hooves, not branches.

"It was strange without you here. Bad strange," Orri said. He dragged one end of the rope to a nearby hemlock and tied it a foot above the ground. After securing the line, he moved on, passing a number of young evergreens before finally knotting the rope to an older white pine.

Sunnifa heard a branch crack somewhere off to their left. "You really think trip lines and bone magic are going to solve all this?" Sunnifa gestured between the two of them.

"Something has to."

Sunnifa watched silently as Orri picked his way between seven more trees. In the end, the clearing was bisected by a nine-sided figure made entirely of rope, a knifeman's line. Sunnifa's line. She was the one carrying the blade.

"Orri, there aren't any wild re'em left in the valley."

"Maybe. How did you manage anyway? In the city?" Orri asked just as though he hadn't been carrying that question for the last three weeks. "You didn't leave with much."

"A friend found me a job."

"Friend?"

The nine unearthed horns kicked up then; their frenzied screams charging even higher.

"A lost little sister," the knackermen called Sunnifa when she first appeared in their midst.

Her re'em-burned arms made her an oddity. Re'em teeth are like a wolf's, meant for tearing. Burne's knackermen had different marks. Sunnifa's knackerman, Jakob, had a line of angry flesh, pointed scars that ran from his neck down below the cut of his shirt.

The re'ems bled red. That's what Sunnifa didn't tell Orri. That first re'em's blood sprayed out from his throat and against his brown hair while strangers stood and watched.

Even with the ropes, the re'em pulled back as she pressed the knife down. His eyes rolled upward and his lips stretched black against his teeth.

"Watch where you're cutting," the foreman called out. "Trust the ropes." He stood just a few feet away on the other side of the stall. Jakob stood next to him. One of Jakob's boots pressed against the side of the pen, while his belly strained against his canvas apron.

Jakob had taught Sunnifa well. After the herd was led up Oreste Street and into the pens, Sunnifa tied the re'em's halter rope to the metal pins. She ignored the looks of the meat tenders who waited nearby. She knew what she was getting into. Flesh couldn't be any worse than a seemingly endless dirge of ghosts.

Before coming to the city, Sunnifa had collected ghost bones and wrapped them tight. She'd laid the skeletons out as though the flesh still held the frame together, then sewn the packages with dried gut.

Blood terror, though, had never entered into it. Sunnifa, it turned out, hadn't understood at all.

After she finished with the knife, she stepped back from the animal's fallen body and with shaking hands held the collecting bowl beneath the gaping wound. The blood of the re'em pooled dark red against the wood while a couple of apprentices, younger than her, shifted the corpse, making sure the animal didn't bleed onto the slaughteryard's cobblestones. Animals, they called the re'em. Nothing but bits of slaughtered flesh to soak the floorboards of newly built homes.

It took Sunnifa six seasons to figure it out. Six seasons before she started her journey home. Family requires sacrifice. Family requires ghosts.

Sunnifa felt Orri's hand twining with hers as they faced the forest. The dig site's nine horns no longer screamed. Instead, they made a soft moaning sound, each one adjusting its pitch to fit with the others.

"Malcolm's got a line on a collector down the coast who likes the older stuff," Orri said. He glanced at Sunnifa. "Just north of where you were. Perhaps you can help negotiate the price."

"I didn't really make it much past the city."

"Mm." Orri sounded distracted. "You really should unsheathe the knife."

Sunnifa could feel his body tense as he tracked the sound of the cracking branches moving closer.

The nine horns' song shifted again, close to melancholy.

In the city, the knackers punched holes through the fresh horns: one or two ragged holes for the whistles, more precise cuts for the reed-and-pipe musicians. On Sundays, when she wasn't at work, Sunnifa would listen to a man at the edge of Caprin Square play two aulos flutes. Both of his hands moved along the dark horns as he adjusted his fingering. Those flutes always put her in mind of the newly dead re'em she'd left back in the knackeryard.

"Why can't you valley folk leave the old things buried?" Jakob had asked, as though unearthed bones weren't spread across his precious city, holding up the city's outer walls.

"It's the work," she replied, not revealing a newly discovered thought: ripened in her forest at least the bones learned to sing their own melodies.

The hunter's moon shone down into the clearing as Orri's hand gripped Sunnifa's. There was a gust of wind, and then the song of the nine horns was echoed by something nearby, just on the other side of the tree line.

Leaves rustled and a few branches snapped against each other. Sunnifa could see Orri's face clearly in the lamplight. He was watching her. "Sunnifa, it's time."

There were many things Sunnifa didn't tell Orri about the city. The early morning echo of hooves on cobblestones. The cries of her knackerman as they made love on his thin, straw-filled mattress. The look in the visitors' eyes as they watched the slaughter.

One more fact she didn't share: the men who looked like Orri were tired, their faces like masks as they pushed those handcarts about town.

Without ghosts, the city was a lonely place.

Sunnifa heard the creaking of tree limbs as something large pushed its way through the branches and on toward the dig site. Then a snorting breath.

"Orri, did you hear that?"

"Yes."

"I'm not cutting anything, Orri Flom." Even to herself, her voice sounded weak. "I'm serious," Sunnifa continued when Orri didn't respond.

She bent down, placing the old knifeman's blade next to the interwoven trip lines, then took a deep breath. "Do you hear me?" she yelled out toward the trees. "It's enough already." Her voice barely quavered. Her hands didn't shake at all. She'd returned from the city. There was no way she was going to recreate it here in these woods.

"Sunnifa—"

"No," Sunnifa repeated, not giving Orri a chance to finish. "Just no."

From beyond the old white pine and its line of rope, a horn appeared, spiraling and black. The creature that followed was covered in brown hair. His red-rimmed eyes glanced from Sunnifa to the knife now lying on the ground, and then he snorted, a sharp blast of air, and started to pick his way over the first of Orri's newly strung lines.

Sunnifa could feel Orri's hand tightening as the re'em bent his horn to a pile of unearthed skins. The re'em tossed his head up, pawed at the hides with his front hooves. The edges of his teeth were now less than two feet away.

Sunnifa smelled the re'em's fetid breath, felt a spray of saliva as the re'em's hooves crashed down against Orri's trip lines. And then a scream rose from the re'em's throat, and still he didn't touch her. And she did not move. Did not move, and did not let go of Orri at her side.

"We could..." Orri started to say. The lantern lay on its side, the burning wick knocked out sometime during the re'em's frenzy. The re'em's attention had moved to the wood-handled knife resting less than a foot in front of them.

"Shh, Orri. I trust you." And then there was a sharp inhalation, her only sign of fear, as the re'em rose up on its hind legs. She should push Orri aside, behind her, do something. But the re'em's legs were already crashing down before the thought was even complete. Once. Twice. *Crack.* Hoof against metal and wood. And still the re'em didn't touch them. Instead, the shattered knife lay in pieces, now nothing more than a ghost knife.

And the nine horns, they had stopped their singing.

"Please," Sunnifa whispered. "I am so, so sorry." Broken. Afraid. Unable to say any of it.

"Sunnifa," Orri said, thinking other unknowable words. Whatever this was, it wasn't as simple as gentle forgiveness.

The re'em showed his teeth one last time before he backed away from the clearing.

And then Orri and Sunnifa were alone, hands still intertwined as they listened to the moan of the wind moving through the trees.

Burne, Orri used to say, was nothing like their valley.

In the Kerill Valley the trees spread wider than any town, and the mountains rise high enough to obscure everything to the south. The people have no need of jellied blood and freshly redded bricks. They no longer need to bury anything beneath the ground. In the Kerill Valley they welcome the ghosts as family.

SIGNAL AND STONE

MAINLAND GIRL

As SOON AS HAZEL STEPPED off the ferry and onto Vinalhaven Island, she felt it. The carved stone eagle, the curb, the granite planter set in front of the fire station: the ghosts of Carver's Harbor were embedded in the building materials of the little town. The other passengers who'd disembarked—even Hazel's mom—didn't seem to notice a thing. In that way the island ghosts were no different from the ones at home. Most people missed their presence entirely.

It was June, not even close to the height of tourist season, but the harbor town's streets were bustling. An old man walked along the sidewalk dressed in a three-piece suit, his expression hidden by both his walrus mustache and the brim of his Trilby hat. A little farther down, a woman with weathered skin and upswept hair stood outside the Davidson Realty storefront. Despite the month, she wore a black skirt that hung just inches from the ground. Meanwhile, two boys in knee-high boots and woolen trousers raced the length of Main Street.

It wasn't just the ghost fragments in the carvings and walls. Ghosts moved about this town, uncontained and seemingly uninterested in the tourists that stepped off the ferryboat.

"Let's go." Hazel grabbed the handle of the wheeled suitcase. "Did I tell you our apartment is the second floor of an old stonecutter's house?"

"Yes. More than once."

The walk to their summer rental took Hazel and her mom all of ten minutes. Hazel trailed behind, while her mom consulted the paper printout of the island map.

"Perfect," Hazel's mom said, stopping in front of a sagging porch with the number forty-seven faded and barely visible above the doorframe. She pushed her long graying hair out of her eyes and tried to smile at Hazel.

"I don't like it," Hazel said, looking over the peeling paint and weathered clapboards.

"You'll see."

"I don't like you," Hazel clarified.

"Ah."

Inside the house, ghost energy emanated from a deep gouge in the staircase banister that led to the second floor and from a dent, not entirely smoothed over, in the center of one of their apartment's kitchen walls. Underneath all that wood and plaster, Hazel could feel the echo of something hard and ugly, the trauma of real living flesh.

Forget graveyards and mausoleums. On the mainland, the only ghosts Hazel knew of lived in cell phones and transmission towers. iPhones and Androids, burners and old-fashioned flip phones: ghost words erupted across them all.

Back home in Bedford, Hazel's Ghost Boy hadn't shown up on her doorstep or tried to hold her hand. Instead, Ghost Boy had reached through her cell phone and its network of electromagnetic waves and stolen things Hazel didn't even realize could be taken.

A break, Mom had said when explaining this summer trip to the island. How could she imagine the solution was so simple? Just because Hazel's cell phone couldn't pick up a signal didn't mean that bastard, Ghost Boy, wasn't pinging, waiting for her reply.

Before Ghost Boy

BGB, Hazel dubbed the time before Ghost Boy. Back in BGB Hazel had lived with her mom and dad in a two-story house in the suburbs northwest of Boston. Her room was a bright turquoise blue with animal sketches on the walls: sailor mice, mountaineer mice, all sorts of happy, pen-and-ink rodents. Instagram and Kik Messenger were full of friends. Back in BGB, Hazel didn't even have a lock screen on her phone.

Perhaps that was how Ghost Boy found his way through.

Good morning, beautiful, Ghost Boy had said. *You've got the sweetest smile. Send me a pic? I've been thinking about that smile all day.* And then his attachment arrived, a smiling boy so completely trusting in her not to let him down.

Ghost Boy claimed his name was Pierceson. Pierceson sent picture after picture: *Here's a flowering dogwood tree, here's a crescent moon, here I am standing beneath the stars. What do you look like, Hazel?*

Parents only talked about stupid stuff when they gave you your phone, like data limits and Facebook and not staying up too late. Hazel had to figure out the truth on her own: the cell network was actually a super highway overflowing with ghosts, secret fragments people had birthed and released into the world's electromagnetic web. It wasn't just trolls and spambots and virtual sockpuppets you had to worry about. As long as the bars lit up the left corner of your phone's screen, the ghosts were watching.

Back before Ghost Boy Hazel had been like any other stupid kid. Of course Hazel had sent Ghost Boy her picture. Sent more than one.

Nice. Wow, he'd texted, *u are so beautiful.* And eventually, after that second topless pic, *we should meet.* Meet and do what, Hazel had started to type before losing her nerve. She definitely wasn't ready for that. Just like she wasn't ready to *send more,* though that didn't stop him from asking. Until, one day, Hazel's pictures started returning home: labeled, curated, re-formed exactly as Ghost Boy saw fit.

HazelWhore, he called her. HazelWhore, do you really want everyone to know?

That's not my name, Hazel typed. But then the next image appeared, followed by the one after that.

HazelWhore loved to smile at the camera with her scratched out eyes and colored in teeth. HazelWhore kept flashing her tits in some stupid-ass animated gif. Up, down, up, down went her red, belly shirt. HazelWhore shared all her most private conversations in speech bubbles: "Sometimes I feel so lonely," "Why doesn't anyone like me?" and worst of all, "I miss my dad so, so much." HazelWhore just didn't know when to shut the hell up "I <3 u. Go ahead and touch them," she said as she lifted up her shirt.

Pierceson, it turned out, had lied. Pierceson wasn't a person at all. The high-speed ghost network of cell towers and transmitters covered almost every speck of land. Of course, Ghost Boy had found his way into Hazel's house and pushed his words through Hazel's phone. That's what ghost boys liked to do.

A Sunday afternoon. Hazel stood with her dad in yet another strip mall parking lot waiting for the weekly parental hand-off, or as she privately termed it, the divorced-parent shuffle. Hazel cataloged the storefronts: CVS Pharmacy, Big Lots, Pizza Restaurant. Pizza Restaurant wasn't even a real name. Slackers. Mom was late, no surprise, and once again Dad was busy boosting the signal, hunched over his phone while Hazel leaned against his shitty car.

"Karen? Where the hell are you? You know I hate it when—no. Damn it. Just get here, okay? Hazel needs you."

As though Dad had any idea what Hazel needed.

Two guys—tall, basketball shorts, black Nike hi-tops—two guys Hazel wished she didn't recognize, exited the CVS and headed straight toward Hazel and her dad. Somehow, out of all the spaces in the parking lot, her dad had managed to park right next to some of her high school's worst assholes.

Hazel watched as the dark-haired one, Tom Gladstone, Tom with the blonde girlfriend and the eyes that always slid off Hazel like she was so much unnecessary, glanced down at his phone and started to laugh.

And then there was nowhere to hide.

"HazelWhore," Tom Gladstone coughed into his hand as he slid past Hazel and into the driver-side door of his Subaru Impreza. "I <3 you, HazelWhore."

How could Dad not have heard that? HazelWhore thought, clutching her phone, palms slick with sweat as it buzzed and buzzed, demanding that she glance down and look.

TOURIST GIRL

Island life had its benefits. For ten cell-phone-free days there wasn't a single Ghost Boy ping. Instead, Hazel walked the rock-lined shore and hiked her way up to the tallest peak on the island—all fifty-nine feet of it. She sat on a sun-warmed length of granite and watched living people plunge off the rocks into the waters of Booth's Quarry, one of the island's two swimming holes.

Stretched out on the warm rock, Hazel could feel the island's stone ghosts somewhere below the surface of the spring-fed pool. While the sun softened her lips and the palms of her hands, while the sun nestled against the hollow of her neck and collarbone and a trio of kids shrieked with each quarry dive, Hazel felt a man's name trying to emerge from beneath the water. A name no one had spoken for almost one hundred years. *Marcus. Edith's Marcus is here.*

Turned out the island's ghosts weren't just wandering the streets. They weren't just embedded above the surface in building plaster and carved island stone. Some of the island's ghosts were buried beneath rock and water: safely hidden. Maybe one day AT&T, Sprint, & T-Mobile would manage to ruin this place, "cell tower" this tiny dot of land and drag Vinalhaven's ghosts into the electromagnetic network, but for now this island ran by its own rules.

From beneath the covers in her second-floor bedroom, Hazel watched the ghost. An old woman with whiskers on her chin paced the room, muttering as she went. *Marcus, please. I didn't understand. Please, I need you.* Next to the room's single window, a mass of wrinkled and red-fleshed babies floated in a puddle of dust. None of these ghosts seemed the least interested in Hazel.

Hazel glanced at the bedside clock: only 7:00 a.m. Outside her window she could see a patch of blue sky and beyond that the harbor. She threw off the covers, grabbed her hoodie, and then it was house key, cash, and out the door. Mom didn't even stir from the pile of blankets on the couch. She'd fallen asleep watching TV—again.

Vinalhaven's Main Street was quiet. The harbor's lobster boats had already left for the day and the ferry's slip sat empty, exactly the same as every other day since Hazel had arrived. Only the eight-foot-tall stone eagle set at the edge of the harbor's parking lot seemed somehow different.

Hazel paused and held her phone up toward the statue's stone eyes and unmoving beak. "Ghost Boy's signal broken. Not even one bar," Hazel called, determined to share her joy with someone, even if that someone was an unknown island ghost. Then she was running down Main Street, past the pier and the pickup trucks and up onto the narrow length of rocky shoreline just beyond. Scrambling across the rocks, Hazel headed up toward the tree line and her favorite spot, an empty length of rock where she could stretch out and listen to the background hum of both island and ocean.

So what if she was fourteen years old and had traded pictures with an asshole ghost? So what if it took a bay full of salt water to keep him away. After almost two weeks of listening to the muttering of Edith and the other island ghosts, after almost two weeks of cell phone silence, Hazel could finally feel it, the island's rock-and-water plan. Step one, the island repeated through the rock and the glimmerings of late June sun: uncover the old stonecutter's tools.

Like so many seemingly daunting tasks, completing step one was easy once Hazel figured out the trick of it: unlock the apartment house's moldering basement door and follow the spiderwebs down.

STEP ONE: FIND

It was cold and damp in the basement. Shadows loomed from the corners. Bits of cobweb clung to Hazel's face and neck. Worst of all, the bedroom ghosts had followed her down and now they wouldn't shut up.

Marcus, the old lady kept repeating. *Marcus, there was no other way. I promise it'll be different this time.*

Whomever this Marcus was, the old lady was definitely obsessed. Probably a ghost thing.

Near the bottom of the stairs, Hazel touched a stack of cardboard boxes, poorly sealed, trying to sense the quality of their contents. The boxes felt entirely wrong. Farther along, at the base of the water heater, she ran her hands along three dented metal tins. Not even close. Another pile of boxes, a plastic shelf, and one wicker basket later and Hazel still hadn't felt the necessary connection.

"Not giving up," she muttered, as something as cold and soft as a dead baby's kiss pressed against her cheek. "I promise." Not saying those other words out loud, about the ever-present network, about loneliness and Ghost Boy waiting on the other side of Penobscot Bay. It would be so easy to go back to how things had been before. "I don't want to be afraid anymore," Hazel whispered to the basement ghosts. "Especially not of myself."

For the first time, the old woman paused and looked directly at Hazel. *Edith, they called me. I hid my tools down here. I didn't throw them out. I didn't forget my other name.* A flicker of half-light and the moment was over, Edith had returned to her pacing. *Marcus. Marcus, it's time to come out.*

Then Hazel felt it: the tug of something hard and tight coming from the far wall where a shadow, rounded but uneven, rested on the floor. Hazel blew back a strand of hair, crossed the dimly lit room, and reached out.

Cold, rough canvas. But so much more. Through the bag, Hazel could feel metal shapes—pointed, narrow, sharp—along with the smoother lengths of wooden handles. She could feel other things as well. Harder things. In addition to the tools, the mildewed bag contained an amalgam of secret rage and bitter-but-necessary desertion.

The island, Dad said that final night, would be good for both her and Mom. The island, Dad said, sounded just about perfect. And then he'd kissed Hazel on the forehead, already checking his phone, making sure all those ghosts knew where his interest really lay.

Hazel was sick of moms and dads, sick of ghost boys who tempted you into forgetting how the story was always going to end. Haunt your own damn lives and leave me the hell alone.

STEP TWO: TRY

Perhaps it was the house ghosts, perhaps the island rock, or perhaps it was some hidden thing inside Hazel nudging her forward. Whatever the reason, the first thing Hazel did after stowing the canvas bag under her bed was turn on her cell phone.

Wi-Fi. How could she have missed that possibility? How could Mom? Or maybe that was why Mom stayed up on the couch late at night. Perhaps, instead of TV, she was sneaking time on the network. Mom had always been the kind of woman to sneak that cigarette or candy bar, flirt with that guy from the office, or gym, or grocery store. Mom, no matter the situation, had never been very good at resisting. Maybe that was how she and Dad had ended up together in the first place—tumbling forward without any real plan.

Like mother like daughter, or so went the cliché. In this case it seemed to be true. Edith's old stone tools and a Wi-Fi link to the mainland's ghost network weren't exactly the best-laid plan, but to Hazel it felt like enough. And, as all those grownup types kept saying, feelings were the important thing. Though none of them ever seemed to notice how Hazel and the other mainland kids were faring inside their networked world.

Well, fuck 'em. Here on Vinalhaven Island, Hazel had a way to fix everything—and the ghosts to show her how.

Hazel tapped the green Kik Messenger icon on her phone and watched as the first text messages appeared.

Tue, June 2, 7:56 a.m.: *How's my sweet niece?*

Sun, June 17, 3:14 p.m.: *Meetup at the mall tonight?*

Wed, July 4, 6:17 p.m.: *What's island life like, honey?*

Aunt Alice, Bethany, even Dad. A screen's worth of messages. None of them Pierceson's. No picture. No request for *more.*

Something tight and dry settled in Hazel's throat, moved to the back of her mouth. Hazel's carefully uncharged phone. Her private, fucked-up tears. This entire trip. All unnecessary. In the end Pierceson had moved on as soon as her signal disappeared.

Or not.

Hazel looked down as her phone vibrated one final time, watched as a blue dot surfaced on the screen: *Hazel? HazelWhore is that you? Are you actually there?*

Yes, Pierceson, HazelWhore texted. *Still here.*

The bedroom seemed no different: polyester floral bedspread, mismatched bedframe and armoire, a single bedside lamp. But the scent of mildew and rot hung in the air, the bag of Vinalhaven tools rested at the foot of Hazel's bed and the old lady, Edith, paced back and forth. *Yes, Ghost Boy, still here,* Hazel typed, and then carefully powered down her phone.

Test complete.

The difference between mainland girls and island girls was such a simple thing: on Vinalhaven Island, for the first time, HazelWhore wasn't entirely alone.

STEP THREE: LISTEN

Ghost stories. Each night, in Hazel's bedroom, her ghost companions shared their secrets. Edith hadn't always been an elderly lady with whiskers. At one time she'd been Edith Carver, sixteen years old. Edith had made sure to tie her hair with curling cloths each night. She'd spent hours sewing and re-sewing her sampler—just as she was supposed to. But what Edith Carver had truly loved was stonecutting tools and island granite.

In her father's stonecutting shed, a thick canvas apron covered Edith's dress, and her arms were in constant motion. As she roughed out a block of granite with her stone hammer and point chisel, the shape seemed to form on its own, without any plan on Edith's part. Unlike most people, the stone knew exactly what it wanted.

Edith did too. And for a long, childish while that was perfectly fine: one Edith sculpture after another appeared on the stonecutting floor.

Her father's first warning came when Edith was ten years old. "Stonecutting isn't really for young ladies, Edith. Nor for girls."

"That's all right, Poppa. My real name is Marcus," Edith replied, glancing up from the half-formed eagle. Poppa loved her carvings. That's what he'd always said.

"Marcus. All right then. No need to tell your mother." Poppa stared at Edith for a long moment before returning to his own tools and block of stone. And then Edith-Marcus was busy with her eagle's first wing. All other thoughts forgotten.

Her father's second warning came when Edith-Marcus was twelve years old and slipping into her stonecutter's apron. "Make sure you do your other chores first," Father said. "Your mother needs help around the house."

"Yes, Poppa. Of course." Though Mother's chores seemed to stretch endlessly out to the horizon, while the stone waited impatiently for her hammer and steady hands.

For another four years Edith-Marcus's chisel found angels, wolves, and lonely women buried within the stone, though mostly what she uncovered were eagles. Eagles flew up and away. Eagles didn't hesitate. Eagles did what was necessary to survive.

Her father's final warning shouldn't have come as such a surprise. "Sixteen is practically a woman, Edith. Time to put away childish things. God made you as you were meant to be. Your mother and I baptized you in His church."

"My name is Marcus," Edith-Marcus replied. Her hands clenched the rock hammer and chisel, her eyes intent on the letters she was carving into the eagle's base. M. A. R. C. U. S.

"No, Edith. It's not. As you and God well know."

"Well, it's not Edith either."

"Don't test me." The fierce look on Poppa's face made him look like a stranger.

Perhaps that was why Edith-Marcus's hand slipped with its next blow. Instead of carving the final S, the sharpened end of the flat chisel bit along the back of her left thigh.

The blood and bandages didn't matter. More shattering was the promise her father extracted while Dr. Jackson stitched her thigh and Mother looked on. There would be no more cutting shed, no more point chisel, no more hammer and island stone.

Chores: besides the sewing and the cooking, and as Poppa put it, "a girl's good learning," there was a never-ending layer of stone dust to wipe from their home's floors and walls. It settled over everything: on the picture glass, the mirror frames, on the silks that Mother loved to sew.

More and more, Marcus felt like something lodged deep in Edith's throat, something heavy and choking that made Edith cry. Only one happy Marcus-thing remained. Like her stone eagles, Edith-Marcus loved the scream of the wind when an ocean storm came in. The promise of flying beyond.

Another cloud-laden April day. Another wearisome morning as Edith-Marcus worked through her morning chores. Mother sat in the parlor.

Poppa worked in the stonecutting shed. Through the kitchen window, Edith-Marcus could see the limbs of two maple trees twisting with the force of the incoming storm. That's when the Godly thought came to her: flight.

Down went the dusting cloth. On went the coat. And then Edith-Marcus was rushing out the back door, following a narrow trail through a stand of wind-whipped trees and a sandy marsh, mud-spattered and damp, until finally she found her way up against the raging ocean. The solution was so simple; Marcus needed to do what he'd always wanted. Marcus needed to fly.

As the wind howled and the waves crashed, Edith screamed her secret, her true name. The name her father had told her no one else could ever know. *Marcus! Marcus! Dear Lord, anywhere else but here. Amen.*

Edith-Marcus took a breath, waited for God's storm to do its job. She could feel the wind pressing into her mouth, her throat, further still, holding Edith down even as it lifted Marcus away. A gasping breath. A choking second attempt at air. Worse than a slap, worse than a chisel strike along her thigh, Edith could feel the battered edges where Marcus used to rest. But finally, despite the pain, she felt lighter than before.

Perhaps God and heaven didn't want a Marcus chiseled from Edith's stone-soul. Perhaps God and heaven needed both Marcus and Edith or not at all. Whatever the reason, in the end Marcus tumbled. With one involuntary intake of air, Edith felt him burrowing down, a sharp, pressing shard. Marcus the ghost, now separate and shameful, lodged deep inside. Edith-Marcus no more.

Hazel wasn't the first girl on Vinalhaven who needed to solve a ghost problem.

Out of all the island ghosts, old Edith in particular had a lot to share with Hazel about stone and cutting tools. And about the death of shame.

QUARRY LESSONS

Early morning. The only sounds were the hum of insects along the side of the road and the occasional noise of a passing car or pickup truck. It took Hazel less than twenty minutes to walk the mile from town to the dirt path that circled Booth's Quarry. On the surface the rock-bound pool looked entirely untroubled.

Edith had explained everything. Hundreds of feet below the surface, the quarry contained a graveyard of rusting bicycles, torn and forgotten swimsuits, syringes, and scorched spoons. For a hundred years people had stood on the quarry's granite edge, tossing away their regrets and shame, including Edith's heart, Edith's shame, Edith's Marcus.

The quarry overflowed with stone ghosts and island power.

Hazel, when her own time came, wouldn't be the first to disappear beneath the quarry's waters. She wouldn't be the first to rise again, diminished and unburdened—stone ghost removed.

Hazel just needed to complete the last few steps.

Hazel knelt on a length of rock, staring down at yet another shattered piece of granite. In her right hand she held Edith's old and well-used hammer, in her left a chisel.

"Each type of stone requires its own strike angle," Edith said. "Granite has very specific needs. Thirty degrees for carving. Ninety degrees to break." Sometimes during their daily carving lessons, Edith's voice sounded no older than Hazel: Edith the stonecarver's daughter. Angry Edith with her secret second name. Other times, like today, Edith's voice sounded old and anxious. Bedroom Edith with no Marcus inside.

There was a third Edith. This Edith never spoke. Each night she sat with Hazel at the kitchen table while Hazel's mother hid behind the TV or her bedroom door. This Edith rested her head against a dent in the kitchen wall—red blood and white plaster—her father's raging words refusing to be forgotten. This was the Edith who had made the final, Marcus-severing cut.

Hazel took another piece of granite from her pile of carefully collected rocks.

"Remember," old Edith said. "Sharp movements, like a whip. Eagle thoughts. No hesitation."

"Right." Hazel raised the hammer and swung, no different from all her other attempts. But instead of the chisel biting into stone, the hammer skittered across the chisel head and landed on Hazel's forearm. "Damn it!" Blood bloomed up along with a sharp pain.

"Try again," Edith said. "Harder."

"Give me a second." Hazel pressed her hand against her jeans pocket and the hard outline of her cell phone. Even with the island ghosts for company, some part of Hazel still felt lonely. None of these ghosts were Ghost Boy. What if she never found that feeling again? What if she ended up like old Edith, anxious and alone? "Why do I only get one shot?" Hazel asked.

"Why do you get any shot at all?" Edith replied.

For that question Hazel had no answer.

It took weeks, but by the end of July, Hazel knew the speed with which the carving hammer had to strike island rock. She knew that tempered steel chisels held their bite much longer than those untreated by heat. She knew that the mason's stroke was for shattering the rock and the letter stroke for creating marks clean enough to form words. She even knew that Vinalhaven granite was Mohs scale eight, tougher than limestone, alabaster, and the town eagle's own marble. In the end Vinalhaven granite would hold whatever form you gave it.

And stone ghosts: after talking with Edith, she knew something about them as well.

LOGISTICS

Hello, Pierceson, Hazel texted. She took a picture of the sunset from her bedroom window, sent it along, ignoring the temptation to take another kind of picture. Though maybe she should. Maybe this time he would actually love her. Someone should.

Hey, kinda busy, Ghost Boy replied.

Right.

Don't be mad.

HazelWhore smiled. Despite the distance, Ghost Boy was definitely not yet ready to let her go. Hazel turned from the window and watched as teenage Edith flounced down on the bed, angry, as usual, and unwilling to talk.

It was old Edith who had explained everything. Soon, Hazel would release one Marcus ghost from his rock-and-water world, even as she bound two new ghosts deep inside the island's stone.

Hey, did you know there are people sort of like you around here? Hazel typed.

There is no one like me, Ghost Boy replied.

Sort of like you. They keep promising me stuff. Some of them seem really nice.

Hazel could feel the bite of Ghost Boy's jealousy—and his interest.

The Final Cut

Out in the darkness Hazel could hear the roll of thunder and the rain pounding against the apartment roof. A real island storm. With less than a week until the end of August and Hazel's ferry ride home, there was no more time. It had to be now.

"Mom, I'm going into town for a bit."

"Sure. Sounds good." Mom didn't open her bedroom door. Didn't ask what the hell Hazel would be doing in Carver's Harbor at night when the town was barely open at midday. These days Mom was keeping as much distance as possible between herself and Hazel's sad little HazelWhore face.

Instead of heading toward the harbor, Hazel started in the opposite direction, following the curving road south toward Booth's Quarry. Goosebumps ran along her arms. Rain trickled down the back of her neck. On one shoulder Hazel carried Edith's canvas bag while Hazel's own cell phone, the final key to the night's planned transformation, was safely lodged in her left jeans pocket.

Hazel had chosen the spot for her stonework days ago. At the eastern end of the quarry, the town had installed a metal railing that paralleled a set of steps carved into the wall. The stairs ended at a ledge about thirty feet long and fifteen feet wide that sat just inches above the waterline. One chance, even with poor lighting, poor angles, wet rocks; Hazel had one chance to get the cuts right.

The rain struck against her face and hands. Below, through the quarry's unsettled water, Hazel could see faces. Shadows of other things as well. *Marcus,* a voice cried. The voice didn't sound like Edith's. Not even close. This was a man's voice, churned up with rage, or perhaps despair. Edith's Marcus.

When Hazel reached the ledge, she pulled out her cell phone, holding the screen close to her face. No bars. If Edith's plan held, that would soon change, along with so much else.

Quickly, Hazel set down the phone, and then off came her coat, her shoes, along with her shirt and bra. HazelWhore was a smart little bitch. HazelWhore knew exactly how to get Marcus's attention. More importantly, she knew how to get her Ghost Boy's. Eagle strikes. No hesitation.

It was time to act, not think.

Hazel grabbed the phone, held her arms high, and slid into the water. Her nipples puckered against the cold. Her eyelashes thickened with rain. Meanwhile, the ghosts, water-and-stone eels, wrapped themselves around her ankles, her knees, made their way up along her inner thighs. Marcus and the other ghosts were inching toward the phone gripped in Hazel's left hand.

Pierceson, she texted. *Pierceson, see what I can do.*

A flash, and then another one: a photostream of HazelWhores standing in the water, writhing, wet, naked, posed. A photostream waiting for the electromagnetic signal boost only Edith's island ghosts could provide.

Pierceson, can you see me yet? Hazel texted, wet fingers pressing against wet screen.

The rain was falling faster now, lashing HazelWhore's face while the phone's flash strobed on and off.

Pierceson! This time Hazel's message was a recorded cry, one word only, followed by the quick press of the send button.

A streak of lightning cracked somewhere beyond the stand of pines. The stone ghosts snaked past Hazel's wrist and along her left palm, finally entering the phone. Ghost energy engaged. Edith hadn't lied. Ghost-powered, the phone now glowed five-bars bright. Booth's Quarry was part of the network. After a lifetime on the mainland, Ghost Boy had finally arrived.

HazelWhore? HazelWhore!!! God, damn it. What the hell do you think you're doing?

That's not my name, Hazel texted.

God, damn it!

Ghost water wrapped around Hazel's breasts, across her lips, pressed along the curve of her lower back. And still Hazel held her phone high. It was almost time for the final step.

God's not my name either.

Hazel!

Hazel scrambled up on to the ledge and set down her phone. With dripping hands, she reached for the chisel and granite hammer, carefully adjusting the angle of the chisel against the quarry stone.

The phone sat less than a foot away, its glowing screen still visible. *Hello, Pierceson.* The words lighting up the screen weren't typed by Hazel's hand. Someone else was texting. Someone who had been trapped in these waters for a very long time. One chance to get it right, Edith had said. So far so good. Ghost Boy and Edith's Marcus were networked together.

Yeah. Hi. Howya doin. Now get the fuck out of here.

I'm trying.

Not fast enough. Shift out of HazelWhore's phone.

Hazel whipped her right arm forward, the granite hammer striking the wet island stone. A hard sharp pain like a shard of rock pressed down against her chest. Hazel rock shattered.

There was no time for hesitation. Hazel raised her arm again.

Boom went the hammer for a second time. Hazel eyes watered, her throat convulsed, gagging, as a wave of quarry ghosts pushed their way inside, forcing Hazel rock, HazelWhore, out of Hazel's body and into the island stone.

Lonely HazelWhore finally safely enclosed.

Marcus's words, meanwhile, continued to flash across Hazel's cell phone screen. He no longer sounded quite so polite.

Touching her, Pierceson. So much better than any words. The water slips everywhere.

The final step. It had to be now.

Another crack of Hazel's granite hammer and another. A flash of ghost-lightning pain smashed through Hazel's throat, holding in her scream. The world had twisted into something new. Marcus was no longer stone-and-water bound. The final step: Ghost Boy, Pierceson, was now buried in his stead, resting next to his HazelWhore.

Hazel's head felt different, lighter, empty. Her legs ached. Gashes, one on each thigh, now mirrored the quarry's fresh stone scars.

On the damp stone ledge, Hazel's phone continued to glow.

Hello, Hazel, the message said. Marcus was free.

Hello, Marcus, Hazel typed. *Edith is waiting.*

Edith, the phone flared up, *can do as she pleases.*

Edith is so sorry, Hazel typed.

Me too. Trapped by my own self. It's my time to fly. Past my time.

That one truth Edith had never considered while she haunted Carver Street with her regret and her sadness: inside the quarry stone Marcus was changing too.

What are you going to do? Hazel typed, not at all sure she wanted to know.

For a moment the phone was silent before Marcus finally responded: *Exactly what I told you. Fly.* Then Hazel watched as text after text spewed out across the network, *ping, ping, ping,* Marcus's messages headed to one unknown number after another.

Hello, the first text said. *You looked so pretty, I had to message you.*

Hey, think you can make it to the party? The next message tried.

Is that you, Gillian? I'm so, so sorry. Can I send you flowers? Make it up to u? Marcus learning quickly.

Just reached the tallest mountain. Look at the fucking view. Marcus now at full speed.

Marcus, I don't want you to go, Hazel thought she heard Edith whisper just before Marcus's final words disappeared from the screen. *Eagle flight. No hesitation.*

Never mind Carver Street, or Vinalhaven Island, Marcus was traveling out in every cell-towered direction before the island's ghost-powered connection broke. Marcus was finally going "anywhere but here," leaving Edith and her regret behind. After more than a lifetime alone, he wasn't going to give up his only chance.

Even after Hazel shut down her phone and climbed the stairs up to the apartment's second-floor bedroom, Edith stood in the Carver Street kitchen by the dented wall, waiting. Reunited a hundred years too late, she was now Edith Simply Left Behind.

ISLAND GIRL

"Marcus," Hazel's mom said, reading the word chiseled at the base of the stone eagle set next to the harbor. "Huh, I didn't know stonecarvers signed their work."

"I guess some do," Hazel replied. "Others probably don't care so much." To Hazel the statue looked like all the other carved blocks of stone on Main Street, empty and kind of dull. It felt weird to think she had ever talked to it or shown it her phone.

The morning ferry's horn blared a warning, coaxing a handful of tanned and freckled travelers out of the coffee shop and toward the ferry slip at the end of the harbor. Other than that, the street seemed empty. As far as Hazel could tell, not even one wool-clad ghost remained.

"Ready to head home?"

Hazel glanced up at her mother and smiled. "Ready." And Hazel's mom—of course; why wouldn't she?—smiled back.

Hazel the changeling. Hazel the girl now freed of her own stone-ghost, along with all others. Hazel her mom's very own happy child.

RAVEN HAIR

SPRING

YOU WERE THE WOLF, the witch, the unnamed monster in the woods. Instead of blood offerings, the townspeople left you woven baskets full of waxy red fruit. I left myself: red cape and fiery virgin blood.

I was the one who lifted my hand and knocked. I had black hair, dark as a raven, and the dress my mother had sewn for me. You saw me just the same: my already-curving hips, my waiting breasts.

My wolf, my witch, my monster: you had yellowed teeth, crooked, with one pointed canine peeking out over your lip. Your clothes were white, crusty, and full of angry stains. You were pretty even so with your salt-and-pepper hair, the sunrise of wrinkles radiating from both eyes. Gray eyes, of course, except on your soulless days when your stare was as blue as an ice-bound ocean. On those days you begged me to be silent, breathless, mute.

Trapped with all my unspoken words, I never felt quiet when I was with you.

SUMMER

Our bedroom was on the second floor. Next to it was your den, carpeted in gray with carefully whitened walls and a scratched closet door you told me not to open.

"It's mine," you said. "A closed door means keep out."

Some days the door's metal handle shook like a cornered snake. Other days it was silent.

On your ice-blue days you roamed the woods while I watched from our bedroom window. Step after step, you bent to examine the forest's undergrowth, searching for the waxy white stalks and scaly leaves of your favorite corpse flower, the Indian pipe. Your favorite was just as elusive as you. I watched until your bent back disappeared into the trees, and then if the closet handle was silent, I stole into your den.

You kept unspooled rolls of 8-mm film in dark green garbage bags stacked against the wall. Your film lacked the black glossy sheen of store-bought. Orangish-brown and subtly dimpled, each length contained a string of tangled images: a felt puppet on a twig broom, a seemingly unending line of girls with freckles or milky-tea skin and sharp-toothed smiles. And that one repeated image—a woman with wolf-gray hair—not you. Words were printed in precise block letters on the bottom of each frame of film, so small I couldn't yet read them. The lettering, I could tell, took hours—a magnifying glass, a steady hand.

It was fairytale time. I pretended the lettering, not the film, was your daytime passion. Your evening passions were easier to ken. Your evenings were spent with me.

I took my time, silent, lips soft against your stomach. Tangled sheets. My hands clutched your narrow hips, then slipped higher until I felt the outer edges of your breasts. I tasted the dampness trickling from between your thighs, salt and musk. Like 8-mm film, my movements took sixteen frames one slow second at a time.

Afterwards, you held pieces of your special brown-orange film up to our bedside light, sharing your work. Each cell was marked, scratched, the original image buried somewhere underneath. Your art, you told me, was about transformation.

Even then I made mistakes. Pointed out a slash mark, an odd corner of red. Left the ghost of a fingerprint behind. "Love me," I cried, finally deciphering the film's tiny words. The long L and five smaller letters suddenly clear.

Yet another transformation: your gray eyes glared, now ice-bound blue. Head bowed, I whispered my own special words: sorry and sorry again while your head nodded its agreement.

I was never as sorry as when I lived with you.

My fairytale monster. My lover. My witch. As with all witches, the kitchen was your domain: bones and gristle, amber syrup clinging to your lips, green herbs disfigured across the chopping board. On late afternoons, heat and flames rose up against the slaughtered flesh. I never asked you where our meat came from, the brown-and-pink flesh so tender as it fell from the bone, curdled bits of blood, gray and glossy, twisting in the gravy.

Afterward, you made sure to tidy the evidence, leaving the countertops snow-blind white, erasing the smell of flesh from the cloth napkins and, later, the sweat-dampened sheets.

Autumn

In autumn the offerings of tribute were fewer than before. The bite of hunger just around the corner, impatient for the last season to begin.

Your Indian pipes, your ghost flowers, your corpse plants, had withered. Now we walked the woods together, collecting what tribute we could find, until finally we entered the village itself.

The townspeople hid behind their wallpapered walls, their curtains, their carefully locked doors. They failed to see the not-so-little girl interred underneath all your scratched and stained clothes. They failed to see your narrow hips that had never birthed a single child, your small breasts with their pale rose-flushed nipples, your shoulders so soft against my nighttime hands.

They missed you entirely.

The Final Season

Hunger. Already lean, your cheeks hollowed once winter came, and your eyes froze into a constant icy blue.

Ravens aren't the only birds that brave the bitter cold. Sharp-eyed finches and crows cawed and spread their wings wide when I ventured beyond our house. I took to sitting on the attic stairs, listening to your slamming closet door. With each thud the metal handle rattled louder than before.

The meat was gone. At night we drank a murky broth that stained my teeth. We ate steaming bowls of melted snow. We left the cloth napkins and the sheets untouched. Even sleeping I was too loud. My heart. My breath. I woke to find your hand against my nose.

"Quiet," you snapped, leaving the darkness of our fairytale bed. But not going far. Just one wall away.

I listened to the creak of the den's opening door, and then the sharp bang of wood closing against its frame. Like a mouse, like a rat, like a hungry deer, I fastened my cape beneath my chin and headed for the stairs. But the landing floorboards creaked. My tread was too loud. It was the final season; the den's door swung wide as the metal handle clattered and shook.

"Come sit with me," you said, grasping my shoulder. "Stay. Speak."

Trapped. Transformed. I was the one who grabbed the handle. I was the one who looked into that finally-open closet door. A hook with a barbed edge hung next to a pretty velvet cloak. A rainbow of red and blue and purple capes. Lengths of black and brown and curling hair. A scalp dangled, the outline of a face clear despite the lack of cartilage and bone. Piles of skin lay heaped across the floor.

Like all your film, each girl had been trimmed down, recreated. Each of your girls now the appropriate eight millimeter width. The evenly spaced perforations along the film's edges were ragged, formed one tooth bite at a time. Surrounding the images, I could see the browned flesh's purple veins. I knew you; this film wasn't yet complete. It lacked the careful words etched along each frame. Love me. Love me. Love me. Sixteen frames per second of begging without any possibility of response. A room full of your blessed silence.

"Love me," you said.

Red-hooded girls can be dangerous, as you well knew.

I stared with eyes of deepening blue. Snarled out, "No." I reached for the metal hook with the worn wooden handle that had clearly been used before, and then my hand and the hook started swinging.

Raven Hair

Raven, the townspeople call me, though my dark hair and red cape were lost long ago. Time has stained my teeth an uneven brown, and coarse white whiskers trail from my chin. Baskets are delivered to my doorstep, and every spring the girls arrive knocking at my door.

Of course, I always open it.

Standing on my stoop, I stare with my ice-bound eyes, measuring the width of each soft round arm, each waist, each thigh. I curl a lock of salt-and-pepper hair round my callused fingers, waiting.

Some girls turn and run. Still more lower their red cotton hoods and show me their raven hair.

I Want to Be Here

AMONG ITS MANY PECULIARITIES, the city hall of Wallington, Massachusetts, contains an actual tax office. Even in the summer, faded green-and-red, crêpe-paper decorations hang down from the ceiling on mismatched lengths of string. Wallington's paper mills and most of its people are long gone. Only the asbestos-riddled infrastructure remains. Forget the internet: web portals and all the rest. If you want to talk to someone, you'd better show up in person.

Francis and I were both in line. I was ahead of him, standing at the counter. He noticed me. Of course he did. In all honesty, I was hard to miss: curling, dark hair and a face termed somewhere between cute and adorable when not overlaid with cuts and bruises in various degrees of fade. I looked like a rough-trade version of the men in Philip-Lorca diCorcia's Hustlers series. Back in the day, I would have tried and failed to offer someone like me thirty dollars for a chance to take a few quick pictures. Then I would have gone home and created my own staged version with Chester, adding in the extra flourishes, the wounds and all the rest, with my bottle of Mehron latex. I don't take those kinds of pictures anymore.

While the rest of the tax-office line, including Francis, watched, I held out my excise tax bill to the woman behind the counter, the third tax abatement in two months.

"They won't stop crashing," I said, trying for a joke.

"Ah."

I heard the cellphone of someone behind me ping. Out of the corner of my eye, I thought I saw a small patch of fog or, perhaps, cigarette smoke lingering near the glass office door. The familiar headache was pressing in against the base of my skull.

"Look," I tried again. "I just want to clear up this fifty-dollar charge. The car's totaled. Crumpled. And that Audi, the other car, just disappeared..." My voice had lowered. I felt floaty, no longer sure of my facts. "The screaming voice was probably just a memory. It's gotta be." The headache made it hard for me to remember. Hard to think.

"Ah," the clerk said again. Crimson lipstick bled into the lines that surrounded her mouth. "We'll still need a copy of the title indicating the car was classified as salvage."

"Oh," I said. "Papers. Yes. I need to get the papers first." I could feel the muscle under my left eye begin to twitch. Another cell phone ping and a rising scent closer to rubber than tobacco smoke. I turned, ignoring the clerk's confusion, and started back toward the office door. I needed to get out of here. Kodo drummers seemed to have taken residence inside my skull. Over the drumming, I could hear steps just a few feet behind me, staying close as I moved through the double doors and out on to the sidewalk. I refused to turn around and confirm that no one was there.

"Excuse me, sir," a voice called out—not *the* voice.

I turned. It was a man: petite with a sharp jawline and narrow nose. He had, I noted, greased-down, blondish hair, parted in the middle, and sleepy eyes that matched his half-smile. A fox-fur stole was tossed across his shoulders.

"Yes?" The Kodo drummers were building to a frenzy.

"Hello," the man said. He reached out and grabbed my hand. "How do you do? My name is Francis. Mr. Francis F. Ahmann."

"Really? Parents can be so cruel." I pulled my hand away and stepped back.

His half-smile didn't even waver. "So...that's a lot of accidents." He tilted his head to one side. "Drugs perhaps?"

"What?"

"Well, you don't look crazy. No tinfoil hat anyway. So I was just wondering...you know, those car crashes. Psychically powered or the result of a dissolute lifestyle. Drugs, darling."

"No drugs," I snapped.

"I'm getting a quivery sense here," Francis held up his hands in a conciliatory gesture. "Transformation via vehicular destruction. It fits right in with—"

"Look," I interrupted and then paused.

"Francis," he prompted with that same half-smile. His lashes were a dark fringe that encircled his brown eyes. There seemed to be muscles under that fox-fur stole. Shoulders. A man's dick. Perhaps not such a clown after all.

"Look, Francis, I've got to go," I said. I scanned the street for the nearest bus stop, slipped my hand into my back pocket and pulled out the contents: four dollar bills and some change, enough to get me home.

Francis glanced at the change. "Do you need a ride?"

I was no fool. The fox-fur could be just a thrift store purchase, but his shoes were made of soft leather. I could see a narrow line of tiny, even stitches holding the pieces together, and he clearly wasn't concerned about the end-of-winter snow and slush. This man had money.

"I'm fine."

"Some cash assistance perhaps?" Francis said.

"No." I turned and headed toward the end of the block and the bus stop. Francis followed. His cane clicked against the pavement in time with my footsteps.

"I feel like my articulation is subpar today. I'm not explaining myself very well. I'm looking for a personal assistant, one who can help me with a special type of experiment. You, dear man," he said, his voice rising with his enthusiasm, "are perfect."

"I'm a photographer, not a scientist—or anything else." I stopped next to the bus stop's white-and-blue sign. No other people were waiting. No pedestrians anywhere. Just me and Francis.

A cab idled by, paralleling the length of city hall. It stopped at the intersection just beyond the edge of the building. If only I had enough cash to flag it down.

"A photographer? How fortuitous. I need one of those as well."

"As well as what?" I turned to face the guy. My head buzz-sawed with dissonant music.

"Science, sir, real science. A portal to the past. Borchgrevink and his sled dogs. Shackleton at the ice floe. My own dear Grandfather Clemens."

"Doesn't the past stalk most people's present?" Christ. Since when did I quote my old therapist to strangers?

A car horn honked. Across the street on the far corner was a Chinese restaurant. Thickening tendrils of fog twined above the snow that lined the street curb. I touched my left jeans pocket, feeling for the familiar cylindrical shape of my prescription bottle. Dr. Banks and his trusty red-and-white pills.

I watched the traffic light change to green. The yellow cab was moving through the intersection. The only vehicle. An icy drizzle began to fall. My coat had no hood, of course. Francis's lips were moving, but the Kodo drummers were drowning him out. And then everything changed.

Please, the voice said, just like it always did. *Please, help me.*

I caught the sound of squealing brakes, then a bus came skidding sideways around the corner, past Mr. Wu's Chinese Restaurant and the snow bank, continuing in the direction of our bus stop and city hall. The bus hopped the curb as it slowed down, finally coming to a halt on the sidewalk, not ten feet away. The number on its display read 314.

Come back, my then-boyfriend Chester cried. I couldn't pretend any longer. Kodo drummers or not, his voice was clear. And scared.

"How much did your last photography job pay?" Francis asked.

"Fourteen dollars an hour." Through the bus's front window, I could see the driver, a middle-aged guy with graying hair and a comfortable middle. His hands still gripped the wheel. A few more feet and he would have slammed right into the granite building. I watched as he reached over and pulled the handle, released the bus's doors, and then stumbled down the steps.

"A VW Jetta came out of nowhere. I drive around that corner at least eight times a day. Eight times a day," the guy repeated. "I passed by not one hour ago. There was no ice then. No parked VW either." He kicked the ice-free sidewalk for emphasis.

"What VW?" Francis asked.

"Where's the Jetta?" The driver turned and stared at the empty street.

"I'll pay you twenty," Francis murmured.

"My rent's due Friday."

"Cash. With a week's pay upfront."

"Deal," I said. Even without Dr. Banks's pills, my headache had disappeared.

"Ian, it's basic neurobiology. Memory is nothing but chemicals. We store our past as a series of delicious little mini-cocktails. The stronger the memory, the stronger the cocktail."

Francis and I were in his car, driving away from City Hall, the bus, and the almost silent street. He glanced at me as though expecting a response, and then sighed when I gave none. The fox head at his neck quivered, almost seeming to sigh as well.

"Look, Ian. In some cases it feels like you're actually reliving the past. Right?"

"I guess. Never gave it much thought." I shifted in the passenger seat of Francis's Audi. If I just out-listened my new employer, maybe he'd finally shut up. Cash or no cash, I was already half-regretting taking the job.

Francis turned and smiled at me, determined, it seemed, to ignore my mood. "I believe some brains, given the right circumstances, can do more than that. They can actually push through to the past. Ian, think of yourself as a chemical transmitter. A special kind of amplifier. You, my dear, have that delicious combination of trauma and, I'm guessing, a mutation in at least one of your serotonin transporter genes." He paused and glanced at me, considering. "What I don't understand is why you haven't hopped back yourself. You're just so ripe. Cars. It seems to be all about cars with you."

I let my left hand slip against his arm and then drop to his lap, anything to shut him up.

We were driving north toward the Hills section of town. Once, the Hills neighborhood had been filled with mill owners and other briefcase types. Carriage houses faced Tiffany glass windows, and manicured lawns topped by flowering Dogwoods. All those stately homes had been carved and re-stitched long ago. Now, the curving streets were filled with sagging, chain-link fences, faded siding, and clapboards covered in peeling strips of Pepto-Bismol-pink paint.

"Your feelings, that's the key," Francis persisted as he paused at a stop sign. "Something about the volume of your left amygdala and the depth of connections with your prefrontal cortex."

The man was definitely beginning to irritate me. "Even at twenty dollars an hour, I don't have mutant superpowers," I said, pulling my hand back from his lap. My headache was beginning to return. "My brain didn't cause those crashes. They were accidents."

"Seems unlikely to me," Francis responded, looking me over very carefully. "You look like a rather sober fellow. If there's no illness, bad eyesight, or illicit drugs, then something else is at work." He nodded in a satisfied way. "A human transmitter."

I can remember every car I've crashed since Chester.

This season's first car was a blue 1998 Volvo, vintage. The interior's dashboard was covered in my collection of super-glued bobbleheads.

The second car came less than a month later. It was my neighbor's little Nissan two-door, also blue. She'd sold it to me for two thousand dollars below fair market value. I'd always liked Mrs. Klaver.

My final car embarrassed me. It was green, which was fine. But it was also big—an old Jeep with a deep dent in the front right panel and a headlight that seemed ready to fall out. The price, however, was right: $750. It's going to cost me a fortune in gas, I thought as I handed over the cashier's check. I didn't even get through a single tankful before the accident with the vanishing silver-gray car.

Now, two months after the Jeep Wrangler's demise, the only car I drove was Francis's. Every day.

Despite the cold, we were outside once again. Francis reclined under his courtyard's sole shade tree, while I sat next to him on a small metal stool. I watched as he exhaled another thread of cigarette smoke. "My loutish father never understood heroic passions. With him it was all fisticuffs. But

Grandfather Clemens, all my research indicates the same thing—a person with whom I can have an actual rapprochement. Time travel seems such a small problem in comparison."

The nicotine cloud from Francis's cigarette traveled upward, climbing the elm's branches before settling back into the deepening under-tree smog. I could feel yet another headache invading my skull. This moment is the present moment, not the past, I tried to tell myself. The haze is just Francis's damn cigarette smoke. Not wisps of fog. There was no screaming voice, no car crash.

Francis, of course, didn't notice a thing.

"Ian, I wonder where I'll land once you push us through. What do you think? Ship deck or deep-sea ice? I'm feeling a wonderfully tingly resonance today. Soon I'll be traveling with dear Grandfather Clemens. I wonder if he'll recognize the family resemblance." Francis glanced at his rumpled linen pants. "I need to get changed, then we'll drive."

"Right. Why don't I meet you at the car?"

For someone who claimed a hatred of the current present, Francis had spent a lot of money on what he termed modern artifacts: a silver Audi A5 coupé, with both a parking system and rearview camera, that was housed in his home's former carriage house.

I watched Francis walk the gravel driveway toward the now-open garage doors, the waiting car, and me, his supposed time-travel chauffeur. He was in his usual sennegrass-filled boots, no socks. Grandfather Clement had done the same when he was down in the Antarctic, Francis once explained. As well as the boots, Francis wore fur-lined mittens over woolen gloves with a thick woolen scarf wrapped around his neck and ears. Despite the sunny day, a small circle of eyes, nose, and mouth were the only visible parts of his flesh.

"Francis, look at the sun," I said. "There's no way we're going to hit any fog or clouds." I regretted the use of the word *hit* the second it came out of my mouth. "Was your father an explorer as well?" I asked, trying to distract him. "Like your grandfather?"

"My father was a drunk. Disappeared years ago. Thank God."

"Okay."

"Let's try some visualizations this time," Francis suggested as he settled into the Audi's passenger seat and fastened the seatbelt. "What were you thinking of when you wrecked the first car?"

"Nothing in particular." I checked both side-view mirrors, adjusting the right mirror by a fraction of an inch. I could still remember the flash of black-and-white images that had risen unbidden just before this winter's Volvo had skidded out of control. Pictures like the ones I used to take. Not my Chester portraits, but the old gray-smoke prints, my dark faerie landscapes.

"All set." I pressed the Audi's keyless starter and then the lock button, manually unlocking each of the doors. If there was an accident, we might need to get out of the car in a hurry. Then I pulled the car forward and paused as a purple Dodge Caravan turned onto the empty street. It was about a hundred yards off and seemingly going slow, but I didn't like to take chances once I was behind the wheel.

Out of the corner of my eye, I could see Francis's finnesko boots, all soft leather and fur, tap against the floor mat, waiting for his voyage to begin.

I let the Dodge pass, hit the indicator, and pulled onto the street. From the side-view mirror, I could see a Ford 450 pull up behind me. The owner was a buzz-cut, ex-military type in his fifties. Both he and the car were probably real. One of my phantom vehicles wouldn't have bothered tailgating. It would have jack-knifed right into me.

I was going twenty in a thirty-mile-per-hour zone. Sunlight, blue sky, and a scattering of puddles where the snow had rested just weeks ago—if I could I would remain in this sunny day for the rest of my life.

Five more minutes, and then the driver of the red Ford revved his engine and plowed around Francis's Audi. When the truck's driver hit the brakes a moment later, forcing me to stop short, Francis's foot went still. I knew what he was thinking: Perhaps he'd get his accident after all. Despite all his talk, Francis still didn't get it. A real accident didn't count, not one caused by a present-day driver.

I continued down the road, ignoring Francis and his irritating enthusiasm while Chester's voice nagged from somewhere in the past.

Don't, Ian. Stay, he'd pleaded.

I'll be right back, I'd told him.

I was here in the present. In the real world. But the sun had slipped behind some clouds. Fog drifted near the edges of the road. Francis was saying something I was having a hard time focusing on. He sounded excited.

"Snow, Ian. Is that snow?"

I squinted against the haze that surrounded us and reached for the headlights.

"No!" Francis exclaimed. "You're avoiding the real path. Break free, Ian. No lights."

I clicked the lights on anyway, but I still couldn't find the edges of the road. I couldn't even find the painted yellow line in the middle. I slapped my right hand against the Audi's circulation button, locking the vents, trying to keep the swirling wisps outside.

Dr. Banks's pills and his worn business card rested in my pocket like a secret lifeline. Pulling over so I could take a pill, that was my current-present problem. Current-present? Francis's ideas were like an infection.

Come back, Chester called.

The car moved steadily forward, despite the past with its swirl of fog and pleading words.

I could hear Francis next to me, hissing in disapproval, demanding his crash through time. Ernest Shackleton and the *Endurance*. The Great Ice Barrier. Mount Gauss. His dear Grandfather Clemens.

"Ian," Chester cried.

The space behind my eyes seemed to explode outward. Pain. Blurred vision. Or was that actual fog? My eyes were closing. My foot felt glued to the accelerator. Where was the brake? I should hit the brake. Francis was roaring something. His words lost in all the noise: the crunching of metal, calipers screaming, glass spraying across the road. The car screeched to a stop—finally. I could feel sharp stings biting into my hands and face. I could smell smoke and the familiar powdery scent of deployed airbags. Francis was fumbling between our seats, the back of his hand pushing against my hip, and then I heard the click as he released his seatbelt.

"Going now," he said. His voice croaked, a raw and troubled thing, as the car filled with cold air. When my eyes cleared, his seat was empty, his door open. Fog rested like a body against the back of the passenger seat, stretched its legs down into the wheel well. The same fog that had risen from the snow bank just before the bus came skidding around the corner. The same fog that surrounded all my crashes, including that very first crash.

Chester.

The tendrils rising from the cane-back chair where Chester sat as I took his picture and later from the car, my car. I was the set designer and Chester was my model.

In this present moment, the Audi's horn blared while Francis yelled from somewhere nearby. "No. No."

And then a bellow, heavy and angry. Someone else's voice. "You little shit! How many times—"

"Father, please. Stop," Francis cried. My employer had finally found the actual past.

Outside the car, shadows were rising up from the fog. Off to my left, a person seemed to be flagging me down or, perhaps, it was no more than swirling bits of smoke.

How could I have forgotten? *Forgotten* was the wrong word: walled-in. Until this moment, at least. Francis had been pushing me so hard into the past, though not the one he asked for. Despite Francis's costumes, his demands for his unknown grandfather, and the icy-cold Antarctic, this was no Disney theme-park ride. Out in this fog, time travel was personal. The paths forged via memories. My employer had landed back in his own life. Of course, he had.

Meanwhile, I was crashing back ten years toward my own past.

Black and white. That's what Chester called my landscapes. Mostly, though, they were neither. They covered the walls of the room we shared, shades of gray trapped behind rectangular glass frames.

"What's with all the fog?" Chester asked. I could feel his hand resting against my left hip. "Ian, you really should show these. You're so damned talented." And then after a pause: "Is that a car?"

"I dunno. Different people see different things." My fog pictures were a sort of Rorschach test. People saw a sled, a mountain, perhaps an ice storm at sea. For me it was always the same bundled figure, covered head to toe. I could never make out his features.

The room's single 60-watt bulb cast strange shadows against the walls. "See that person? Kind of skinny? She's got furry boots on and one of those crazy-big scarfs."

"Nah," Chester said, leaning in closer. He pulled me in toward him. "It's a rocking chair, man, or maybe a polar bear. That's possible too." He let out a breath of laughter. The bastard could never keep a straight face for long.

"Right." I wriggled out of his grasp and turned, pressing my body against his, running my hand down the length of his jean's zipper. Hard already.

"No way is she a polar bear," I said after a moment, still thinking about the picture.

"No way is that a she," Chester said.

Chester and I sat side by side on the brown plaid sofa, our feet resting on the coffee table.

"You see," Chester said. "Time is the real issue. Past. Future. Our minds get to travel but our bodies are totally stuck in the present."

"I guess," I said. Something about the corners of the room felt off, like half-visible ghosts or visitors from another time. It was probably just a reflection from the TV screen. I took another sip of my half-warm beer.

"Almost sunrise," Chester said after a long stretch of quiet. "Still want to take those pictures?"

I shrugged.

Chester slid off the couch and settled into the old cane back rocker. The chair moved back and forth, back and forth as one of Chester's feet slowly pedaled against the floor. A small wisp seemed to rise from Chester and swirl up toward the ceiling.

"Yeah, why not," I said. "Sure you're up for another modeling session?"

"Yeah. I'm sure."

My car, a VW Jetta, was parked just a couple houses down on the other side of the empty street. The sky was a golden-edged gray. The street was empty. Only the windows from all the stacked-together houses were watching.

"We'll have to hurry with the setup, or we'll lose the light," I said after I unlocked the car.

Chester slid into the passenger seat and flipped open the makeup case while I checked the light meter. It was cold. Wisps slipped from my nostrils. It felt like I was breathing one of my pictures out onto the world.

"How deep should the wound go?" Chester called as he leaned his head out the passenger side window.

I glanced at the digital readout on the meter and frowned. We hadn't brought the reflectors this time.

"Ian?"

"Damn it, Chester," I started. I could feel the tension building. The shot was probably already fucked.

"Ian, you know you're just gonna get pissed if I don't get it right."

"This one is all about the light. And the goddamn light is almost gone."

"You know, I don't have to pose for these bullshit accidents. It's fucking creepy."

"What, you like it better when I make you look pretty?"

"Everyone likes it better when I look pretty."

It happened in an instant. No past. No present. No future. The bus slammed around the corner and against the right side of the car.

I could hear Chester crying, screaming out "Oh, my God" again and again as my fingers pulled uselessly against the crushed door handle.

"Help. We need help," I screamed. Where had the bus gone? "Chester, it's gonna be okay. I promise. I just need to go get help. Okay?"

"Please, don't leave."

"It's okay. I promise."

And then I was running. Away from the car, and the screams, and Chester's body covered in wounds that had nothing to do with any makeup kit.

"It's okay. It's okay." I kept chanting all the way to the nearest house. All the way up the stairs. Pounding on the door. Yelling.

"Ian. Please. Come back," He sounded so scared. And then Chester wasn't crying anymore.

I could hear the bus's horn screaming somewhere out in the fog, stuck, while steam hissed from the Jetta's cracked radiator, white-and-gray streaks rising up.

No more black-and-white pictures after that. No more conversations and hours spent alone in our room, though the wisps of fog never entirely let go. The worst was this winter: all that snow and the gray skies that followed. It was like living inside a glass frame as the swirling gray of my old photographs tried to get out.

"It was an accident, Ian," the man said. He wore a doctor's white coat. "Just an accident." He reached out and took my hand, not even commenting on the scattering of bruises and scars. "My name's Dr. Banks. I'm here to help you. They found my number on a card in your pocket."

I sat in a bed with metal rails and white sheets. A curtain hung across the window, blocking out whatever was on the other side.

"Where am I?" I asked, not sure I wanted to know. Through a crack in the curtain, I could see the other bed was empty. No Francis. No Chester either. Both my arms were bandaged. My face felt stiff.

"This is McLean Memorial Hospital," Dr. Banks replied.

I could feel tears, wetness, on my cheeks.

Dr. Banks picked up a small paper cup from a nearby tray and held it out to me. "Ian, the pills will calm down the serotonin receptors," He held my gaze. His scruffy salt-and-pepper eyebrows reminded me of an elderly cat, hairs sprouting up like whiskers. "You'll feel better again. I promise." He pressed the paper cup into my unresisting hand.

"Chester." I tried to focus on the bed, the cup, the white hospital curtain. This is the moment I am in now. This is the present moment. I am inhabiting the real, physical world.

"You just need to calm down."

I nodded, raised Dr. Banks's cup to my lips, and swallowed the pills. At least for a little while, time would flow forward once again.

Come back, Chester cried whenever I let my guard down. *Please.* Private truth time: Despite Dr. Banks's pills, most of the time I wanted to do exactly that. Go back.

Previous Publications

"Everyone Gets a Happy Ending" Originally published in *Interzone* #268 (January–February 2017)

"The Woman in the Woods" Originally published in *Necessary Fiction* (January 2016)

"A Pinhole of Light" Originally published in *Black Static* #54 (September–October 2016)

"One Thousand Paper Cranes" Originally published in *Kaleidotrope* (Winter 2017)

"The Thirteen Tuesdays of Saint Anthony" Originally published in *Farrago's Wainscot* Issue 16 (October 2015)

"Raising Babies" Originally published in *Crack the Spine* #145 (April, 2015)

"Holes in Heaven" Originally published in *Isthmus* #4 (January 2016)

"Florida Miracles" Originally published in *Interzone* #261 (November–December 2015

"The Faces Between Us" Originally published in *Interzone* #254 (September–October 2014)

"Idle Hands" Originally published in *New Haven Review* Issue 019 (February 2017)

"Finding Your Way to the Coast" Originally published in *A cappella Zoo* Issue 9 (September 2012)

"Pretty Little Boxes" Originally published in the Resurrection House anthology XIII (March 2015)

"The Re'em Song" Originally published in *Interzone* #258 (May–June 2015)

"Raven Hair" Originally published in the *Cream City Review* 41.1 (April 2017)